Look what people are saying about Vicki Lewis Thompson…

"Ms Thompson does a wonderful job of blending the erotic with romance that is sometimes tender, sometimes funny, and always exciting."
—Diana Risso, *Romance Reviews Today*

"Vicki Lewis Thompson has reached a whole new dimension in laughter. A big...*bravo!*"
—*A Romance Review*

"When you pick up a book that bears the name of Vicki Lewis Thompson on the cover, you can expect a great read. She... will make you laugh, cry, need a cold shower and most important fall in love."
—*Fallen Angel Reviews*

"Vicki Lewis Thompson never fails to deliver a book filled with intense chemistry, sexy heroes, and just a little bit of naughtiness."
—Missy Andrews, *Fallen Angel Reviews*

"Ms Thompson continues to set the romance world on fire and keep it burning."
—Diana Tidlund, *WritersUnlimited.com*

Dear Reader,

When I was a little kid in Tucson the local paper published rhymes as part of the weather report. One of mine got accepted. *Sky is blue. I am not. I love the sun. I love the hot.*

A few (ahem) years have passed since then, but some things never change. I still love the hot, whether we're talking about the heat rising from the desert floor or the heat rising from a Mills & Boon Blaze novel. To set a Blaze – pun intended – in my hometown of Tucson was a no-brainer.

For one thing, it's so toasty in southern Arizona that we don't have to bother with layers upon layers of clothes. I'm sure you can see the obvious advantages to that! Plus there's something about the starkly beautiful landscape that inspires lusty, primitive emotions. At least, that's my excuse, and it seems to work for my characters, Jess and Katie.

So come spend some time in my favourite city in the world and let me tell you a story. Oh, and you might want to bring one of those little electric fans. It gets hot down here.

Warmly,

Vicki Lewis Thompson

TALKING ABOUT SEX...

BY
VICKI LEWIS THOMPSON

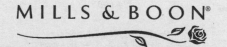
MILLS & BOON®

To my parents, Doc and Randy.
Thanks for bringing me to Arizona.

*First published in Great Britain 2006
by Harlequin Mills & Boon Limited, Eton House,
18-24 Paradise Road,
Richmond, Surrey TW9 1SR*

© Vicki Lewis Thompson 2005

*ISBN-13: 978 0 263 84612 6
ISBN-10: 0 263 84612 1*

14-0906

*Printed and bound in Spain
by Litografia Rosés S.A., Barcelona*

1

JESS HARKINS WAS TOO OLD for fix-ups. But he'd forgotten that fact in a moment of insanity and now was stuck with the woman sitting in the passenger seat of his Jag. Suzanne Dougherty, friend of a friend, billed as *lots of fun and just your type*…wasn't.

They'd struggled to make conversation over a very expensive dinner at Anthony's and were currently en route to the Flying V for dancing because it would be an insult to take her home at nine on a Friday night. God. Why hadn't he nipped this idea in the bud?

Gabe should have known better than to set him up with somebody like Suzanne. The guy had been Jess's construction foreman for five years. Plus they'd hung out watching sports and had spent a bunch of Sunday afternoons hiking their favorite mountain trails. Gabe should know by now what kind of woman Jess would like.

Maybe Gabe wasn't a great judge of character. Or maybe his girlfriend had pushed him into setting up the blind date. In any case, it wasn't working.

Suzanne reached for the power button on his sound system. "Let's listen to the radio."

"Good idea." Anything to fill the awkward silences.

She punched the button. The minute she did, he remembered where he'd last set the dial…and what came on after the nine-o'clock news Monday through Friday nights.

"Hi, there! Crazy Katie for KRZE, 'crazy' talk radio in Tucson, home of that marvelous phallic symbol, the saguaro cactus! It's Friday, October seventh, and we're Talking About Sex!"

Suzanne's shrill laugh bounced around inside the air-conditioned Jag. "Hey, I totally forgot it was nine o'clock."

"Maybe we should go with some music." Jess reached for the channel switch.

"No, leave it." Suzanne caught his hand. "I like her show. Haven't heard it in a while."

Jess used to like it, too. He'd made a habit of switching it on weeknights wherever he happened to be—in his foothills home or driving around town. Her sassy voice took him down memory lane and her topic interested him more than a little.

He'd even thought about stopping by the station to ask her out for old time's sake. It certainly wasn't out of his way now that he was building a high-rise right next to KRZE's studio, located in a quaint little adobe dating back to the forties.

He'd considered leaving her a note on his way home from the job site. Wouldn't she be surprised to hear from him, a blast from the past? She might be seeing someone, of course, but it was worth a shot.

Then, as he'd been about to make his move with a clever little note referencing days gone by, she'd started lobbing grenades at his project. She'd been doing it for a couple of weeks now, egging on the handful of Value Our Roots picketers he continued to deal with. The project had attracted dissenters from the start, with VOR being the most vocal. But once the zoning board had ruled in favor of the high-rise, the protests had mostly died down. Except for Katie's.

Okay, maybe construction caused a few traffic problems for KRZE's employees. But soon that wouldn't matter because the station would have to relocate anyway. Livingston Development Corporation was negotiating with the station's owners to buy the property.

KRZE was sitting on land that could be put to better use, simple as that. The rest of the properties in that block were already in escrow, and plans had been approved for a shopping mall several stories high. Jess expected to get that contract, too. This development was the most high-profile project he'd ever landed. When it was finished, Harkins Construction would be *the* big-deal company in Tucson. Jess wanted that kind of job security.

Plus he was having fun. The new buildings would bring more business downtown and add an interesting silhouette to the skyline. They would not be the *eyesore devoid of all redemption* that Katie had called them on Wednesday night or a *testimony to human greed and excess,* which was the phrase she'd used last night. They would look nice. Impressive. Worthy of Harkins Construction.

He should have stopped listening after the first time she'd dinged him, but he'd had some perverse need to know what she was ranting about. Still, he didn't relish being insulted in front of Suzanne. No help for it, though. If he insisted on changing the station he'd look defensive.

"On this show, we're all sex, all the time," Katie said. *"And here's your nightly tip from the* Kama Sutra. *Tired of the same ol', same ol' with the woman on top? Ladies, try this—squat down, settle yourself on that bad boy of his, close your legs and use a churning motion. Let me know if it works for you, okay?"*

Jess coughed to hide a groan of dismay. Suzanne had been giving him sexual signals all night. This should throw her into high gear.

"Interesting idea," Suzanne said. "Ever had a woman try that?"

"Not exactly."

"I think it sounds like a lot of—"

"Work," Jess said. "It sounds like a lot of work."

"Wait a minute. I wasn't going to say that. I think—"

"Tonight we welcome Dr. Janice Astorbrooke." Katie's voice drowned out whatever Suzanne might have said. *"Dr. Astorbrooke is the author of* Thrusting Skyward: Sexual Symbolism in Architecture."

Jess ground a millimeter off his back molars as he gunned the Jag through an amber light. As if the *Kama Sutra* tip hadn't caused enough trouble, now he had to listen to a discussion of high-rise buildings as phallic symbols. He could smell it coming. Katie must have combed the Internet looking for this crackpot.

"Let's get right to it, Dr. Astorbrooke. Surely on your way here you noticed what's happening next to our charming little studio. A pit that large means a foundation for a very tall building. Forty stories, to be exact."

Dr. Astorbrooke had the deep voice of a heavy smoker. *"Katie, as long as we allow men to design buildings, we'll see structures climbing ever higher. At forty stories, this one is modest."*

"Well, we are in Tucson, not Manhattan," Katie said.

"I've noticed you have precious few tall buildings, but you have some, and the motivation is definitely the same, whatever the size."

Jess braced himself. He wasn't going to like this.

"And what would that motivation be, Dr. Astorbrooke?" Katie sounded so sweet. So deadly.

"Compensation for sexual inadequacies."

"Watch out!" Suzanne yelled.

Jess slammed on his brakes and barely missed hitting the car in front of him. "Sorry." The apology came automatically as his brain continued to deal with what he'd heard. *Sexual inadequacies?* Shitfire. He was making damn good money building a viable office complex. He sure as hell wasn't *compensating* for a goddamn thing.

"Absolutely fascinating," Katie said. *"So it's a bit like driving powerful cars?"*

Katie couldn't know he had a Jag. But he winced all the same.

"Like that, but even more revealing, Katie."

Suzanne laughed again, an eardrum-piercing sound. "I just realized something. That's *your* building she's talking about, isn't it?"

"My company's constructing it. I didn't design it." *Way to go, hotshot. Blame the architect.* "But I like what the architect has done," he forced himself to add.

As Dr. Astorbrooke launched into a detailed explanation of her theory, Jess noticed that Suzanne kept glancing at his crotch. Hell.

At long last Katie broke for a commercial. Jess had never been so happy to listen to an ad for Jack Furrier's Western Tires.

"You've built several high-rises around town, haven't you?" Suzanne's tone indicated she was definitely on a fishing expedition.

"It's our speciality." Yeah, he liked working on tall buildings, but it didn't mean anything sexual. He liked sex. He was good at it. Sex was one thing and work was another. Two separate subjects.

"And why did you make it your speciality?"

"I like the challenge of multistory buildings." He wasn't about to go into his fascination with steel girders or his love of Erector sets when he was a kid. That would be misinterpreted for sure. If he had to say why he liked working on tall buildings, he might admit that he liked the power and prestige implied in them. He'd had very little of that as the son of a mom working the cash register at Target and an absentee father perpetually on the run from the law.

"So what do you think of this theory?"

"I think it's bull." He stopped at a red light. He could have made it through another amber, but he wanted to demonstrate that he was in complete control and this discussion hadn't rattled him at all.

"Of course it's bogus." Her voice had a new quality, a decidedly sexual quality. "You're obviously a very virile guy."

Damn it. What if she thought he should prove it to her? He looked over, and sure enough, she seemed ready to rock and roll. He had no such inclination.

With a sigh he drove through the intersection and into a turn bay that would take him back in the direction of her apartment. "Suzanne, you're an amazing person, but—"

"There's a reality-show quote if I ever heard one."

Guilty as charged. He'd heard it on one of the *Bachelor* shows and filed it away for future use. Apparently it only worked on those shows. "Okay, bad line." He sat in the turn bay waiting for traffic to clear while he tried to come up with something better.

"You're taking me home, aren't you?"

He sighed. "I just don't think you and I are meant to be."

That sounded equally lame. He was no good at dishing out rejection. Sappy as it sounded, he didn't like to hurt a woman's feelings.

"You were fine until sex came into the conversation."

He hadn't been fine. He'd been faking enjoyment. Apparently she couldn't tell, though, and he didn't want to make things any worse by explaining that.

Suzanne tossed her head. "Maybe this Dr. Astorbrooke is onto something, after all."

He'd have to take a blow to his manly pride. It was either that or say something hurtful to Suzanne. It wasn't her fault they hadn't clicked. "Maybe she is."

"I guess you'd better take me home then. I'm not in the market for someone with inadequacy issues."

With a great sense of relief, Jess pulled into traffic. "I'm sorry it didn't work out."

"You could get counseling."

"Yeah, maybe I should." He managed to hit a bunch of green lights and had Suzanne at her doorstep in no time. A handshake later, he was back in the car.

In a roundabout way Katie had done him a favor tonight, but he wasn't giving her any credit for that. She was out to get him, and he planned to put a stop to it.

Primed for battle, he headed for KRZE.

KATIE PETERSON ESCORTED Janice Astorbrooke out of the studio during a commercial break for Cialis. After the good doctor left, Katie returned to the studio to tidy up in preparation for Jared Williams, whose program *Sports Nuts* filled the ten-o'clock slot. As she gathered her notes, she basked in the glow of accomplishment.

The walls of the small adobe building she loved might

quiver from the rumble of earthmovers during the day, but she'd gotten in her licks tonight. She felt like a warrior defending her turf. This was her house, even if she didn't own it.

She'd understood why her grief-stricken grandfather had sold it after her grandmother had died when Katie was in high school. She'd understood why her suburban parents hadn't wanted it either, although losing her grandmother and the house in the same year had been very tough to take. She'd hated the feeling of having no control over major events in her life. When the construction had been proposed and she could see the building was threatened, she'd vowed to do what she could to save it.

Dr. Astorbrooke had been a real asset to her campaign. Judging from the number of callers during the second half of the show, the topic had stirred up plenty of controversy, which was Katie's bread and butter. Boosting the ratings even higher while taking potshots at Harkins Construction made for a fine evening's work.

At ten on the dot Jared ambled into the studio. A tall, lanky guy with glasses, he loved his wife Ruth and weird sports statistics, in that order.

Katie got up and turned the microphone over to him. "Did you catch any of my show?"

"Absolutely." Jared grinned at her as he sat down and reached for the headset. "Just for the record, I have no urge to construct tall buildings."

Katie laughed. "I didn't think so. Ruth seems like a very satisfied woman."

"Yeah, she got a kick out of your show tonight. She was still listening when I left home."

"Tell her I appreciate the support. Every listener counts."

"Will do." Jared glanced up at Katie as he adjusted the headset. "Have a good weekend."

"Thanks." Katie gave him a wave as she slipped out the door and walked down to the hall to the station's modest lobby.

"Great show," said Ava Dinsmore, KRZE's most recent intern from Pima College. Interns worked well for KRZE, which operated on a tight budget.

Ava obviously understood tight budgets. On her twenty-second birthday she'd decided to go back to school and climb out of the minimum-wage rut. She favored multiple piercings and an ever-changing rainbow of hair colors, so radio was a more logical venue for her than TV.

Besides being a general gofer, she covered the switchboard in the mornings and every evening until the station signed off. "You had lots of calls," she said.

"I know! Wasn't the response terrific? We even had to bleep out some language. I loved it."

"You got a few personal calls, too." Ava picked up several slips of paper.

Katie made no move to take the messages. Ava lived for moments of drama, which included reading messages aloud instead of handing them over. From the beginning Katie had admired Ava's ability to talk clearly with her tongue stud.

"First priority, Edgecomb called. The owners are pissed about tonight's show. They're afraid the negotiations with Livingston Development will go south."

"Good! Then Livingston can build its precious parking garage somewhere else."

"Yeah, like on the lot on the other side of us, with the station sandwiched in between. Our signal will be ruined, regardless."

"That's why we have to stop *all* the construction! I'm not accepting defeat yet."

"Edgecomb wants you to accept defeat. He wants you to go back to the original format—sex toys, foreplay techniques, stuff like that."

"Last night I reviewed two adult videos and interviewed a topless dancer."

"I know." Ava's spiked hair didn't move when she nodded. "But in between you've been dissing the construction. And tonight the whole show was about that. Edgecomb wants you to cut it out."

"We'll see." On Monday night Katie had a guest scheduled who would talk about the sexual significance of hardware items like bolts, screws and nuts, which would give her an opening for more anticonstruction comments. She really wanted to do that show.

"As Edgecomb put it, you can rag on this project all you want—on your own time." Ava's grin was framed by purple lip gloss. "I have to give you credit, though. I never would have dreamed you'd find a way to connect sex with construction."

"Google is a girl's best friend." But the leap had been an easy one. Jess Harkins and sex were forever linked in her mind, although she'd take splinters under her fingernails before admitting to anyone at the station that she had a personal grudge against the general contractor for the project.

"I would love to be a fly on the wall when somebody tells that builder about tonight's show. Can you imagine some manly construction dude being called a wimpy-dick on the air? Good thing your phone number's unlisted."

"I didn't call him a wimpy-dick." Katie smiled her secret smile. "That was Dr. Astorbrooke's theory, not mine." She hoped the word would get back to Jess, though. Served him right.

"Yeah, I noticed that you protected yourself nicely." Ava's dimples flashed. "So are you gonna ease up on the smear campaign?"

Not on your life. "I'll talk to Edgecomb." Katie checked the clock on the wall. "What were the other messages?"

"One was from Cheryl, who said—" Ava paused to read from the message *"—'Give 'em hell, Katie. Let's go for margaritas at six tomorrow. Usual place.'"* Ava looked up. "She said a bunch more stuff, but that was the gist."

"Got it. Thanks."

"Can I come?"

"Sure, why not?" Katie suspected that Ava was outgrowing her regular crowd of slackers and wanted to find a different group to hang with. Katie and her best friend Cheryl, a trial lawyer, might look pretty good to Ava right now.

"Great! Thanks."

"It'll be fun. Any more messages?"

"Uh, yeah. Your mother wants to know why you're picking on that nice Harkins boy."

"Oh." She heard the sound of a second shoe dropping. Obviously Ava had saved that message for last. She was like a bloodhound when it came to sniffing out juicy gossip. Doggone Mom anyway.

Cheryl knew better than to leave any incriminating messages with Ava, but Mom…well, she'd always liked having Jess around. She'd been upset when Katie had broken up with him. She might even *want* people at the station to know he was an ex-boyfriend.

Ava eyed Katie with interest. "I'm assuming she means the guy who runs Harkins Construction."

"Um, yeah."

"Your mom knows him?"

Katie thought quickly. She hadn't wanted anybody at the station to figure out her connection with Jess, but thanks to dear old Mom, Ava already had an idea there was one. If Katie didn't come clean, Ava might start to speculate, which could be worse.

Moving closer to Ava's desk, Katie lowered her voice. "Listen, this can't become common knowledge."

"You can trust me." Ava's dark eyes gleamed.

"I'm serious. If this information gets out, it could be really bad for me."

"It won't get out."

"Good." She had to hope that Ava was highly motivated to continue the friendship and be invited to future happy hours with her and Cheryl. "Back in high school I dated Jess Harkins my senior year."

Ava blinked. "No shit. Wow. I guess it didn't work out, huh?"

"No, it didn't."

"Um, are you into revenge or something?"

"No." She kept telling herself it wasn't revenge. Justice was more like it. Protecting what was rightfully hers. "It's one of those crazy coincidences."

"But you said he was sexually compensating by putting up that high-rise. That sounds like you have an ax to grind."

"Remember, I didn't say he was. Dr. Astorbrooke—"

"I know, I know. But you're the one who invited her to be on the show. Was he that bad in bed?"

"Ava, I'm not going to answer that." Katie realized that in trying to prevent gossip, she might have made things worse.

Ava slumped back in her chair. "Which means you're not gonna tell me why you guys broke up."

"Nope. Sorry."

"Damn. I suppose your mom doesn't know either, or she wouldn't be saying he's a nice boy."

Katie wasn't so sure about that. A high percentage of mothers, including hers, would have been deliriously happy with Jess's prom-night decision. But Katie had been wounded beyond belief.

She'd thought she was over it, but then the Harkins Construction sign had popped up next door. The developer's long-range plan to demolish this entire block that included her grandmother's house was bad enough, but having Jess be a part of it added insult to injury. She wondered if he even remembered that her grandparents had owned this house.

She might not have told him. They'd been too busy making out in his old Ford Galaxie to talk about family history. She remembered feeling in control of her life again, recovered from the blows of losing her grandmother and the house she'd loved. She'd been sure she could make it all happen—become a disc jockey just like her grandfather, stay in Tucson where her friends were and lose her virginity to Jess on prom night.

But Jess, her first love, the boy she'd counted on to be crazy about her in the same way her grandfather had been crazy about her grandmother, had declined to cooperate with that last part. Once again she'd experienced that horrible loss of control over something important to her. She never wanted to feel that vulnerable again.

"I can see why you don't want anybody knowing he used to be your boyfriend," Ava said. "Don't worry. I'll keep quiet."

"I appreciate that more than I can say."

"No problemo."

"Thanks." Katie had no choice but to trust Ava with the volatile information. At least they hadn't gotten into the nitty-gritty of her sexual history with Jess—or rather, her lack of a sexual history. "Well, I'm outta here. See you at six tomorrow at Jose's. You know where it is, right?"

"Of course."

"Maybe we can sit outside on the patio."

"If I get there first, I'll snag a table for us." Ava sounded overjoyed to be included, so maybe she would resist the urge to gossip.

"Sounds good." Katie headed for the door, an antique that had been hand-carved in Mexico. Her grandfather had hauled it back from Nogales in the back of his pickup, along with several carved interior doors, as a special present for her grandmother. He was always doing things like that to show how much he loved her. And she'd been the same—baking his favorite desserts and haunting garage sales to find the old LPs he collected. They'd had something special going on.

Before Katie could reach for the knob, it turned with a soft click. A thrill of premonition ran down her spine as the door opened. A second later she was looking into a pair of angry brown eyes that brought a jolt of recognition. Her heart raced exactly as it used to back in high school.

Jess Harkins had caught tonight's show.

2

JESS HADN'T SEEN KATIE in the flesh in years…thirteen, to be exact. But he'd passed her picture hundreds of times while driving around town. A giant version of her gazed down from at least three billboards that he knew of. He'd had a few wet dreams involving Billboard Katie, and he probably wasn't the only guy.

Billboard Katie reclined on a red velvet couch while wearing tight black pants and a black blouse with a plunging neckline. Her blond hair hung from a center part and framed her face, which wore an expression that promised incredible sex. If she'd looked at him like that on prom night, he wouldn't have been able to resist her, but at eighteen she hadn't had the sophistication to pull it off.

Real-life Katie wore a sedate gray pantsuit and her hair in some girly arrangement on top of her head. There wasn't a hint of sexiness in her expression. Alarm would be more like it. Good. She should be alarmed.

A few minutes ago she'd sounded so carefree that he'd almost lost the urge to create a potentially ugly scene. A window at the front of the building had been left open, and as he'd approached, he'd recognized Katie's voice as she'd made plans to go out for margaritas tomorrow night.

Then his name had come up and the volume of the conversation had dropped considerably. Knowing she was discussing him with the receptionist had riled him up all over again.

But now that the moment was at hand, finding the right words was more difficult than he'd expected. He should have anticipated that. Making speeches had never been his long suit. Katie, on the other hand, had always been extremely verbal—she'd been senior class president and captain of the debate team.

But now the opening sentence had to be his. "We—" He stopped to clear his throat, irritated with himself for having to do that. "We need to talk."

"So talk," said a spiky-haired woman sitting behind the receptionist's desk. "Don't mind me."

Jess had completely forgotten someone else was there until she'd spoken. Apparently Katie still affected him to the point that he blocked out everything but her. That was an unwelcome discovery. He wanted to keep the upper hand in this interaction, and going gaga over Katie wouldn't help.

Katie glanced at the receptionist. "Ava, this is Jess Harkins, an old friend from high school. Jess, this is Ava Dinsmore, our intern from Pima College."

"Nice meeting you," Jess said.

"Same here." Ava studied him with interest.

"I think I left some files in the conference room," Katie said to Ava. "Would you check and see if they're there?"

"I'd be glad to, but I'd better watch the phones. We always get a bunch of calls for Jared's show on Friday nights."

"Good point. Then I'll go check. Jess, why don't you come on back with me so we can discuss this on the way?"

"It won't take long." Jess looked into Katie's eyes and was rocketed back thirteen years.

She'd been his first love, and he'd had so little to give her back then. He and his mom had moved their meager belongings from Globe to Tucson his senior year in high school. He'd been the new kid, the one with no money and big dreams, a quiet guy who'd been fascinated with Katie's gift of gab and her blond good looks. He'd envied her sense of belonging.

When she'd taken an interest in him, he'd been thrilled. They'd been a good combo because she'd done enough talking for both of them. To compensate for not saying much, he'd written her poems.

One he happened to remember now had compared her eyes to every blue thing he could think of, including his favorite stone-washed denims. God, he'd been pathetic. And a lousy poet. But her eyes still had the power to make him lose his train of thought.

"Just come with me," she said. "I need to take those files home tonight and we can talk on the way, kill two birds with one stone."

"That's not necessary. I just—"

"I think it is." She turned and started toward a hallway.

He wasn't about to deliver his ultimatum to her back, so he had no choice but to follow her like an obedient lapdog. This was not going the way he'd scripted it in his head. He was forced to pass the receptionist, who took no pains to disguise her curiosity.

"I think she still likes you," Ava said in an undertone.

He stared at her. Surely she didn't know that he and Katie…surely not.

Ava met his stare and shrugged.

Then again, no telling what Katie had revealed and to whom. But if she'd made her life an open book, she wouldn't be trying to keep this discussion private. He was confused, not a good state of mind for accomplishing his mission.

Katie paused at an open door and glanced back at him. "Jess?"

Instinct told him not to go in there. His plan had been simple—confront her at work and threaten legal action if she didn't stop her attacks on his project and on him. Especially on him. But now that he was here, his threat seemed silly and belligerent. Defensive. As if he'd taken the sexual-inadequacy thing seriously.

He should have thought of how it would look, him storming over here to demand better treatment. Instead he should have ignored the whole business. But he was into it now, and leaving without saying anything would make him seem even more idiotic. A firm stand was called for.

He walked toward the door Katie held open. She maintained her position, which forced him to walk past her into the room. Anyone would think she'd initiated this meeting with the way she'd taken charge. He needed to reverse the dynamics, but one whiff of her perfume—the same lemony scent she'd worn in high school—and his brain took a major hit.

Instead of planning his line of attack, he was wondering if she was seeing anyone. She wasn't wearing a ring—that much he'd noticed right away, though he shouldn't have taken the time to notice. Her comments on the air made it clear she considered him pond scum.

Focus, Harkins. He was good at that. Harkins Construction, built from scratch in only seven years, was a testament to his powers of concentration and his ability to bring others around to his point of view. Although he wasn't much of a talker, he'd somehow convinced loan officers to take a chance on him when he'd had no collateral except his will to succeed.

Maybe that's where he'd gone wrong. He'd barreled over here to issue demands instead of trying persuasion first. His temper had taken control. Katie had always had the power to arouse strong emotions in him—anger, joy, passion. Reasonable discussion wasn't normal with them, but that insight had arrived about thirty minutes late.

The conference room had a couple of windows covered with wood-toned plantation shutters, and a desert mural decorated one wall. The large oak table in the middle looked as if it had come from a Spanish hacienda. He could imagine how much Katie enjoyed working in this old adobe house. She'd always loved anything Southwestern.

When the door closed, he turned around. He and Katie were alone for the first time since the night of the senior prom. And just like that night, he couldn't figure out what to say to her.

As THEY STOOD FACING EACH other, close enough that they could reach out and hold hands if they chose to, Katie's heart hammered like a set of bongos. She'd always been fascinated by Jess's mouth. His full bottom lip had been so much fun to nibble on, and when he'd chosen to use that mouth on her breasts, she'd experienced a little bit of heaven.

She looked away from that tempting mouth. Now was not the time to be thinking of how much she'd loved making out with him. Being alone in the backseat of a car with

Jess used to make her forget where they were and what time it was. She'd blown her curfew more than once because of that.

She needed to take a deep breath, but that might telegraph her nervousness, so she made do with the small amount of air in her lungs. As a result, her voice sounded more breathy than usual. "I take it you're upset about my comments on the air recently," she said.

"Yeah, especially tonight's comments. You're making this personal and I don't like it."

Although she met his gaze, she was trembling and she didn't want him to notice. She gripped the back of a mission-style chair to steady herself. "Too bad. I call 'em like I see 'em."

"I'm not compensating for anything, Katie."

"That's not the way the experts see it."

He sighed. "Please just tell me why you're doing this."

That sigh almost defeated her. When they'd dated, that kind of heartfelt sigh had made her want to gather him into her arms and make everything better. At times Jess had seemed to carry the weight of the world on his shoulders, and she'd wanted to soothe away his cares.

But sigh or no sigh, he was still the man involved in destroying her legacy. "I want to save this beautiful old adobe building from the wrecking ball," she said.

"It seems like more than that." He paused and cleared his throat. "I think you're still upset with me about prom night."

"Of course I'm not," she lied. "That was ages ago." And she could still remember the thrill of parking with Jess. Her body remembered, too.

His eyes narrowed. "But your attack tonight was against

me, not the construction project. Don't tell me you honestly believe I'm building a high-rise because I have sexual hang-ups?"

She felt backed into a corner and said the first thing that occurred to her. "It's always possible, isn't it? Not that I care anymore, but I have personal knowledge that you won't finish what you start."

He took a step closer. "You don't know what you're talking about."

"I most certainly do." She refused to retreat and let him see that he was intimidating her.

With the kind of sexuality Jess projected, she didn't really believe he was compensating for anything by constructing that building. To be completely honest, it was very possible she'd unconsciously hoped that tweaking his male ego would bring exactly this result—Jess to her doorstep.

He moved even closer and his voice deepened. "Look, contrary to what you might think, contrary to what happened thirteen years ago, I don't have a problem with sex."

"Couldn't prove it by me." She could barely breathe, but what little inhaling she was able to do brought with it a heady combo of spicy aftershave and fresh soap. Her nose remembered how good he used to smell.

"What exactly do you want from me, Katie?"

She wanted him to kiss her, which was really stupid. What would that accomplish? "I want you to stop construction."

"That's not going to happen and you know it. You and VOR lost the fight. The building's going up, and taunting me isn't going to change a thing."

"Public opinion can be a powerful force. I'm working to sway it in my direction."

"Good luck. I plan to erect that building."

Gazing up at him, she remembered how silky his brown hair used to feel when she'd run her fingers through it. She had to white-knuckle the chair to keep from reaching for him. "Can you hear yourself? You plan to *erect* that building. If that isn't sexual symbolism, I don't know what is."

"It's only a building." Heat flashed in his eyes. "This is sex." He grabbed her by the shoulders and kissed her. Hard. Then he let go so fast she staggered.

She vibrated from that kiss like a plucked guitar string. Unable to form words—an unusual state for her—she stared at him and struggled to breathe. They simply gazed at each other for a long moment.

"Damn it, Katie." His voice was soft as a caress.

She matched his tone. "Damn you, Jess."

"You used to drive me crazy."

She gulped. "But not…crazy enough."

He studied her in silence for several seconds. "So this *is* about prom night."

She couldn't very well deny it now, not when all she wanted was another kiss. More than a kiss. She wasn't over him, not by a long shot.

"Katie, it wasn't the place. And now that I think about it, neither is this." He backed away and fumbled for the doorknob.

She leaned against the table for support. "You're leaving?"

"Damn it, we're in the KRZE conference room."

"And the door has a lock."

He hesitated, as if thinking that over. Then he shook his head. "But I'd like to see you again. I think—"

"What, so you can set me up and knock me down? Not bloody likely!"

He gazed at her mouth. "I'm sorry. I didn't mean for that kiss to happen."

"Don't worry, I'll never let it happen again." She folded her arms and hugged herself to stop the quivering. "I should have known nothing's changed."

"Of course it has. Everything's changed."

"Not when it comes to you and me. For some fiendish reason, you love to tease me with possibilities and then leave."

"We were kids then! It's different now."

"Is it?"

He gazed at her for a long moment. "Yeah, it's different. And I'll find a way to prove it to you." He turned and opened the door, then walked out and closed it softly behind him.

Shaken, Katie stared at the carvings on the heavy door without seeing them. Dear God, if Jess had been willing, she would have kissed him again. She might have done more than kiss him. Talk about stupidity squared.

This room wasn't soundproof, and Ava was down the hall, curious as hell. She might have heard something, although probably not. The door was heavy and the walls of this old building were thick. But if Katie and Jess had gotten carried away, Ava would have known.

Katie had been ready to commit professional suicide, and only Jess's refusal to continue had saved her. Edgecomb would cancel her show in a Tucson minute if he ever found out something like that had gone on in his conference room, especially involving the owner of Harkins Construction. And he'd be justified.

So Jess had made the right call, but that didn't mean he wasn't a rat. He should have tried to follow through and let her be the one to stop them. Which she might not have done, but that was beside the point. She was finished with him.

He might be the guy who could start her engine with only a feather touch. He might be more gorgeous now than he had been as a teenager—his body had filled out and his voice had a deeper, sexier timbre that gave her goose bumps.

But none of that mattered because he couldn't be counted on to need her beyond reason, the way her grandfather had needed her grandmother. Men were supposed to be victims of their hormones, not ruled by logic. Why did Jess have to be the exception?

Yep, she was through with him. And as for her comments on the air, they would only get more scathing. She'd talk Edgecomb out of worrying about the negotiations. And as for Jess, he could just deal with it.

JESS KNEW HE HAD TO TAKE bold action if he expected to square things with Katie. After that interlude in the conference room, he wanted things to be more than square. He wanted to finish—finally—what they'd started so many times before. She wasn't going to make that easy for him, though.

Tonight's episode told him she'd never forgiven him for refusing to have sex with her on prom night. She couldn't know how much that refusal had cost him, was still costing him. Countless times he'd cursed himself for being so damned noble. And he'd never found a woman to equal Katie.

But he hadn't wanted to cheapen their first real lovemaking by doing it in the back of a car. His mother had told him he'd been conceived that way. She didn't regret having him, but she thought sex should be conducted in better surroundings. He'd never forgotten that.

Make-out sessions with Katie were okay because they'd only been fooling around, indulging in heavy petting. But when she'd asked him to take her virginity, that was serious stuff. He'd wanted it to be special, and back then he hadn't had the resources to make it special.

On top of being broke, he'd underestimated the importance she'd place on his refusal. He hadn't expected her to take it as a rejection, but obviously her expectations of prom night had been huge. He'd let her down.

Apparently he'd done it again tonight by kissing her and leaving. But damn it, he wasn't about to take that kind of chance with either of their reputations. It was bad enough that he'd lost control and kissed her in the first place.

If things had progressed and word had gotten out, he might have weathered it. But the double standard was still around, and she might never have recovered her status in the community if anyone discovered she'd had a hot rendevous in the KRZE conference room.

He hadn't meant to tick her off, but when passion of the Katie kind gripped him, he didn't dare spend time discussing why he was going to leave. He had to get out of the situation before his control snapped and he actually did something dumb.

Katie hadn't understood that thirteen years ago, and she hadn't understood it tonight either. He'd have to pull out all the stops to convince her to give him another shot.

He planned to start by breaking into her apartment tomorrow night.

3

BY SIX O'CLOCK ON SATURDAY NIGHT, the temperature on the patio of Katie's favorite Mexican restaurant hovered around seventy-five degrees—perfect for sipping frozen margaritas. In the desert she might not have colorful autumn leaves to enjoy, but she had warm October nights and lime-flavored tequila.

Ava sat at a table by the fountain. For the occasion she'd dressed in a black scoop-neck shirt, long black skirt and combat boots.

"Good call, getting this table." Katie sat across from Ava. "This is my favorite spot, where you can hear the water splash."

"Splashing water produces negative ions," Ava said. "Negative ions elevate your mood."

"I could use that." Katie signaled a waiter. "Plus a margarita."

Ava nodded. "I could tell you were bummed when you left last night."

"Yeah, sorry I was so abrupt."

"It's okay. I understand."

"It was a tough situation. I—" Katie paused as the waiter approached.

The waiter did a double take. "Aren't you Crazy Katie?"

"Yes." Katie was used to being recognized once in a while, but it had happened a lot today. Everybody wanted to comment on her Friday night show, which had helped distract her from thinking about Jess.

"My friends and I think that big building is stupid, too." He winked. "We're not the kind of guys who have to prove ourselves, if you know what I mean."

"Glad to hear it. The more support I can round up, the better."

"I know a lot of people are behind you," the waiter said. "Anyway, I wanted to let you know. So what will you ladies have to drink tonight?"

"Two margaritas," Katie said. "And Ava, it's my treat."

"Aw, you don't have to do that," Ava said. "I invited myself."

"And you're also putting yourself through school. I remember what it's like to be twenty-two and broke. When you're pulling in the big bucks you can buy me a drink, okay?"

"It's a deal." Ava looked very happy at the prospect of an extended friendship with Katie. After the waiter left, she leaned closer. "Do you get recognized a lot?"

"Not a lot, but it happens. Today more people than usual have stopped me to say something about the show, which is good. I need ammunition for Edgecomb."

"Yeah, you do. And what's the situation with your ex? Is he still a turd?"

"Yep." Katie had figured the subject of Jess would come up, so she was prepared. "He didn't react well to Dr. Astorbrooke's theories, to say the least."

"Most guys wouldn't."

"What about our waiter? He seemed to agree with me."

"He's young. He's antiestablishment."

"Jared was fine with it."

Ava waved her hand. "Jared's a mensch. You couldn't ruffle his feathers if you hit him with a fire hose. But your guy—"

"Not my guy," Katie said.

"A figure of speech. Anyway, you're hitting this Harkins dude right where he lives. And he doesn't strike me as being that easygoing."

"He's pretty intense." *And girl, can he kiss.*

"I know looks aren't everything, but he's kind of cute in a Jude Law sort of way."

"I suppose." Jess was more than cute. He had a heart-throb quality that made her go all gooey inside. She'd had that reaction the minute she'd caught a glimpse of him in her senior English class and she'd been battling that same reaction ever since he'd kissed her nineteen hours and forty-six minutes ago. Not that she was counting.

Mooning about Jess had affected almost half of her weekend, but she was determined it wouldn't affect the second half. Having drinks with Cheryl and Ava was a good start. And speaking of Cheryl, she arrived at that moment, all smiles and curly red hair.

"Hey, guys!" Cheryl snagged a chair and settled her curvy little body into it. "Sorry I'm late. I played tennis this afternoon with this yummy-licious new guy from the law firm and I lost track of the time." She barreled on without taking a breath. "I would have called but my cell's acting weird. I need to trade it in for a new one, but I hate going through that, you know? New phone, new options, more buttons to figure out. So, I'm thinkin'—" She paused and looked at Katie. "What's so funny?"

"You." Katie was so glad she'd agreed to spend happy hour with Cheryl. Nobody could stay depressed with Cheryl around. "You have more energy than a four-month-old Chihuahua. By the way, this is Ava, the person you always get when you call the station."

"Hi, Ava! It's good to meet you at last! As for the Chihuahua thing, please don't tell me I look like one." Cheryl fluffed her short hair. "A Lhasa Apso's okay. You can compare me to a Lhasa Apso any old day, but a Chihuahua looks so sort of naked, you know? Which is cute in its own way, but I like to think that I have more— oh, here come your drinks." She batted her eyelashes at the waiter. "I'll have one exactly like that, please. Are you a student at the U of A? I ask because lots of the students wait tables here."

As Cheryl turned to launch into an animated discussion with the waiter, Ava leaned across the table toward Katie. "Is this normal?"

"Completely normal."

"I was afraid she was on something."

"No, she's just being Cheryl. Her courtroom rep is that she wins cases by talking the jury to death."

Cheryl swung back to them. "You're explaining me to Ava, aren't you? Ava, you might as well get used to my motormouth. I've been this way ever since I was fourteen months old and I'm not likely to change now. Katie and I recognized each other as soul mates in first grade and we've been involved in a conversational marathon ever since."

"Oh, you won that race a long time ago," Katie said.

"Hey, you hold your own, DJ girl. The point is, Ava, that Katie's used to me, but you're not. If you have something you need to say, just holler *shut up, Cheryl* and I'll do my best."

Katie laughed. "I just want to know if you passed up drinks and dinner with the yummy-licious lawyer so you could meet us for happy hour."

"I did, but that's a good thing. I liked being able to tell him I had other plans. It's good to have them thinking you have a full social schedule, you know? But in any case, I wouldn't have canceled this to go out with him, because I think that's just wrong. Men come and go but girlfriends are forever. Am I right?"

Both Katie and Ava nodded.

"Of course I'm right." She didn't break stride as her margarita arrived. "Listen, Katie, that show last night was dynamite. *Thrusting Skyward.* I loved it. What a zinger. I'm going to start field-testing the guys I date to find out how they feel about high-rise buildings. What a great litmus test. I hope that Je—I mean someone from Harkins Construction caught that program. I mean, the whole *crew* at that job site should be required to listen to that program. They think they're so macho with their hard hats and their tool belts, but every last man-Jack of them needs to reevaluate their—"

"Cheryl, it's okay." Katie didn't want Cheryl working herself into a lather trying to cover up her little slip. "Ava knows about Jess. In fact, he came to the station after the program last night."

Cheryl stared at her. "He *did?* What did he say? What did *you* say? What did he look like? Is he still hot? Is he married? Was he—"

"Cheryl, shut up." Katie grinned at her friend.

"Right. I'll drink my margarita. Start talking. Tell me everything."

Katie wasn't about to do that, but she sketched in the outline of the visit without supplying the detail about the kiss. She said they'd agreed to disagree and parted ways. His final vow that things were different and he'd prove it to her didn't make the edited version she gave Cheryl and Ava.

Cheryl obviously knew she was holding back. Katie could see it in the tiny smile that Cheryl hid behind the rim of her margarita glass. And when Ava left at seven because she'd promised to catch a movie with her usual crowd, Cheryl dropped all pretense of believing Katie's story.

"First we're going to order dinner and another margarita," she said. "And then you're going to tell me what *really* happened."

"I told you what happened!"

"Yeah, right. First we order, then you spill." Cheryl motioned the waiter over and they each chose a taco salad to go with the second margarita.

"Okay, you can begin anytime," Cheryl said after the waiter left. For once she didn't elaborate on that thought or spin off onto a million other somewhat related topics. Instead she sat looking at Katie with that same tiny smile, waiting.

They'd been friends for a long time, and Katie knew that Cheryl would get the truth eventually. She always did. Most of the time she talked a blue streak, which was her natural state, but once in a while, like now, she could create a silence so welcoming, so in need of being filled, that a person felt obliged to confess all. That tactic had also served Cheryl well in the courtroom.

"I'm..." Katie drained her margarita glass and set it down on the glass table with a solid click. Between Cheryl's open invitation to tell all and the tequila fogging her brain, Katie couldn't hold her tongue. "I'm still into him, Cher."

"I know."

Katie sighed. "I figured you would. So when he showed up, I was all quivery, like I used to get in high school. I didn't want Ava to hear what we said, so I brought him into the conference room and closed the door." The memory of that got her hot all over again.

"Who made the first move?"

"He did. He…kissed me." She tried to breathe normally, but telling Cheryl made her relive the moment when his lips had crushed hers, and all the powerful emotions created by that contact came rushing back.

"I take it you didn't run screaming out of the room. No, you don't have to tell me how you responded. I can see it in your eyes."

Katie groaned and covered her face with both hands. "I'm sure he could see it, too." She lifted her head and looked at Cheryl. "But he did the same damned thing as prom night! Got me going and then walked out the door, saying it wasn't the place!"

"Well, it wasn't! You could get fired for a stunt like that!"

"I know, but I wish I'd been the one to call a halt instead of him. I hate that I want him more. It's humiliating."

Cheryl fingered the stem of her margarita goblet. "If you should decide to give it another try, I'll bet you could turn the tables on him. You're not some shy little virgin now, are you? You have some experience and you—"

"You make it sound like I know all about sex. I don't. I do research for the show, but that doesn't mean I have a ton of practical knowledge. It's not like I've tried all those *Kama Sutra* tips, you know."

"I said *some,* not a ton. We've both had some, and I like to think we have a few tricks up our sleeve that can turn the average man into a groveling fool willing to do anything to keep us happy. You need to take the offensive with Jess if you want to regain some control. When are you going to see him again?"

"I'm not!" Katie thought the conversation was getting way out of hand. "He's too hot to handle, Cher. I lose my head when I'm with him. And besides, he's putting up this hideous building next to the station. How can I get involved under those circumstances? I'm putting him completely out of my mind."

"If you say so." Cheryl held Katie's gaze. "But I wonder how you're going to do that. With that building going up, he'll be in your face and on your mind for the next few months. You haven't gotten over him in thirteen years, so what makes you think you can get over him now?"

"I just will, that's all."

"I have a suggestion, but it's only a suggestion, mind you. Don't act on it unless it makes sense. But it seems to me that a better course of action would be to make some moves on this guy—on your terms. Get into bad-girl mode and tease him until you have him eating out of the palm of your hand."

"I don't want to—"

"For one thing, it would make you feel a whole lot better about past events," Cheryl said, pushing on, "and for another, if you end up having to tolerate that building next door, at least you'll have some compensation for the pain. I think it sounds like a fun project, personally. Jess is easy on the eye, and if you could pin him down, he might be one hell of a lover. That intensity of his tells me that he could give a woman—"

"Shut up, Cheryl." Katie hadn't interrupted because she had something to say. She had nothing to say. But the longer Cheryl talked, the more Katie wondered if she could pull off such an outrageous maneuver. And that was dangerous thinking.

JESS GOT KATIE'S ADDRESS from her mother, who was thrilled to hear from him and apologetic about the things her daughter was saying about his building. Jess told her not to worry about it, that he and Katie were in the process of working things out. Then he proceeded to Katie's apartment near the university.

Jess didn't let too many people know he could pick a lock in under five seconds. He'd learned that trick from his father, one of the few things his dad had taught him during his rare trips back to Globe. By the time Jess had hit puberty and wised up about his dad, Mel Harkins had stopped coming to see him.

That was just as well. Jess's mom had never admitted that her ex-husband was a thief, but Jess had figured it out by himself when she wouldn't let him keep the portable DVD player his dad had brought him. His mom had left that perfectly good piece of equipment at a bus stop because she'd said keeping it might get them in trouble.

Since his mom didn't talk about his dad, Jess didn't either. If anyone asked, Jess said his parents were divorced and his dad wasn't around anymore. But Jess had vowed to be the exact opposite of his father—steady and true. Picking the lock on Katie's apartment door made him feel uneasy, but he couldn't figure out any other way to guarantee he'd have her attention.

AS KATIE UNLOCKED HER apartment door, she heard music and wondered if she'd left her CD player on. Then she stepped inside and her adrenaline level spiked. At least a dozen thick tapers threw flickering light over her living room.

And there, lounging on her sofa, was Jess. She'd been thinking about him so much that she wondered if she'd conjured him up.

"Hi," he said softly.

That was the voice of a real man, no matter how much he looked like a fantasy. Jess Harkins, the guy who revved her up like no other, was actually sitting in her living room. Heart pounding, she backed up against the door. "How did you get in here?"

"Your mom gave me the address, and—"

"A *key?* If my mother gave you a key to my apartment, she and I need to have a serious discussion. I can imagine her telling you where I lived. I realize that she always liked you, but giving you a key goes way beyond—"

"She didn't give me a key. I wouldn't have asked for something like that, and I'm sure she wouldn't have given me one either. That would have been way too weird."

"And this isn't? You somehow appearing in my apartment without a key?"

"My, uh, dad taught me how to pick locks when I was a little kid."

"Cute." She never would have pictured Jess doing something like that. As her eyes adjusted to the dim light, she noticed a bottle of red wine and two crystal goblets sitting on her coffee table. "Did he also tell you that breaking and entering was illegal?"

"No, but I figured that out. I'm reasonably sure my dad was a thief. Probably still is."

That tidbit knocked her back some. In high school Jess had claimed his dad was a loner and a drifter, but he'd never offered this particular factoid. She had a feeling he didn't mention it very often, if at all. It wasn't something to boast about.

But he'd told her now, as if finally willing to trust her with the news. She fought the warmth of his subtle flattery. She didn't want to fall in with his plan—and there was obviously a plan. Candlelight and wine sent a definite message, and she was vulnerable to that message, too vulnerable for her own good. "I should call the cops."

"Don't."

"I don't know why I shouldn't. You have no right to break into my apartment and light a bunch of candles."

"That's true."

"Besides that, you have solid brass ones, buddy." *And solid muscles to go with them.* Even in the soft light from the candles she could tell how perfectly he filled out his knit polo. His biceps stretched the ribbed cuffs of his shirt-sleeves in a most satisfactory way. "For all you know, I could have brought a date back here tonight."

"I didn't think that was likely."

"What, you can't imagine me with a date?" In truth, she didn't go out much. Lately it had seemed so pointless. She'd begun to wonder if her sexual drive was diminishing now that she could see thirty in the rearview mirror, but Jess had dynamited that particular theory last night.

"I'm sure you have dates, but I—"

"Damn straight. I have so many guys hanging around I was forced to order date-tracker software last week so I can keep them all straight. I could have been out with one of a number of men tonight, and wouldn't that have been awkward—to come back home with someone and find you sitting here with all your candles lit, so to speak."

A smile touched his mouth. "I suppose candles are a phallic symbol, too."

"*Those* certainly are. Just look at them. They're penis-size. They're even flesh-colored!" And the subliminal message had been working on her ever since she'd laid eyes on them. She'd seen those fat tapers in a mall speciality store. They'd looked erotic at the time, and now, thrown into this Jess mess, they seemed blatantly sexual.

"The minute I saw them I knew you'd think that. That's why I bought them."

It occurred to her that he'd had to buy more than the candles, which wouldn't fit in ordinary holders. He'd been forced to add three wrought-iron candelabra to hold the thick tapers. Then there was the wine. She couldn't tell for sure but the label looked pricey. And those weren't her goblets either.

"You went to a lot of trouble and expense," she said.

He didn't respond. Instead he simply gazed at her with those brown eyes that had the power to melt the steel barriers she was frantically trying to build around her heart.

She took a deep breath. Cheryl had advised her to take control of the sexual dynamics, to get into bad-girl mode, but Cheryl had no idea how potent Jess could be. Katie was afraid that if she let herself surrender to this campaign even slightly, she'd be swallowed by a wave of sensuality that would rob her of all power.

No, she couldn't allow herself to be tempted by this man. "I'm afraid all that trouble was for nothing, though. I'll have to ask you to leave, Jess."

He stood, and for a minute she thought he might actually walk out the door. She would be relieved if he did that. Of course she would. As she'd told Cheryl, he was too hot to handle. She'd get burned.

But instead of leaving, he came around the coffee table until he was only about three feet away. Candlelight played over the strong planes of his face, and his powerful chest heaved. The years had been good to Jess, maybe because he had a job that required him to be active. His body was fit and tanned.

Thirteen years ago she'd only imagined what sex would be like with him. Now she had more experience to feed her active imagination. It didn't take much effort to picture getting naked with Jess. She grew moist and pliant as she thought about it. The trick was to stop thinking about it. Immediately.

Yet that was easier said than done. She'd never rejected a man as gorgeous as this. She didn't want to do it now, but it was for her own good. She had to be strong. "I mean it," she said. "I don't want to play whatever game you're playing."

He gave her another long look. When he spoke, his voice had a husky quality that spoke volumes about his state of mind. "Are you going to make me beg?"

As his words sank in, hot desire slid through her veins. Maybe she'd miscalculated. Maybe her own needs had blinded her to the force of his sex drive and they were more alike in their desires than she'd thought. It was a fascinating theory.

Did she dare test it? Could Cheryl be right, after all, that Katie had the ability to make him grovel? Now that would be sweet.

In the end, the chance to put him at her mercy was too irresistible to pass up. "Yes." Her heart beat wildly at the prospect. "I do believe I'm going to make you beg."

4

JESS SWALLOWED A SMILE of triumph, not wanting to push his luck. He didn't care how or why Katie was letting him stay, just so he got to. Just so he finally put an end to thirteen years of longing and frustration. The thought of making love to her nearly had him moaning out loud, but he swallowed that, too.

"Shall we have some of that wine you brought?" she asked.

"Great idea." He walked back to the coffee table and picked up the bottle.

Earlier he'd uncorked it and closed it again with a silver stopper that he planned to give her along with the crystal goblets. Maybe it was ostentatious, but he needed her to realize he was no longer that poor kid who'd worked long hours at Home Depot after school to help his mom financially and buy gas and tires for his old Ford.

"While you're pouring the wine, I'll change into something more comfortable."

He almost dropped the bottle. He'd never dreamed she'd be this cooperative. "Uh, sure. That would be terrific." Wow. This was turning out to be the best move he'd ever made. Breaking and entering had its advantages, after all.

After she left, he poured wine in both goblets and sat on her sofa wondering what *more comfortable* meant to her. Ads for Victoria's Secret swam through his fevered brain and he shoved his hand into his pocket to make sure the condoms were still in there.

If he didn't want to get an erection while he was waiting for her, he'd better concentrate on something neutral, like furniture. Earlier he'd prowled around her apartment and discovered a Southwestern theme throughout, with old pots and Native artifacts scattered everywhere.

Her coffee table and end tables were trimmed with saguaro cactus ribs, and she'd hung several small Navajo rugs on the walls. The turquoise sofa he was sitting on was the single spot of color in a room dominated by earth tones.

He wasn't particularly surprised. Her parents' house looked like this, and she'd told him how much she liked being immersed in Southwestern culture. He could relate. Now that he was able to afford the trappings, so did he.

But he still couldn't understand why she'd fought so hard to keep KRZE's adobe house from falling to the wrecking ball. Personally he couldn't see the point. By the time KRZE had finished modifying the place for its purposes, the place had lost whatever historic value it once might have had.

There were plenty of other structures like it, even a few with actual historic significance. He could think of several that would be ideal for KRZE's new location and weren't in danger of being bulldozed any time soon.

Maybe in the course of getting close to her—very close—he'd learn what made her such a passionate opponent of his project. It wasn't the main motivation for his decision to break into her apartment. His hormones were mostly in charge on that one. But as a side benefit, it wasn't bad.

And here came Katie wearing something filmy and

black. He was such a sucker for black, especially on a blonde like Katie. The outfit consisted of billowy harem pants that rode low on her hips and gave him a view of a black thong underneath, plus a low-cut black bra and a wispy jacket that might as well not have been there for all it covered up.

He began to sweat. As much as he wanted her, sitting here casually sipping wine would be torture. But then, maybe that was the idea. She had said she'd make him beg. He was ready to start with the begging ASAP.

Choosing a spot on the opposite end of the sofa, she settled into the plump turquoise cushions.

He picked up both wine goblets and reached over to hand her one. "Here's to renewing old acquaintances."

She raised her glass in his direction. "To settling old scores."

He blinked. Maybe she wasn't going to be as cooperative as he thought. "You're still upset about that prom-night thing, aren't you?"

She eyed him over the rim of her wineglass as she drank. Then she lowered her goblet. "I chose you to be my first. I was curious and excited and eager…but you didn't wanna. How do you suppose that made me feel?"

"Not good, but I had my reasons. I didn't—"

"Reasons you weren't able to share with a heartbroken girl, unfortunately. You'll be happy to know I found another candidate, though."

Now there was an unwelcome conversational thread. "I'd rather not hear about it, if you don't mind." He moved a little closer to her. Talking about her other lovers wouldn't help get this seduction under way.

"I'm sure you don't want to hear about it." She took another swallow of her wine. "But I think I need to talk about it."

"Why?"

"You're the only person in the world I ever thought of telling, and here you are, sitting in my living room. Of course, you don't have to stay and listen. You could always leave." She lifted her eyebrows.

"I'm not leaving." If she wanted him to suffer a little, he'd suffer. The payoff would be more than worth it.

"It was during my freshman year at the U of A. He was a jock, a basically nice guy but sort of clumsy. Still, he got the job done, and presto, I was officially a nonvirgin. You see, I wanted sexual knowledge." She paused. "I would rather have gained that knowledge with you," she added softly.

"Damn it, Katie, I know that! But I didn't want it to happen in the back of a car. You deserved more."

"So what do you think of an upstairs bedroom in a frat house with a party going on down below?"

Jess closed his eyes as if that would block out the image of Katie with some idiot college kid who didn't know what a treasure he had. Closing his eyes only seemed to make the picture more vivid, so he opened them again. "Obviously I screwed up and I'm sorry. I should have found a way to pay for a nice hotel."

"Were you a virgin, too?"

"Yeah. Yeah, I was. Clueless and scared I wouldn't make it good for you."

She cradled her goblet in both hands. "I'm assuming you're not a virgin anymore."

"No." He thought of his first time, which hadn't been particularly memorable either. Since then, he'd taken several women to bed and each time he'd tried to convince himself he was falling in love. It had never happened.

"I'm glad you're not a virgin. I wouldn't want to shock you."

He grew uneasy. After all, she did have that radio talk show. Last night she'd seemed like the woman he remembered, soft and eager for his kiss. But tonight she'd morphed into someone more experienced and sure of herself. She'd become Billboard Katie.

For all he knew, in the past thirteen years she'd turned into a wild thing who'd had more lovers than he'd had. Once upon a time they'd been equally green, equally ignorant of the nuances. Since then, she might have outstripped him.

"Changed your mind, Jess?" Her blue eyes issued a challenge.

He looked at her in that filmy black number and knew he'd never be able to live with himself if he walked away from this chance. He'd be a damned coward if he allowed himself to be intimidated and left now. "No, I haven't changed my mind."

"I'm glad." She finished her wine and held out her glass for more. "Because I'm looking forward to this."

His hand was unsteady, but he managed to pour her wine without spilling any on her turquoise sofa. "So am I." He resisted the urge to top off his own glass. He could use the Dutch courage, but more wine might dull his senses. Dulled senses wouldn't serve him well in the hours ahead. He had to stay sharp.

"So how did you happen to hear my show last night?"

He wasn't about to confess that he listened to her show almost every night. "I was out. I had the car radio on."

"Driving around by yourself?"

"Uh, no. I had a date."

She put down her wine. "Please tell me you didn't have a date waiting out in the car when you came to the station. If you did, then I don't know you at all, and this night is so over."

"I didn't have a date in the car. I drove her home before I came down to KRZE."

"Is she...someone special?"

"No." He took comfort in the way she'd asked that. She didn't want him to have a steady girlfriend any more than he wanted her to have a steady boyfriend. Once they got past the stage where she felt the need to hiss at him every so often, they would be fine. Once he could hold her in his arms, they would be even better.

"That's a relief," she said. "I don't want to poach on another woman's territory."

"I wouldn't want to poach on another guy's territory either." He wanted confirmation of what he suspected—that she wasn't serious about anyone.

"Oh, don't worry. You won't be poaching."

He could take that two ways. Either he had clear sailing...or she'd keep him moored at the dock. He'd go with the clear-sailing image. "Okay. Good." He edged closer to her. "You know what? You're too far away."

"Hold your position, Harkins."

He frowned. "What?"

"Stay where you are. It's been thirteen years, and I want us to have a chance to get to know each other before we start with the physical stuff."

That totally bewildered him. "Like what? You want to go out to dinner first?"

"I've had dinner, thanks. I think we should sit and talk."

"Well, okay, but at the station last night you seemed ready to—"

"Old tapes playing in my head is all. I'm conditioned from our high school make-out sessions to go up in flames the minute you kiss me, so I reacted that way last night, like Pavlov's dogs. But we're starting fresh, like you said. We never did much talking back then."

He remembered how they'd steamed up the windows with heavy breathing, not conversation. "No, we didn't." And he wished she'd save herself some work and continue with that earlier conditioning instead of trying to reprogram herself. Going up in flames when he kissed her sounded A-okay to him.

"So let's talk," she said.

"About what?"

"I'm curious to find out how much you know about sex."

He gulped. "I'm not sure what you mean by that. Besides, I'm more a man of action than words." Sweat began to trickle down his spine. He might be in way over his head with the new version of Katie Peterson. "If you're asking me to list techniques, I'd rather show you than try to describe them."

"Maybe it would help if I asked a few questions. For example, what's your favorite way to make a woman come?"

His chest tightened. He had a feeling she was going somewhere with this, but he couldn't figure out where, and that put him at a big disadvantage. He struggled to breathe normally. "Depends on the woman," he said.

She nodded. "Good answer. You don't have a one-size-fits-all approach to female orgasms. I like that."

"I hope you would…like that." Maybe she was putting him through some kind of test.

"Mmm." She ran her tongue over her lower lip. "I do

like to come. Sadly a girl can't always count on a man to take the time she needs, though."

"I would." He was getting hard, which might be what she'd had in mind when she'd suggested this conversation. "You'll have all the time you want. We can take it slow or we can take it fast. Whatever feels good." And he'd like to get started. Now.

"Are you in favor of oral sex?"

"Yes." He was in favor of it immediately. If she'd let him settle his head between her thighs in the next five minutes, he'd put an end to this conversation and replace it with her satisfied moaning. "I have an idea. Let's move the discussion to your bedroom."

"Not yet. First I need to convince myself that I'm going to have a climax with you."

"Trust me, you will. As many as you can stand. I'll be happy to take care of that." He didn't know if she could achieve multiple orgasms, but he'd give it his all. And his all was currently feeling very restricted inside his briefs. He had on far too many clothes. So did Katie.

"I like a sure thing." She put her empty wineglass on the coffee table.

His pulse rate jumped another notch. Maybe she was ready to head in the direction he wanted at last. He set his glass on the table, too. "I'll make you come or die trying."

"That sounds a little extreme." She turned and reached for one of the candles stuck into the candelabra behind her. "I wouldn't want to put that much pressure on you."

"I'd welcome the pressure." He glanced at her holding the lighted candle. "If you want candlelight in the bedroom, you might want to bring the whole thing. Those are a specialty size. They won't fit just anywhere."

"I know." She blew gently on the wick. The flame fanned out sideways and went out. "I know exactly where it would fit."

A possibility skittered through his brain. But she wouldn't really do that. Would she?

"These candles really do have an interesting shape." She turned the candle over and examined the blunt end.

Jess stared at her. She seemed to be almost caressing the thing, as if—no, surely not.

Then, looking straight at him, she slid the blunt end of the candle into her mouth.

His entire groin ached as she sucked on the candle. "Okay, I deserve that. I bought them." His voice cracked. "And in case you can't tell, you're getting to me."

She took the candle, shiny and wet, out of her mouth. "That was for my benefit, not yours."

"I don't—" He caught his breath as she leaned back against the cushions and opened her thighs. He'd missed a significant detail of the harem pants. They weren't stitched at the crotch.

Now he understood her diabolical plan, one that was sure to drive him out of his mind. And he'd been the genius who'd introduced candles into the equation. He had no one to blame but himself. He swallowed. "Katie, please…"

"Relax, Jess. Relax and enjoy the show."

TWO GLASSES OF WINE HELPED, but Katie still couldn't believe she was doing this. Some alter ego seemed to be whispering in her ear, urging her to be a very bad girl, bad enough to have Jess completely in her power, as Cheryl had suggested. From his expression, she was almost there.

In the process, she was arousing herself beyond belief. She'd never tried anything this daring with a man. "I'm not the little virgin you remember, Jess."

"No." His voice was a hoarse croak, and he clenched the sofa with both hands. "So I'm supposed to just…sit here?"

"That's the idea. Unless you want to leave."

Slowly he shook his head.

"Then let's get this party started." Her black thong was soaked as she pulled it aside. She'd begun planning this while she was changing clothes. Her harem outfit, bought in a moment of craziness more than a year ago, had never been on her body until now. Yet it was perfect for what she had in mind.

Using one of the candles he'd brought seemed like the perfect touch. He'd wanted her to think of them as sexual symbols, so could she be blamed for imagining the possibilities?

"Katie…I wish you'd let me…"

"I'm letting you watch." She barely recognized her own voice. It had turned sultry, the kind of voice that belonged to a woman who was teasing herself with the blunt end of a penis-size candle.

He groaned.

"Consider this a tutorial." Her breathing quickened. "Pay attention." She held his gaze as she pushed the smooth wax taper deeper. "You might learn something." *She* was learning that being a bad girl was more exciting than she'd ever dreamed. One slide of the candle and she was ready to come.

"All right." His tone was strained. "Now I'm begging."

Her words came out in a breathy rush. "For what?" She stroked slowly with the candle, wanting to prolong the moment when she had Jess completely enslaved.

"Don't make yourself come like that." His dark eyes glowed with an unholy fire. "Let me touch you…please." He made a move toward her.

"No. Stay there."

"I want to satisfy you, damn it!"

Her thighs started to quiver. "But this is guaranteed satisfaction."

"So am I!"

"I don't know that." She jiggled the candle faster.

His breath grew tortured. "I do! Katie…God…*Katie.*"

"I'm going to come, Jess." She moaned as the spasms started. "And it's good…so very…good…." Clutching the candle in both hands, she shuddered and slumped back against the sofa cushions.

Through half-closed eyes she gazed at him. He was a wreck. Her tender, caring side felt sorry for him and wanted to invite him back to her bedroom for the fun and games he'd hoped would happen.

But she needed to remember that he'd broken into her apartment expecting to seduce her. The wine and candlelight had been part of a carefully constructed plan. With the old Katie, it would have worked beautifully.

Instead she wanted to change the dynamics, and inviting him to her bedroom this soon would destroy all the progress she'd achieved so far. A bad girl wouldn't make things that easy for him. A bad girl would expect him to wait a little longer.

She took a calming breath and laid the candle on the coffee table.

Jess glanced at it before refocusing his gaze on her. "Now what?" he asked quietly.

"We make a date for tomorrow night."

Disbelief flashed in his eyes. "You're *sending me home?*"

"It's been a lot of years, Jess. I think we need time to get reacquainted, don't you?"

"Like this? With me watching you masturbate? What kind of ridiculous idea is—"

"You don't have to come back tomorrow night if you'd rather not."

A muscle worked in his jaw. "Maybe I won't."

"Suit yourself. But if you decide to, make it about six. I'll have some snacks for us. Maybe something...interesting."

"I'd expect cucumbers and bananas, at this rate." His gaze burned with frustration.

"I'm sure I can think of something more creative than that."

"No doubt you can. But you'd better know now that I plan to take part in whatever you dream up. Sex isn't a spectator sport, you know."

"You don't think so?" Her research for the talk show was really coming in handy. "Don't you ever use mirrors?"

"I—no."

"You should try it sometime. Mirrors give a whole new dimension to the action." She didn't know that from first-hand experience, but she had no trouble imagining it.

He studied her, his jaw tight. "I don't know what to make of you, Katie. I thought we could just have sex."

"It's not that simple."

"I can see that."

Maybe now was the time to dangle a carrot in front of Jess's nose. "In any case, if you decide to show up tomorrow night, I'll make you a promise."

"What's that?" He looked wary.

She smiled. "You won't be just a spectator."

5

JESS DIDN'T GIVE KATIE a firm answer as to whether he'd
show up at her apartment on Sunday night, but he was certainly firm in one specific area. He drove home with an
erection that refused to wilt. The image of Katie mastur-
bating with the candle followed him the whole way back
to his town house, which explained his continuing problem.

Once he was in the privacy of his own shower, he took
care of that immediate situation, but he still wanted Katie.
He would go back tomorrow night. No matter how much
he'd like to stay away and salvage his pride, he wouldn't
be able to do it. She had him hooked.

Besides, tomorrow night would be different. She'd said
so, and even if her plans didn't include full participation
from him, he'd make that happen. He wasn't going through
another session where he only watched while she brought
herself off.

But even as he ranted against her treatment, honesty
made him admit that he'd never been so aroused in his life.
She'd raised the bar on sexual excitement with that trick.
And when he finally made it to the major attraction with
her, the rewards would be greater because he'd been forced
to wait and required to suffer extreme frustration.

So, yeah, maybe her technique wasn't all bad. Once

was enough, though. She'd proved her point and he'd gone along for the sake of future benefits. He expected those benefits tomorrow night. Either they'd indulge in the whole enchilada or he was outta there.

KATIE WOKE UP AT DAWN the next morning feeling wired even though she hadn't slept all that well. Wearing her faded KRZE sleep shirt, she wandered into the living room to see if she'd dreamed Jess had been here. But the candelabra with the penis-size candles told her that he'd been there, all right, and she'd acted like a very bad girl.

Thank God she was scheduled to meet Cheryl at Sabino Canyon this morning for a run. She needed to work off some of her excess energy. After changing into shorts and a sports bra, she grabbed a water bottle, her cell phone and a visor before heading out of the apartment. Now that vehicular traffic had been banned from the canyon, the road into it made a perfect walking and jogging trail.

Cheryl was late, as usual, but Katie didn't mind. Strolling the parking lot at the entrance to the canyon, she listened to the birds and watched the sunlight move down the granite cliffs. She loved Cheryl, but her constant chatter tended to drown out the beauty of any natural surroundings.

"Here I am!" Cheryl's cheery greeting sailed across the parking lot like a kite in the breeze.

"Let's go." Katie set off at a jog. She still wasn't sure how much she wanted to say about last night, so she let Cheryl talk.

That was never a problem for Cheryl. She'd built up her lung power over the years and could carry on a conversation even when running. "I set my alarm," she said, "but it's a new Zen kind with a chime instead of an annoying ring, and it turns out that the cute little chime doesn't do squat to wake me up. I sleep like the dead, you know."

"I know." They'd roomed together in college. Some mornings Katie had resorted to a glass of water in the face to get Cheryl out of bed.

"I love to sleep. Do you know how important those REMs are to your overall health? People in this country are sleep-deprived, I tell you. Why, the SATs would probably go up amazingly if high school kids could only get enough sleep."

"Probably." Katie jogged up the trail and listened to Cheryl's dissertation on sleep, which morphed into a diatribe about lack of productivity in general before moving on to the values of massage, which continued with a list of the best places in town to get one.

Then unexpectedly Cheryl threw in a question. "Any word from Jess?"

Katie had been lulled into complacency by Cheryl's monologue and stumbled with her answer. "Uh, yes. He…when I got back last night, he…was in my apartment."

"*What?*" Cheryl stopped in the middle of the road. "What do you mean, *in* your apartment? Did you leave a window open?"

"No, he sort of…picked the lock."

Cheryl stared at her. "Jess? Our Jess?"

Katie explained about Jess's father while Cheryl stood there, uncharacteristically speechless. Then Katie added the info about the candles and the wine. After that she wasn't sure how much she wanted to tell, so she suggested they continue on up the trail.

Cheryl went along with that, but she kept glancing over

at Katie and shaking her head. "I still can't get my mind around Jess picking your lock. That's bizarre."

"I guess he figured if he knocked on the door like a normal person, I wouldn't let him in."

"Obviously! And he had seduction on the brain. So did he succeed?"

"Not exactly." Katie felt flushed, and it wasn't only because of the run. "I...teased him a little, pretended I would go along with him, but then...I didn't."

"Good for you! That's excellent. He had some nerve coming over there, breaking in and then expecting you to fall into bed with him. I mean, after his past history, he can't expect you to welcome him with open arms. I don't care if he floats your boat or not, you have to be careful with a guy like that. So now what?"

"I sent him home hot and bothered and told him he could come back tonight if he felt like it."

Cheryl whooped with laughter. "You are *such* a bad girl. That's awesome. Are you gonna do it tonight or make him wait?"

Good question. "I don't know if I should ever do it at all."

"Sure you should, once you've turned him into a quivering puppy eager for whatever you're willing to give. You'll be able to judge that when the time comes. But you need your reward after all he's put you through."

"I said I'd provide snacks tonight." Katie was already regretting that. "I'm no cook. Assuming he shows up—"

"Oh, he'll show up."

"What should I serve him?"

Cheryl jogged along in silence for a few seconds. "Fondue."

"Like what our parents used to make when we were kids?"

"Exactly. It's back in fashion. I'm sure you can find a couple of fondue pots at the mall. And melted stuff can be used for all kinds of interesting purposes."

"Omigod. Food sex." Katie got hot just thinking about it.

"See? I knew you could do the bad-girl thing."

"Yeah, but he might not even show up."

"If he doesn't, invite me over." Cheryl pulled her water bottle from her fanny pack and took a sip without breaking stride. "I love fondue."

JESS AND GABE SANCHEZ spent most of Sunday hiking the Finger Rock Trail in the Santa Catalinas. Over the years the relationship had gone way beyond employer and employee. They shared a love of strenuous hikes where the climbs were challenging and the conversation was kept to a minimum.

Jess hoped that pattern would continue, because he didn't want to talk about his ill-fated date with Suzanne, considering Gabe had arranged it.

No such luck. At the first water break Gabe brought up the subject. "You haven't said anything, so I guess Friday night was a dud, huh?"

"Pretty much." *Except for what happened later.*

"I don't get it. She's smart and she has a great body." Gabe took a swig of water. "If I hadn't found Tanya, I'd be asking Suzanne out. Did she do something to turn you off?"

"No." Jess wasn't going to mention that her laugh irritated the hell out of him. That was such a subjective thing. Someone else might think nothing of that laugh. "We just didn't connect. Maybe it's a lack of pheromones."

"Too bad. With all the trouble you've had with this job we're on, you need an outlet, man. I mean, first the protesters and now you've got Crazy Katie on your back."

"Yeah." Jess glanced away, afraid Gabe would pick up on his reaction to hearing Katie's name. "She's crazy, all right."

"Did you…uh…hear about her Friday night show?"

"Yep." Jess took a drink of water and worked to keep his cool. Talking about Katie made him think about tonight, which sent his pulse into overdrive and messed with his breathing.

"Me and Tanya heard it, too. Tanya likes the show because of all the sex info, but I told her we couldn't listen anymore after the way Katie insulted you Friday night. That was just wrong."

"Maybe she was only insulting the architect."

"Maybe so." Gabe repositioned his Diamondbacks cap. "I took it that she thought any guy involved in a high-rise project had issues. Including me, I guess." He grinned. "Fortunately Tanya said I have nothing to be compensating for."

Jess laughed. "I'm sure you're quite the stud, buddy."

"So she lets me believe. Anyway, I thought that program was cold, man."

"There's no point in taking that kind of crap seriously."

"I guess you're right." Gabe stuck his water bottle into his backpack. "But it would be awesome if you had a chance to show Crazy Katie that her theory is all wet." He hoisted the backpack onto one shoulder. "If you know what I mean."

"Um, yeah." Jess had in mind to show Katie that tonight, in fact.

"Not that you'd want to crawl in bed with a smart-mouth like her. But it would be sweet to make her eat her words, wouldn't it?"

Jess couldn't agree more. "It sure would."

KATIE HAD NEVER SPENT SO much time shopping for groceries in her life. First of all, the groceries she bought took some thought, considering she was planning a bad-girl episode. Second of all, people kept stopping her to talk about her Friday night show. That was gratifying, but she really wanted to concentrate on her purchases.

She came home with two fondue pots, various kinds of cheese, a loaf of French bread, fudge sauce, chocolate bars, whipped cream and strawberries. She'd also picked up another bottle of the wine Jess had brought the night before. In the process she'd discovered that it was indeed pricey.

By five-thirty she'd showered, dressed and begun cutting the French bread into cubes for the fondue pot. She'd lit the Sterno underneath both pots sitting on the coffee table in her living room. With cheese melting in one pot and chocolate simmering in the other, her apartment smelled great.

If Jess decided to show up, she was prepared. She'd never been so prepared in her life. Tonight's activities would also take place in her living room. The bedroom seemed like such a cliché, anyway, and she didn't have a good place to set up for fondue...or the activities she'd planned would go along with the fondue.

She'd dressed for maximum titillation—a short flowered skirt with a thong underneath and a white halter top with nothing underneath. No shoes either. Sensuous music with a faint tribal beat played on her sound system. The blinds were closed and the candles—Jess's flesh-colored penis candles—were lit. She'd created quite a little den of iniquity, if she did say so.

How strange to be planning a night of seductive pleasures for the man whose current project she hoped to torpedo. But judging from the wine and the silver stopper he'd left, Jess was obviously doing very well. He could replace this project with another one. Katie's grandmother's house was irreplaceable.

At some point she'd probably tell Jess why this little house was so important to her, but she didn't think it would make any difference. Jess was bound by contract to finish the high-rise. The only way he would not finish it was if Livingston Development halted construction because the project was getting too much bad PR.

Realistically Katie knew she could be shooting in the dark on that one. But she had to try. Once the high-rise was built, the station's signal would be gone and the owners would definitely sell. Sure, she could continue to do her show from another location. Being a DJ suited her perfectly and she wasn't about to give that up, but she also wouldn't let the little house be demolished without a fight.

In the meantime she planned to take Cheryl's advice and find a way to ease her pain. She didn't know if she and Jess had a future or not. After living on her own for so many years, she'd grown fond of being single. No man had tempted her to think in couple terms.

No man had been Jess either.

And he was due to arrive in a matter of minutes, if he arrived at all. She'd told herself that it didn't matter, that she'd be fine with spending the evening with Cheryl watching a rented video. But that wasn't exactly true.

As she carried the basket of French-bread cubes and the fondue forks into the living room, she was well aware of the time. She went back for the wine and the goblets he'd brought over. Five minutes would tell the tale. He wouldn't be late, unless he'd changed drastically from the punctual guy she'd known.

Her tummy felt jumpy and her pulse rate was definitely faster than normal. She surveyed her living room, checking all the details as the minutes ticked slowly by. Besides the groceries today, she'd stopped at Target for two tan-colored beanbag chairs, which sat next to the coffee table. The vinyl surface should be perfect for, well, anything.

Now that the moment had almost arrived, she couldn't decide if she wanted the doorbell to ring or not. Tonight would be another test for her to see if she could maintain her bad-girl persona. If Jess stayed away, she could convince herself that she would have passed that test. But if he walked through that door...

The bell chimed at exactly six o'clock. Katie forced herself to take a long, slow breath before going to answer it. She was shaking, but maybe he'd be so busy taking in the scene she'd created he wouldn't notice.

She opened the door to find him in jeans and a white dress shirt unbuttoned at the neck. And he was holding a single yellow rose. Just like that, she was a puddle of emotion. Thirteen years later and he still remembered.

On their first date he'd brought her a yellow rose. Then he'd spent five minutes apologizing because all the red ones had been gone when he'd stopped by the grocery store, which was the only florist he could afford back then. He'd had to settle for the yellow one or downgrade to a carnation, which had seemed tackier.

She'd raved so much about that yellow rose that it had turned into their private joke. After that he only brought her yellow roses, including the last time he gave her flowers— when he'd presented her with her prom corsage. Even today, she couldn't look **at a yellow** rose without thinking of Jess.

"Thank you." She **took the rose,** noticing that this flower had probably never **seen the in**side of a grocery store. The bud was barely starting to open, and not a single petal was torn or bruised. The thorns had been expertly clipped.

Yet today was Sunday. Florists weren't normally open. Maybe he had a friend in the business and he'd called in a favor. To think he'd gone to that much trouble boosted her ego quite a little.

She stood back so he could enter and then closed the door again. "This is really beautiful, Jess."

"It seemed appropriate."

So he'd intended to boost her ego. Maybe he planned to use that to his advantage, too. She'd have to stay on her toes with this guy, who knew all the right buttons to push. His self-confidence seemed to be back in spades, and he obviously expected her to have sex with him tonight. She could see it in his eyes.

But she still wanted to know how he'd scored this rose today. "If you don't mind my asking, where did you get such a perfect rose on a Sunday?"

He shoved his hands in the pockets of his jeans. "Out of somebody's backyard. Where else?"

She wouldn't have believed him, except that he had broken into her apartment the night before. "Are you saying you actually stole it?"

"Believe me, the owner doesn't care." He gazed at her in total unconcern, as if stealing roses was something he did all the time.

"Well, *I* care. That's something we once would have agreed on, Jess—respecting other people's property. This is a very sentimental thing to do, but I hate to think that you vandalized someone's rosebush in order to make this gesture."

"Want me to return it?"

"That wouldn't accomplish anything, now would it? You can't exactly tape it back in place now that the damage is done."

He laughed. "Okay, okay. My backyard. My rosebush."

"Oh." How interesting. She shouldn't ask, but she couldn't help it. "Did you plant it?"

"Yeah, as a matter of fact."

As she gazed at him, she told herself not to read too much into that. But it was hard not to see the significance. "Any particular reason?"

He shrugged. "I'm partial to yellow roses."

She still didn't know if that had anything to do with her or not. She might have started him down that path, but that didn't mean he'd thought of her when he'd picked out a rosebush for his backyard. Or that he thought of her every spring and fall when it bloomed. It could be a giant coincidence that he had a yellow rosebush blooming in his backyard. But he was no dummy, and he could be working that yellow rosebush angle for all it was worth. Therefore she shouldn't allow herself to be too bowled over by his gift.

"Something smells good," he said.

"Fondue." She swept a hand toward the coffee table. "Have a seat in one of the beanbags while I get a vase for the rose. You can pour us each some wine if you want."

He glanced at the beanbag chairs. "I don't remember those from last night."

"Good memory. I didn't have them last night. I bought them this afternoon."

"For tonight?" He looked a little less sure of himself.

She lifted the rose and took a deep sniff to hide her smile. "Yes. For tonight. They're perfect for eating at the coffee table and they have the kind of surface that will take...anything."

He swallowed. "You mean if we spill food and stuff." He looked decidedly wary.

"Right. And stuff." She walked back to the kitchen, afraid if she stayed any longer she'd start to laugh. She was much better at this bad-girl routine than she'd given herself credit for. She'd knocked Jess off balance again, and it had been so easy.

6

JESS THOUGHT HE'D PREPARED himself for the sexual impact of being back in Katie's apartment. But no guy could really prepare for this barrage of—how could he describe it?—bordello lite.

Sure, he'd set the scene last night with music and wine and candles, but he was an amateur compared to Katie. She's bought *beanbag chairs,* for crying out loud. Who would think of them in connection with sex?

Yet put them together with the coffee table full of goodies and that short skirt and skimpy halter she was wearing, and the beanbags seemed to be all about sex. They were moldable. He'd never considered that before.

Beanbags were the ultimate surface for sex, come to think of it. You could bunch them any which way you wanted to get the best angle for…almost anything his heated imagination could think up. And speaking of *up,* he was getting there fast, and he'd only just arrived on the scene.

That could be a problem. They had the whole evening ahead, and from the looks of this setup, Katie planned to drag out the action. He wanted to prove to her that he was cool with the leisurely approach to sex. She might not believe him if he sat there with a constant woody.

Women had it easier. They could practically have a climax and nobody would be the wiser if they wanted to disguise their reaction. A guy couldn't hide bubkes, especially while sitting on a beanbag next to a coffee table.

So instead of sitting, he poured the wine and decided on a stroll around her living room to see if that helped mellow him out. He already knew the territory but had been too nervous to examine it closely.

She had a shelf system against one wall that held woven baskets, clay pots and kachinas. A framed picture of her folks was there, too. The light was dim in the room, but he still recognized them. Don and Joanne Peterson, nice people. This must have been taken recently, because Joanne had looked a lot like this when he'd seen her yesterday and asked for Katie's address.

After staring at the snapshot of Don and Joanne for a while, he was in better control of himself. Nothing like the smiling faces of a woman's parents to kill the sexual urge. Beside that picture stood one of Katie's older brother, Dennis, with a pretty brunette and a little baby.

So she was Aunt Katie now. He wondered if she'd ever thought of settling down herself. Come to think of it, she could have been married and divorced. Most of their classmates from high school were married, and some were on second marriages by now. Whenever he ran into high school friends, they always asked him what he was waiting for.

It might be more a question of *who* he was waiting for. Until seeing Katie at the station Friday night he hadn't realized how much she'd influenced his choices in women. After her he'd dated primarily blondes, but none of them had seemed quite right. Then he'd come face-to-face with Katie and it felt as if a gear had finally meshed that had been out of alignment for years.

He honestly hadn't thought about his motives for planting a yellow rosebush until today, when he'd looked at it and realized that he should take her one of the buds. Unconsciously he must have planted that bush because of his memories of her.

"Dennis married a girl from New York, so they live back there now," Katie said as she walked into the room and set the vase on an end table. Then she came over to stand beside him. "That's Dennis and Julie with my niece, Emma."

"Cute kid."

"Adorable." Katie reached out and turned both pictures facedown on the shelf.

There went Jess's sexuality damper. "Why did you do that?"

She glanced up at him and smiled. "Makes the room less crowded, don't you think? Let's go have some fondue."

Although Jess had a feeling they would enjoy more than fondue sitting in those beanbag chairs, he pretended that they were pulling up ordinary chairs for an ordinary snack. "Why not?" But as he lowered himself onto the pliable surface and began to imagine the possibilities, he must have groaned or whimpered or something.

"Are you okay?" Katie sat in the chair next to him.

"I'm just dandy." The graceful way she eased into the scrunchy seat reminded him she was once a cheerleader who could do the splits like nobody else on the squad. The guys at school used to make bawdy jokes about that, which had caused Jess to get in a couple of fights to defend her name. Everyone on campus might have thought he and Katie were having sex, but he'd known differently.

Now he was debating the wisdom of his course of action back in high school. If he'd accepted Katie's offer on prom night, he wouldn't be here feeling at a decided disadvantage with a woman who'd become extremely worldly. If he'd had sex with Katie thirteen years ago, they might have stayed together.

And yet…staying together might not have been the best thing for them. He could have done something stupid and asked her to marry him before either of them were ready for that. They'd both needed time to spread their wings.

Katie picked up her wineglass. "Here's to old friends…and new experiences."

"Sounds good." He touched his glass to hers and took a long swallow of the wine. "I've never had fondue before." He didn't think that's what she meant by *new experiences*, but he'd play dumb.

"Not even when you were a kid?" She gave him a long fork and passed over the basket of bread cubes.

"I don't think so." He would make book on it. His mother hadn't had the time or money for froufrou grocery items. They'd been lucky to have a half pound of ground beef and a box of Hamburger Helper.

But if he ever had fondue again, he'd associate it with Katie sitting in the beanbag chair, her skirt hiking up each time she moved and her nipples outlined against her halter top as she handed over the fork.

Wait a minute… It wasn't even slightly cold in this room, and the soft, seductive light from the candles made everything hazy. If he could see her nipples against the cotton material, then she was definitely excited. He felt better knowing that. He took the fork and stabbed a bread cube from the basket.

"My parents had a fondue pot when I was a little kid." She speared some bread and leaned toward the one holding melted cheese. "Then the craze ended and they sold the pot at a garage sale. Now fondue is in again. I thought we should try it."

Jess caught about half of that speech because mostly he was watching what happened when Katie leaned over. Her halter top gaped open, and he was ready to forget fondue and go for something more satisfying.

"The idea is to swirl your piece of bread through the cheese." Katie dragged her fork through the creamy yellow mixture.

Jess could sit and watch her do that forever. As she moved, so did her breasts. Then she picked up the bread cube dripping with cheese, leaned over the pot even more and opened her mouth.

She was putting a cheese-saturated bread cube in there, not a candle, but Jess associated her mouth with sex all the same. She'd apparently permanently imprinted the message in his brain, so that anything to do with her mouth equaled sex.

While they'd been dating, he'd never had the nerve to ask her to go down on him. Now, after last night's question about oral sex followed by the candle incident, he couldn't seem to think of much else. The candles burning in the room didn't help, and the music she'd chosen was even sexier than the CD he'd put on the night before. The faint sound of jungle drums seemed like the perfect rhythm for thrusting.

"Mmm." She chewed the piece of bread and swallowed it. "Not bad. Try it."

He wasn't the kind of guy to leap on a woman and start tearing at her clothes, but this atmosphere was rapidly changing his normal disposition. In spite of that, he'd restrain himself. He'd always been proud of his self-control.

Time to spear a bread cube and fondue something. While bending closer to the melted cheese, he was reminded that sweats would have been a better choice than jeans. The denim pinched, especially with the ever-present swelling going on underneath it.

With Katie watching, he stuck the bread in the cheese and swirled. "It feels like dipping a brush in a bucket of high-grade enamel."

She laughed. "I hope it tastes better than paint."

He wondered if she had any idea what he longed to taste right now. It wasn't a cheese-laden bread cube, that was for sure. Leaning closer, he managed to get the dripping cube in his mouth.

"How do you like it?"

He chewed and swallowed. "Not bad. A plate of nachos would have been a more efficient delivery system, but this is decent enough."

"Spoken like a typical guy. Maybe I should have bought beer instead of wine."

"Right. And then we could power up your TV and watch the Cardinals play football."

She looked crestfallen. "Do you want to?"

"No, Katie. Not even slightly." *I want to strip you naked and kiss every inch of your body—a fantasy that's haunted me for years.*

"Okay." Her expression brightened.

"I'm not much of a sports fan. Maybe it's because I never had time to play." Indoor sports, that's what he was talking about. Bouncing together on an innerspring. There was a event worth training for.

"But you came to most of the games in high school."

"As many as I could with my work schedule. The thing

is, you were a cheerleader." He could still picture her in that short skirt, about the same length as the one she was wearing now.

She'd had some sexy moves out there on the sidelines. He wondered if she could still rotate her hips the way she could back then. Before the night was over, he intended to find out.

She paused in the act of spearing another bread cube. "You only came to the games because of me?"

"Pretty much." He took another drink of his wine. "You didn't know that?"

"I thought…well, I thought you liked sports and seeing me was a bonus." Her fondue fork remained poised in midair, apparently forgotten.

"I liked *you* and seeing the game was a bonus." Actually he'd loved her desperately. Because he tended to use words sparingly, he probably hadn't told her often enough. Broadcasting his teenage passion now seemed kind of sappy, so he'd modified the wording to save them both embarrassment.

"I…liked you, too."

For a moment, as he gazed into her eyes, he imagined regret lurking there. Well, she could join the club. He should have been her first lover. He should have worked it out so that had happened.

Then she smiled, and the regret seemed to disappear. "Come on, Jess. Have some more fondue."

KATIE HAD NURSED HER grudge against Jess for so long that trying to see him in a different light was giving her mental eyestrain. She'd convinced herself that she hadn't been all that important to him.

His refusal to have sex with her on prom night had seemed like solid evidence that he hadn't wanted to get tied down to her. The way his life had turned out since then had given her more proof that he'd had big goals for himself after graduation. She'd imagined that his personal plans hadn't included a close relationship with her.

Maybe she'd been wrong. Maybe she'd been far more important to him than she'd imagined. She'd pictured herself as the most invested of the two of them. What if that hadn't been true?

In any case, she was in a great position to find out. A desperate man would be more likely to bare his soul, so turning Jess into a desperate man was still in her best interests. She'd already learned some things. She wanted to learn much more.

Telling her that he'd gone to high school games only for her had made her dangerously warm and mushy inside. But if she allowed herself to think about that too much, she might become too cooperative and make everything easy for him. Cheryl had counseled against that.

He might not be the louse she'd wanted to believe, but he was still showing signs of traditional male thinking, expecting sex would automatically happen. She'd allowed him to lapse into his comfort zone while eating cheese-covered bread cubes and drinking wine. He might be under the impression that this would morph into a typical bedroom scene.

She wasn't nearly ready for that. Frankly it scared her a little. One taste of bedroom sex and she might transform from a kick-ass bad girl into his willing slave. Thirteen years ago she'd been heading down that road, and she wasn't about to let history repeat itself.

Time to shake things up. "Let's switch to chocolate," she

said. "That's where the strawberries come in." She pushed herself out of the beanbag. "I bought some whipped cream to go with this, too. Let me get it."

"All right." The wary look had returned to Jess's dark eyes.

Good. Cheryl would approve of her keeping him off balance. Last night she'd had him begging, but she wasn't nearly there tonight. She'd been way too easy on him so far. With this next stage she'd turn up the heat and see how Mr. Self-Control handled her newest suggestive behavior.

In the kitchen she grabbed the can of whipped cream from the refrigerator and a bowl from the cupboard. She returned to the living room shaking the can vigorously. She knew that created a great breast shimmy and she wanted him to get an eyeful of jiggle. Men were notoriously susceptible to that, which she'd counted on when she'd chosen to wear the halter top.

Sure enough, his eyes grew wider the longer she shook the can. Then his throat moved in a quick swallow and he ran his tongue over his lips. Excellent. He was primed for the next step.

After walking over to the coffee table, she set the bowl down and stood between the two beanbags so that he'd have no trouble looking up her skirt when she leaned over. "Are you ready for this?"

He swallowed again. "I…guess."

"Here goes." Bending at the waist so her skirt rode up good and high, she popped the top on the whipped cream and squirted a high, fluffy mound of it into the bowl. "There." Still holding the can, she turned and eased back into the beanbag.

Jess looked hypnotized. She had the urge to snap her fingers under his nose to see how startled he'd be. But she had a better way to get his attention.

"This is a great brand of whipped cream." Facing him, she ran her tongue around the nozzle. "It tastes so good that sometimes I suck it straight from the can."

Instantly his gaze was trained on her.

"There's always a little left in there after it squirts out." Rounding her lips, she sucked gently as the sweet cream slid over her tongue.

Jess was transfixed, not moving a muscle.

And that was exactly how she wanted him. "If I crave more, and I often do, then I can suck and press the nozzle so the whipped cream comes right into my mouth." With a little whoosh of compressed air, she filled her mouth with whipped cream. "Mmm." She let some dribble out and caught it with her tongue.

"Katie." His voice rumbled low in his chest.

She adopted an air of innocence. "What?"

"You know what."

She held out the can. "Want to suck on it a little while yourself? It's fun to do."

He ignored the outstretched can. "You're something else."

"So I've been told. Let's each have a strawberry, shall we?" After setting down the can, she picked up her fondue fork and stabbed the biggest, plumpest strawberry in the bowl. As she dipped it into the warm chocolate, she glanced over at Jess.

He still hadn't moved, and his stare was hotter than the Sterno flame.

She pretended not to notice. "What's the matter, lost your fork?"

"No, just my mind when you pulled that last stunt."

"It bothered you?"

"Hell, yes, it bothered me. You know perfectly well what you were doing with that can of whipped cream."

She lifted the strawberry from the chocolate and turned it gently until it stopped dripping. "I certainly do. I was enjoying it." She dunked the chocolate-covered strawberry in the mound of whipped cream.

"You were mimicking something else."

"Was I?" She licked the whipped cream and chocolate off the strawberry.

"You want me to imagine what it would be like if you…did that to me."

"Did what?" She held his attention as she sucked on the tip of the strawberry.

"That." Waves of intensity rolled off him as his gaze bored into hers. "And you're not going to do it either, are you? You're going to drive me crazy thinking about it, but you're not going to actually—"

"I might." She nibbled on the strawberry.

He groaned.

"If you ask me nicely."

"You mean if I beg, don't you?"

She finished the strawberry and stuck her finger in the bowl of whipped cream. "Something like that." Then she licked the whipped cream from her finger.

"Well, I won't."

"No?" She gathered more whipped cream on the tip of her finger and sucked it off. "Too bad. You look like you could use some relief. But if you're not interested, I'll just have another strawberry." She speared one from the bowl. "You should try this. They're great."

"Damn it, Katie, it seems backward to start with you

going down on me. I think we should have regular sex and then—"

"You know what, Jess?" She dipped the strawberry in chocolate and then in the whipped cream. "Maybe you should just relax and take what comes your way."

7

JESS HAD NO FRAME OF reference for what was happening. He was used to being in charge of what went on between him and a woman. Oh, sure, he'd been seduced before, but not like this, without body contact. With no kissing or fondling, he had zero leverage for influencing the action. That took him way out of his comfort zone.

And speaking of discomfort, Katie had used the power of suggestion to produce the most painful erection of his life. Something had to give—either his ego, his pride or the stiff denim constricting his penis. Possibly all three.

He could see now that she'd been setting the stage for this the night before, when she'd sucked on the candle. She'd focused his attention on that particular activity, then and now, until it seemed like the next logical step for them to take. Never mind that he'd never before imagined such a sequence of events.

And he was in desperate need. Still, saying the words wouldn't be all that easy. He drained his wineglass while she continued to make love to a strawberry. Finally he set the glass on the coffee table and took a deep breath. God, he ached.

"Katie, please come over here."

She put down her fondue fork. "You need something?"

"Yes." The thought of what she was about to do made him shake. "Yes, please."

She slid from her seat and onto her knees in front of his chair. The move positioned her very conveniently between his legs. "Asking for what you want can be liberating."

He closed his eyes. "Then liberate me, Katie. Please liberate me."

"By doing what?"

He opened his eyes to gaze at her. "You're going to make me say it?"

"I want us to be clear."

"I…" He couldn't go back now, not with this kind of pressure building up in his groin. "I want…" Pausing to clear his throat, he started again. "I want you to unzip my jeans." God, he was trembling like an aspen in the wind.

"I can do that." But as she reached for the tab, she paused. "This would be easier if you'd lean back."

He hadn't been aware of hunching forward, straining eagerly toward her. Maybe he needed something else before she pulled that zipper down. "I want you to kiss me."

She glanced up at him. "On the mouth?"

"Hell, yes, on the mouth. What did you think I…oh."

"Okay. On the mouth." She rose up on her knees and clasped his face in her warm hands. "One kiss, coming up."

"You'd better believe it." He covered her hands with his and leaned forward, aiming for that mouth tinged with strawberry juice, that mouth that had sucked down a whole helping of whipped cream, that mouth which would soon—no, he couldn't think about that yet or he'd go crazy.

She drew back. "Jess, I'm supposed to be kissing you, not the other way around."

He groaned in frustration. "Do you have to call all the shots?"

"Wouldn't that be fun for a change?" She looked into his eyes.

He could easily get lost in the hot blue depths of her eyes, but he wanted to work this out in his head, so he forced himself to concentrate on the matter at hand. "Why can't we just let things happen?"

"*We* never just let things happen. *I* was the one who let things happen. You were the one who directed everything, the one who decided what came next or what didn't come next."

"I was only trying to—"

"It doesn't matter if your intentions were noble or not. The result was the same, with me in the passive role. If you want to have sex with me now, after all this time, I want you to take the passive role. Those are my terms."

The jungle drums in the background coaxed him to abandon the argument and let her have her way. But he'd been born with a stubborn gene. "You're making a simple thing complicated."

"That's what you say." She smiled. "I say I'm making a complicated thing simple...for you, at least. You don't have to do anything or think about anything. Just enjoy."

"What if I *enjoy* taking a more active role?"

Her smile broadened. "Oh, I'm sure you do. I'm sure you love making things happen instead of having them happen to you. But that isn't the way this will work."

"Ever?" As he heard himself say it, he realized the implication of that one little word. So far he and Katie had lived this from moment to moment. Neither of them had anticipated more than a few hours into the future. He'd just done that.

She paused as if assessing the meaning of that word. "I don't know," she said at last. "We'll have to see how this goes, won't we?"

And that's when he understood exactly where they were. She needed to find out whether he could allow her to be in charge. If he could, then they'd go from there. If he couldn't—he would be out the door.

He'd come over here tonight with a different idea. In his version, he'd give Katie some teasing room but then he'd take over and press the advantage he'd always had—the ability to make her want him. Instead she was pressing her advantage—the ability to make *him* want *her*. It was a subtle difference he'd missed until now.

"Can you handle it?" Still cupping his face in both hands, she gazed into his eyes. "You can still back out."

"That's not an option. Not now."

"Then hold still. I'm going to kiss you."

Not meeting her halfway wasn't easy, but he did it. As her lips settled over his, he closed his eyes and forced himself to do nothing aggressive. To his amazement, being kissed was a whole different thing from kissing.

She controlled the pressure of her mouth against his. She decided when to use her tongue and when to invite him to use his. Because he wasn't supposed to think of his next move, couldn't even make the next move if he wanted to, he was free to appreciate.

And appreciate he did. He savored the softness of her lips, the sweetness of strawberries, chocolate and whipped cream, the playful glide of her tongue. How he'd lived the past thirteen years without kissing Katie was a mystery.

If she needed to be in charge in order for him to enjoy the privilege of being kissed, then she could be in charge forever. Well, maybe not forever. For a long time, though. Several hours, at least.

Because this woman could kiss like no other. How could he have forgotten the joy of kissing her? Why hadn't he sought her out long before this? Because he was an imbecile, that's why, too busy caught up in making a success of himself to remember the happiness he'd once found with Katie. From now on he'd pay attention to what was important.

She lifted her mouth from his way too soon. Or maybe not. He'd been aware that the more she kissed him, the harder he was getting. He was fast approaching system overload.

Her breath was warm on his face. "Now lean back," she murmured.

Closing his eyes, he did as he was told. With the bean-bag molded to his body and the rasp of his zipper blending with the beat of jungle drums, he felt the unfamiliar aphrodisiac of surrender pour through him, heating his blood.

"What next?" Her voice floated to him on a stream of sensation.

He had no modesty left. He wanted everything she was offering. "Pull down my briefs."

Soft hands fumbled with the elastic band. Cool air touched his unrestrained penis. He gripped the pliable sides of the beanbag and fought for control over the one variable left to him. He would not come yet. Not yet.

She drew in a sharp breath. "And now?" Her voice trembled.

"Touch me. Please touch me."

Her hands felt cool against his hot skin as she began to caress him. "Like this?"

He groaned. "Yes." Such pleasure should be illegal.

"What else do you want, Jess?"

What else, indeed. He wasn't sure he could take the *what else* he had in mind, but after she'd taunted him so thoroughly, he had to have it. "I want you to...use your mouth."

"I thought you'd never ask. But first...I'm going to play."

He wasn't sure what she meant until he felt something warm and slippery being smeared on his penis. Opening his eyes, he was greeted by the sight of Katie finger painting his buddy with melted chocolate.

"How does that feel?" she asked.

He couldn't possibly answer her when he was fighting not to come. But the incredible sensation of her fingertips smoothing chocolate up and down was worth a clenched jaw.

"I thought this was a better idea than asking you to dip yourself in the fondue pot."

Laughter rattled in his throat, and he choked it back, afraid it would break his iron control.

"Is it too warm?"

He shook his head.

"Too cool?"

He shook his head again.

"Just right?"

He nodded.

"We'll call this the Fondue Fondle."

He would not laugh. He would not. A snort escaped anyway.

"And here goes the main event." She started giving him a tongue bath in time with the primitive drumbeat in the background.

Dear God. His breath came hard and fast as he absorbed the ecstasy without allowing himself to climax. She lapped him like an affectionate puppy, putting his brain on tilt and his body in such orgasmic readiness he doubted his ability to hold back.

But he would hold back. He would hold back until…ah, there. Her lips closed over the tip while her tongue continued its sensuous dance.

"More." He was starved for air, hoarse with lust. "Deeper."

She took him in by slow increments—sweet torture that nearly drove him over the edge. Still he maintained a tenuous grip on his control. Then she retreated, and he moaned in supplication.

"Please," he whispered. "Please."

She responded by taking him deep into her mouth. This time when she pulled back it was only for a fraction of a second. Then she took him in again and again, sucking vigorously until he was gasping and clutching the beanbag so fiercely he was afraid he'd rip the thing in two.

He didn't last long after that. In no time she'd mastered him as efficiently as she'd mastered a can of whipped cream. He heard her proud murmur of satisfaction right before he erupted. His strangled cry of release filled the room, drowning out the sound of jungle drums.

Eyes squeezed shut, he rode the whirlwind of his climax. She stayed with him through the last shudder. Then she slowly drew away, and he lay spent, sprawled in the beanbag chair unable to move, unable to speak.

He was vaguely aware that she adjusted his briefs and zipped his jeans. Then he felt the movement of air as she shifted position. Her lips brushed his cheek. "Take as long as you need," she said. "Lock the door behind you when you leave."

His eyes snapped open. *Leave?*

She blew out the Sterno under the fondue pots. Then she began blowing out the candles.

"Katie?"

"Mmm?" With one candle left to go, she lifted her head to gaze at him. The candlelight flickered over her flushed cheeks and her mouth, rubbed free of lipstick.

His tongue felt thick and unwieldy. "What...what are you...doing?"

"Closing up shop."

"But you can't."

"My shop. My rules." She smiled at him. "Besides, you look finished for the night."

"No, I'm not." He struggled upright and used the coffee table to steady himself as he got to his feet. "Give me a few minutes—twenty, tops. I'll be fine. I'll be ready to go again. We've only just started here. I haven't even touched you."

"Oh, but I've touched you."

"Yes, I know." Gratitude welled in him. "And you did a fantastic job of touching me. I loved every second of it." He moved toward her. "Now it's time for me to return the favor."

"How quickly we forget."

"Forget what?" With the orgasm he'd had, remembering his name was an accomplishment.

"I'm the one calling the shots."

Oh, yeah. That. "You can call the shots. We'll go into your bedroom and you can tell me exactly what you want me to do."

"I didn't invite you into my bedroom, now did I?"

He rubbed a hand over his face. In this new world he was a stranger who didn't speak the language. "Okay, forget the bedroom. You choose the place. And you can tell me exactly how you want me to touch you. You'll be in charge of everything, I promise."

"I don't want you to touch me. Not tonight. Maybe tomorrow night. We'll see how I feel about it then."

"Katie, you have to be feeling sexually frustrated."

"I'm a little hot and bothered, now that you mention it."

"Then why are you making me leave?"

"I can take care of it myself."

He felt like throwing something. "*Why?* Why not let me give you an orgasm? I'll do it any way you want!"

"I'm not ready for that to happen yet, Jess. So go on home, and if you're still interested tomorrow night, you can come back then." She looked so approachable in the glow of the candle.

Yet she was sending him away. It made no sense. "There's not as much time tomorrow night. You have your show until ten."

"Is that past your bedtime?"

"Not if I can go to bed with you."

"I'll think about it between now and then. Come by about ten-thirty and we'll talk about it."

"Talk? Damn it, I want to do more than talk! We have unfinished business, you and I."

"That's not entirely my fault, is it?"

He ground his teeth. "Will I ever stop paying for that decision?"

"You can stop paying anytime you like. Nobody's forcing you to come to my apartment. That's up to you."

"You are a very frustrating woman, you know that?"

Her expression was calm, her smile gentle. "You don't have to show up again if it bothers you so much."

"Maybe I won't."

"Your call. I'll be here." She leaned down and blew out the last candle. If not for a faint light coming from the kitchen, they would have been in complete darkness. "Good night, Jess. Sleep tight."

He mumbled a swear word under his breath. He'd been dismissed. She'd had her way with him and now he was banished. But a woman had never had her way with him in quite so spectacular a fashion. A guy would be twenty kinds of a fool to turn his back on that kind of pleasure. He would come back tomorrow night and they both knew it.

SENDING JESS HOME WAS one of the toughest things Katie had ever done, but she knew it was the right move. With every moment that passed she felt more natural in her new role. It boiled down to a question of power. Thirteen years ago she'd given hers away, but she wouldn't do that again.

Now she was reclaiming her power. In the process she'd gifted him with incredible pleasure. That had been obvious. And gratifying. Also extremely arousing.

She'd told him that she'd take care of the situation without him, but that had been mostly to torment him with a mental image. In reality she had no taste for it. She wanted Jess, naked and willing, to climb into her bed.

He would have been happy to oblige, too. But what she'd told him had been completely honest. She wasn't ready for that yet. When she allowed him the freedom to make love to her, she had to be sure of herself, confident that the balance of power wouldn't shift again.

As she finished cleaning up the fondue pots, her cell phone rang. It wasn't a ring she'd programmed into it, which meant it could be…Jess. Although she hadn't given him her number, her mother probably had.

She let it ring and waited long enough for him to leave a message before she picked it up. Sure enough, the caller had been Jess.

"I can imagine what you're doing right now, since you're not answering your phone," he said. *"That's partly why I called, just to remind you that I could be giving you that orgasm you're currently having if you'd let me stay. You're not the only one good at oral sex, Katie Peterson."*

It was a long speech for Jess. He sounded riled up, and she had to admit that excited her. When she finally turned him loose, he could get a little wild and crazy. So long as she had herself together and could match his forcefulness with her own, they'd have a great time.

"The other reason I'm calling," he continued, *"is to invite you to lunch tomorrow. I think we should see each other in broad daylight. I can meet you at the station at twelve-thirty. Let me know."*

After allowing fifteen minutes to go by, she did a few jumping jacks to get her heart pumping and her breathing accelerated. Then she called him back.

"Hi!" She sucked in a dramatic breath. "I got your message."

He groaned. "Are you calling me before, during or after?"

"Before, during or after what?" Good. Her act had worked.

"You know perfectly well. From the way you're breathing, I know exactly what you've been doing. You could go blind, you know."

"I disproved that years ago. I'm proud to say that I still

check out twenty-twenty in both eyes." She couldn't help grinning. This was fun. "Too bad you believe that old myth, though. What a drag."

"I don't. I was kidding."

"Or maybe you do believe it and are too embarrassed to say so. That would explain why you were so desperate tonight."

"I was not desperate, damn it!"

"Were so. But that's okay. I enjoyed myself." She paused. "I'm still enjoying myself." *By yanking your chain, hot stuff.*

"You're doing it *right now?* While you're talking to me?"

"Why not? Is there a law against that?"

"I can't believe you're talking to me while you're... well, yes, I can. That would fit your pattern of trying to drive me nuts."

"So how am I doing, Jess?"

"Too damned well."

"You're getting hard again, aren't you?"

"Never mind." His voice had that low, husky quality that gave him away. "At least I know you're not using a vibrator. I can't hear anything humming."

"Want to guess what I'm using?"

"No."

"Not a candle. Been there, done that. I believe in variety. Come on, take a guess."

"Katie, I'm hanging up now."

"But I haven't told you whether I'd meet you for lunch. I thought you wanted an answer."

"I did, but now I wonder if lunch is such a good idea. No telling what you'll try."

She smiled in triumph. She'd thoroughly convinced him

of her bad-girl status. "But if we don't meet for lunch, you'll never know, will you?"

"So you'll come?"

"Interesting choice of words. Yes, I'll definitely come."

"I meant to *lunch*."

"That, too."

"I'm really hanging up now. I'm not about to stay on the line and listen to you having an orgasm."

"That's fine. I was going to hang up myself. I need two hands."

"Katie."

"'Bye, Jess. Think of me." She took the phone away from her ear and pressed the disconnect button. She was having a blast.

8

As Jess steered his truck around the barricades and past KRZE Monday morning, anticipation tightened in his gut. He remembered that feeling—he used to get it every weekday morning when he'd drive to Katie's house to pick her up for school. Knowing he would see her again today made the sun shine a little brighter. Even if she was a pain in the ass.

No doubt about it, she was a challenge to deal with. In high school she hadn't hassled him like this. He shouldn't be surprised that she'd changed in thirteen years, though. A radio personality had to become gutsy or give up the business.

Jess kind of wished she'd picked a different show format, though. Why sex? Why not politics or the environment? Then she wouldn't have done all that research, research that was making him sweat bullets every time he thought about climbing into her bed. No doubt she knew more than he did.

Well, too bad. He'd have to deal with it. His only alternative was to give up on Katie, and he wasn't about to do that. After all she'd put him through, he would by God enjoy the fruits of his labors.

He parked the truck and noticed that the number of picketers marching back and forth in front of the tall chain-link fence seemed to have increased. The signs had been updated, too. He shaded his eyes so he could read the closest one, lettered in lipstick-red.

Don't Put It Up 'Cause You Can't Get It Up.

Wonderful. Value Our Roots had latched on to Katie's pet theory. He couldn't imagine she'd ever seriously had that opinion of him. Most likely she'd done it for the sound bite. She especially wouldn't think of him in those terms after last night. His problem was more along the lines of keeping it down.

But she'd caught the imagination of the protesters and breathed new life into their campaign. Damn. After clapping his yellow hard hat on his head, he picked up a set of plans and climbed out of the truck.

"Hey, Harkins!" called one of the picketers. "Get a girlfriend, man!"

Jess ignored him and headed for the construction trailer. Wouldn't that guy be amazed to know where Jess had been last night and what had happened inside Katie's apartment?

That's when it dawned on him that he had the power to bring her down if he chose to do that. He could blow her credibility out of the water by exposing their personal interactions of the past three nights. Obviously she didn't think he would. He didn't know whether to be flattered or irritated that she was so sure he'd keep their secret.

Gabe met him before he made it to the trailer. "Some of the guys are ticked about the signs," he said. "You might want to talk them down. I'd hate to see a fight break out."

"You and me both. We need to laugh this off. If the guys take it seriously, that'll just give VOR more ammunition."

"I've heard through the grapevine that the Livingston

Development brass are unhappy, too." Gabe stepped into the shade of the trailer and took off his sunglasses. "They're leaning on the KRZE station manager to clip Crazy Katie's wings. I just hope it's not too late. The protestors seem to love this new angle. Did you see the helium balloons?"

"Balloons?"

"It's like performance art. They're down at the far end of the fence. Not too far from KRZE."

Jess turned back to look. "I don't see—oh, wait a minute. They're blowing one up now." He watched as a large tubular balloon in Day-Glo pink began to inflate. After it reached a height of about eight feet, it began losing air. As it grew limp, a second pink balloon began to swell.

Jess sighed. "Now isn't that special?"

"Uh-oh. Here comes a TV van. Looks like the balloons might make the six-o'clock news."

"They wouldn't put that on the six-o'clock news." Jess gazed at the TV crew piling out of the van. "It's too suggestive. Kids could see that."

"Maybe they'll save it for the ten-o'clock news, but somebody's here to get a story. They might look for an angle that won't offend viewers. I suggest we make ourselves scarce before they spot you and try to get an interview."

"Oh, shit." Jess made a beeline for the trailer. "I didn't think of that."

Gabe followed at a brisk pace. "Personally I'd like to wring Crazy Katie's neck. I wonder if the Livingston guys can get her fired. Wouldn't that be sweet?"

"It would be overkill." Despite his irritation, Jess's stomach clenched at the thought of Katie losing the job she loved. Back in high school she'd told him this was her dream, and she'd achieved it. "I still think we ought to treat this whole thing as a joke and ignore it," he said as he climbed the metal steps to the trailer and went inside.

"Good luck telling that to the guys." Gabe closed the door after him. "Their machismo is being challenged, and with some of them, that's major. If they didn't catch Katie's show Friday night, they've heard all about it now, thanks to the balloons and the protest signs. If Crazy Katie showed up here, she'd be in some serious trouble."

Jess braced his hips against the battered desk at the far end of the trailer and looked at Gabe. "Maybe I can get her to retract that theory she promoted Friday night."

Gabe stared at him. "How?"

Jess wasn't sure how, but he wanted to try and defuse this situation. "Well, I can—"

"Hold on. I was kidding yesterday. I mean, you can't exactly force yourself on her to prove you're a manly man. Guys get jailed for that stuff, dude."

"No, I'm not talking about that." Although in a roundabout way he was. A night of lovemaking might cause her to reconsider her views, although that wasn't his main motivation for wanting that. "I know Katie from high school." He hesitated. "I'm taking her to lunch today."

Gabe's mouth dropped open. "No kidding?"

"I'm meeting her at twelve-thirty at the station."

"And you think you're going to buy her lunch and talk her out of messing with us? Good luck, buddy. That is one tough cookie. I think you'd better wear your cup."

Jess had to laugh. Protective gear wasn't a bad idea, but not for the reason Gabe was thinking of. What Jess needed was a male chastity belt.

Gabe shook his head. "I mean it, man. That woman might take a notion to kick you in the nuts."

"Not if I handle the situation right."

"You're gonna sweet-talk her?"

"There's that old saying, 'You can attract more flies with honey than vinegar.'"

"I never got that saying, because who wants to attract flies in the first place? Anyway, I admire your cojones. And I hope it works."

"Yeah, me, too. In any case, it'll be interesting." Jess thought that might be the understatement of the century.

KATIE ARRIVED AT THE station at eleven so she could talk to Herbert Edgecomb. Ava had called her at home an hour before, gleeful about the new VOR signs, the helium balloons and the TV coverage.

When Katie walked in the lobby, Ava gave her a thumbs-up. "Edgecomb's digging this publicity," she said. "He thought you didn't have a chance of stopping that construction before, but now he's not so sure."

"Good." Katie allowed herself a moment of satisfaction. That was followed by a flicker of concern for Jess. Yes, he was putting up a building she hated and his company probably had the contract for the parking garage, too. But she didn't want him to crash and burn because of her. At lunch she'd find out how high the stakes were for him.

"Edgecomb told me to send you in as soon as you got here. He said something about forming a strategy."

"That sounds promising. Thanks." Katie walked back to Edgecomb's office.

"Katie, Katie, come in!" Edgecomb, a balding little guy with a booming voice, looked even smaller sitting behind the huge mahogany desk he was so proud of. With his big nose and thinning hair that stood up in wisps from his pink scalp, he looked like a newly hatched sparrow.

Whenever Katie stepped into this room she felt like Dorothy finally catching a glimpse of the little man who was the Wizard of Oz.

"Well, now, Katie." That big voice coming out of such a small instrument was startling. "Sit down, sit down."

She did, knowing how Edgecomb disliked anyone towering over him. He'd placed low-slung chairs in front of his desk which put visitors at his height.

"You caused quite a stir with your Friday night show," he said.

"So it seems."

"I'm sure you got the message that I was concerned, especially after the owners called me at home."

"Ava told me. But under the circumstances, I think—"

"We're not worried about the negotiations on the sale of the property at the moment," he said.

"Oh?" She picked up on his use of *we*. Whenever he did that, he was speaking as if he and the station's owners were part of a tight group of insiders. When he used *we* he was feeling extremely pleased with himself.

"The ratings for Friday night's show were…very good."

"I'm glad to hear it." She had to believe the ratings had gone through the roof for Edgecomb to admit to *very good*.

"And then this added publicity with the VOR getting TV coverage—even if they have to edit it carefully for sexual content—well, it's good news for KRZE. By positioning ourselves against this building and parking garage, we could increase our market share considerably. Everyone loves an underdog."

"So you'll back me?"

"All the way, Katie. Full speed ahead. Even if you don't succeed—"

"I will succeed." Katie wished her grandmother were alive to share this victory. She would understand why Katie was fighting for the little house, even if Katie's parents thought it was misplaced sentimentality.

"I think there's a chance you might, but even if you don't, the station will reap the benefits. We'll have our pick of alternate locations because everyone will want to be associated with the little station that battled for its place in the world."

Katie nodded. "I can see how that would be, but I want us to stay right here, if it's all the same to you."

"That would be wonderful. But until you brought forth that outrageous opinion on Friday night, it wasn't a remote possibility."

"It does seem to have struck a chord with people."

"It absolutely has, Katie." Edgecomb steepled his fingers. "So what do you have in store for your listeners tonight?"

"I found a sociologist who did a study of the evolution of fastening devices like nails, pegs, screws and nuts. He draws a parallel between the devices and male and female anatomy and he even maintains that's why men relish working with those items. I couldn't bring him here for the show—he lives in Washington—but I've arranged for a phone interview during the first segment of my program."

Edgecomb smiled. "Phone interview, huh? So is there really a sociologist or are you making him up? It seems almost too perfect."

Katie's jaw dropped as she absorbed the implication. "You think I'd create a fake expert to further my cause?"

"Well, it's not like anybody's going to try to track down your Washington sociologist to see if he's real. And this is great theater, so—"

"I would *never* do something like that, Mr. Edgecomb." Indignation made her quiver. "That's dishonest."

"Okay, okay." He held up both hands, palms out. "Didn't mean to upset you. Obviously you've done a lot of research to find these people. That's great."

"Thank you." Katie's respect for Edgecomb slipped several notches. He obviously didn't care if she made up her sources just so the ratings were good. That was disheartening.

"And I'm expecting those ratings to go even higher tonight," he said. "Congratulations."

"I'm glad it's working out." She'd like to have a more ethical boss, but life wasn't perfect.

"Me, too. Now I'll let you get on with your day. I'm sure you have more research to do."

"Yes, I do." And she liked to think that was part of the reason she'd done so well as a DJ and why she'd continue to increase her listener base. Syndication wasn't out of the realm of possibility someday.

She admitted to a certain amount of ambition. It would be a kick to reach even more people and educate them about the fun parts of sex. Besides, if she became famous enough, the little house that contained the radio station would become famous, too, and less likely be destroyed.

As she left Edgecomb's office, she allowed herself some nostalgia. She'd been allowed to spend many weekends here with her grandmother and grandfather. Every morning she'd walk down this hall from her bedroom to the kitchen, drawn by the scent of coffee brewing and pancakes sizzling on the griddle. She no longer had her grandmother with her, but thanks to this campaign, she might be able to save the place that held such poignant memories.

ALTHOUGH JESS TALKED TO his crew, he didn't think he made much headway with them. Finally he'd been forced to threaten firing any guy who picked a fight with the protesters. In today's economy, money should count more than machismo to them. At least he hoped to hell it did.

At twelve-thirty he drove his truck over to KRZE. Originally he'd planned to walk over and take her somewhere close by. The inflating/deflating balloons and the growing number of protesters made that seem like a bad plan.

He collected his share of suspicious looks from the picket line as he cruised around to the KRZE parking lot on the far side of the station. He wondered how they'd react when he came out the front door with Katie. With luck, it would confuse the hell out of them. This lunch date might serve more purposes than he'd thought.

When he walked into the lobby, Katie was standing by the receptionist's desk, her back to the door as she talked to Ava, the same multipierced woman who had been sitting there Friday night. What a contrast—Ava with her spiked hair streaked green and her tongue stud flashing as she laughed, Katie in a slim-skirted suit of cobalt-blue and her hair a sleek waterfall of golden silk.

Sexual heat hit Jess the moment he saw Katie. As she turned and met his gaze, a picture of her kneeling in front of him came back with full force. He could smell the chocolate, feel the press of her fingers as she smeared it on, the flick of her tongue as she licked it off. He couldn't speak for thinking about what she'd done with that mouth and those soft hands.

"Hi, Jess."

"Hi." With great effort he tore his attention from Katie so he wouldn't appear rude. "Hi, Ava."

"Hello." Ava looked at him as if he were a specimen under a microscope.

"I'm ready to go if you are," Katie said.

"Great." He tried to decide if she was really as cool and calm as she acted. Her smile seemed relaxed and her body language didn't suggest any tension except…she was gripping a pen so tightly in her right hand that her knuckles showed white against her skin.

"I thought we'd take the truck and get out of the downtown area for a while."

"Far, far from the pink balloons," Ava said.

"Um, yeah." Jess had told the guys at work this should be treated as a joke, but he was no expert at laughing it off.

"Let's go then." Katie picked up her purse from the receptionist's desk. "See you later, Ava."

Jess held the door for Katie and she thanked him.

That was a relief. He'd met some women who thought holding the door for a woman was an outdated chauvinistic gesture. But it was how he'd been raised and he couldn't help it.

On the way to his truck he didn't look to the left, although he would have loved to know if anybody from VOR was watching. "I hope your supporters don't think I'm kidnapping you," he said.

"Now there's an interesting idea. Maybe you're kidnapping me and taking me away in your big old truck so you can have your way with me."

"Never mind." Him and his big mouth. Or maybe she would have taken *anything* he'd said and turned it into a sexual reference.

"Where are we going, by the way?"

He hadn't decided until this minute, but now that he knew she was liable to say anything at all and get them both in trouble, he wanted some out-of-the-way spot. "There's a little place I like called Casey's Club, about two miles away. Great sandwiches."

"Quiet?"

"Yeah, pretty quiet." He opened the door and held it while she climbed in. He tried not to look at her legs while she did that, but a guy would have to be lobotomized not to. She had great legs, and she hadn't covered them up with panty hose either. Tonight he wanted to be wedged right between those bare thighs.

He'd be wise to keep his mind off that topic, though. Lunch today was supposed to be for talking about something besides sex.

Taking a deep breath, he walked around the front of the truck and climbed into the driver's seat. Katie was rustling around in her seat, and ten whole seconds sped by before he realized what was going on.

Opening her purse, she tucked a pair of lace panties inside.

His brain reeled. Even in the face of the evidence, he couldn't believe she'd done it. "What the hell is that all about?"

She turned her blue gaze on him, and the taunting fire was back. "I thought I'd add a little zing to our lunch hour by going commando."

9

IF ONLY KATIE COULD PULL out her picture phone and snap Jess's expression, she'd have a prizewinner. She'd gotten the drop on him...again. If he'd imagined that taking her to lunch in his truck to a place he'd chosen would put him back in charge, then he'd just found out how wrong he was.

"Changed your mind about going to lunch?" she asked.

He blinked. "Uh—"

"Because that's okay if you have. Not every man is game for this kind of adventure."

A look of resolution replaced the dazed expression. "We'll go to lunch." He sounded calm, but he jabbed at the ignition three times before he got the key in. Then he spun the tires on the way out of the parking lot.

She'd been right that he would go along with her move. No doubt he was keeping his eye on the evening ahead, and bailing on the lunch challenge would obviously mean no nooky later on. She still hadn't decided how to handle their interaction tonight either.

Cheryl had advised structuring more detours so Jess wouldn't get everything he wanted yet. That probably made sense. Unfortunately that meant that Katie wouldn't get everything she wanted either.

Her dreams last night had centered on penetration of the

Jess variety. She was ready to welcome that fine piece of equipment he carried around and test it for compatibility with her system. She had an inkling the fit would be outstanding.

But in the back of her mind lurked the fear that once she allowed that to take place, she'd lose all the ground she'd gained. She didn't trust herself to experience full-out sex with Jess and not become totally infatuated with him. Then he'd be holding all the cards...again.

Riding in his macho construction truck with the manly leather seats wasn't helping. He looked rugged and commanding as he negotiated the lunch-hour traffic. Good thing she'd taken off her panties to freak him out or he'd be totally in charge right now.

"Your protesters seem to have picked up speed," he said.

"I need to warn you, Jess, that we might win this one. My station manager is behind me, and as you can see, we have more support than before."

"The building's in progress. Livingston Development isn't going to back out now. They'd lose too much money."

Not if it turns into a PR nightmare and they stand to lose even more by finishing it. "All right. But humor me here. Let's say the building is no longer a viable investment and the developers call a halt to construction. What would happen to your company?"

"They have a contract with us. They'd have to find a way to honor that. If we've acted in good faith, then they'd have to compensate us."

"So it wouldn't really hurt you all that much."

He glanced at her. "I don't know how you expect me to carry on a discussion when I know you're sitting there bare-assed under your skirt."

"So it's getting to you?" She thought she'd detected some movement under the fly of his jeans.

"What do you think?"

"I'd be worried about you if you *weren't* thinking about it."

He cleared his throat. "I'm thinking that you had the panty move in mind from the time I invited you to lunch."

"Maybe."

"You're killing me, Katie."

"Am I really?" She doubted it.

"Really."

"Come on, be honest. This is more sexual fun than you've ever had in your whole life."

The corner of his lips twitched, as if he might be trying not to grin.

"It *is*. And don't try to deny it."

His laugh gave him away. "All right," he said. "I'll admit that I've never experienced anything quite like the past few days. Sex has never been so complicated."

"Or so exciting," Katie added. "Anyway, I'm glad your company wouldn't suffer if Livingston stops construction. That eases my mind."

"I didn't say we wouldn't suffer. I happen to take pride in what I do. Leaving a project unfinished, especially such a visible one, wouldn't be a good feeling. The people I hire think the same way. We're invested in putting up something we're happy with."

Katie controlled the urge to comment. Beauty was in the eye of the beholder. "I can understand that, but your building is threatening the adobe house KRZE calls home. Abandoning that house to the wrecking ball wouldn't be a good feeling for me or the people who work there."

Jess pulled the truck into the parking lot of a small restaurant with no windows. "KRZE could find another location even more historic, one that wouldn't be right in the path of progress."

"I don't define your high-rise as progress."

He turned off the motor and glanced at her. "So I noticed." He rested his arms on the steering wheel and stared out the windshield. "I should be furious with you, considering the problems you're giving me with that building."

"I should be furious with you, considering that you're the one putting up that monster next door."

He turned to her. "The thing is, I'm not furious with you, Katie. But I intend to *erect* that building, no matter what you throw at me."

"I'm not furious with you either, Jess. But I'll do whatever I can to keep you from *erecting* that building."

"Including taking off your panties before we go to lunch?"

That stopped her cold. She would never use sex as leverage against Jess's project. In all her life she'd never been a dirty player. She believed in a fair fight. "Maybe we need to establish some ground rules."

"If this is about you being in charge of anything sexual between us, I get that."

"No, this is about us being on opposite sides of the fence but still attracted to each other."

Amusement flickered in his eyes. "Is there a knothole in this fence?"

That made her laugh. "There could be."

"Good, because I'm battling some powerful urges."

She held his gaze. "So am I."

Amusement turned to hunger. "We could forget lunch. I can have us in a hotel room in fifteen minutes."

"No." A hotel room would make the decision for her as to whether they'd have sex. Faced with a bed, cool sheets and drapes drawn against the world, she'd give it up in no time. "We should have lunch, like you said. And we'll set some ground rules. Let's go eat."

He studied her for a moment longer. "Okay."

GROUND RULES. JESS THOUGHT about that as he escorted Katie into the dim interior of Casey's Club. He wasn't surprised that Katie wanted ground rules. He'd admired her ethics ever since she'd had a chance to win the state debate tournament by cheating and had taken the loss instead.

Maybe that's why he'd never believed she was jacking him around sexually in order to mess with this construction project. She must have a similar opinion of him, considering that she trusted him enough to have this sexual involvement in the midst of the building battle.

And it was his building, damn it. Maybe he hadn't designed it and maybe his personal money wasn't tied up in the construction process, but once he'd taken over from the architect the structure had become his.

When it was finished—and it would be—red-and-gold sunsets would set the western windows on fire. At night the lighted windows would glitter like diamonds in a debutante's bracelet and the city's silhouette would be forever changed by something he'd built.

Not many people knew how much he loved his work. He let them think it was a job, a way to earn a buck. But it was much more than that. If he thought Katie would understand, he might tell her. But he wasn't sure she could get beyond her objection to high-rises, or worse yet, she might start believing that construction really was a sexual thing to him.

Maybe it was. The process was creative and satisfying, and those were the same thrills he expected from good sex. Maybe building high-rises was an expression of sexuality, after all. He'd never agree that it was a substitute, but it might be another outlet.

"Looks like we can sit pretty much where we want." Katie surveyed the restaurant's dim interior. One couple occupied a booth near the door and two men were finishing up at a table by the kitchen. Otherwise the place was empty.

"There's more traffic on weekends, but I like it better on weekdays because it isn't crowded."

Katie glanced back at him. "Booth or table?"

"Booth." He wasn't sure what to expect from her, and the high-backed wooden booths gave them some degree of privacy. Then again, if they took a table, she wouldn't be as likely to try something outrageous.

"A booth it is." She headed toward one in the far corner.

That's when he admitted to himself that he wanted her to try something outrageous. He might be on a runaway train bound for disaster, but he was loving the ride.

Katie sat down and plucked a menu from a holder mounted on the wall. "Will somebody come?"

The line was too tempting to pass up. "Interesting question. What do you think?"

Her gaze snapped to his. Then a smile spread across those kissable lips. "Jess Harkins, are you turning into a bad boy?"

"In self-defense."

She laughed. "This could be fun. Maybe we should set those ground rules before something...comes up."

"All right. You're the one with the ground-rule concept. Me, I'm just here to...eat." If she could play these word games, so could he.

She fanned her face with her menu. "I see."

"I recommend the turkey club."

"Is that what you're having?"

"For starters." He loved watching the heat build in her eyes. Maybe he could trade loaded comments with her, after all. She'd set the stage for it, and he could finally see the advantages to her approach.

A Hispanic waitress whose name tag read Lupita approached the booth. She was new, which was a relief to Jess. No telling what might happen here today, and being anonymous would serve him well. But he'd forgotten to factor in Katie's celebrity status.

"You're Crazy Katie, aren't you?" the waitress asked.

Katie smiled. "Yes."

"I listen to your program all the time!" She glanced at Jess, turned slightly away from him and lowered her voice. "You know the tip you gave everybody on Friday night?"

"Sure."

Lupita made a circle with her thumb and forefinger. "Awesome. My boyfriend and I were at his place listening to your show, so I got to test it out, like, right away."

Jess tried to remember what the *Kama Sutra* tip had been for Friday night, but he'd been too distracted to file it away for future reference. He should have been filing all those tips away now that he planned to take Katie, the woman who gave out those tips, to bed.

"Glad it worked out for you," Katie said.

"And are they really going to tear down that house where KRZE is located?" the waitress asked.

Jess was beginning to think the regular server would have been better. She hadn't been nearly this chatty.

"Not if I can help it," Katie said.

"My mother used to clean house for the lady who lived there," the waitress said. "I went with her sometimes and I got to play with her granddaughter. I—"

"Lupita? You're *that* Lupita?"

"Omigosh! *You're Katie?* The one with the *Star Wars* action figures we used to play with in the backyard?"

"Yes!" Katie leaped to her feet and the two women hugged. "I can't believe it," Katie said. "What a small world."

"Isn't it?" Lupita beamed at her. "I always wondered what happened to you, but little kids don't think about last names, and so it never crossed my mind that Crazy Katie could be you."

"It's me." Katie turned to Jess. "This is Jess, a friend of mine."

"Nice to meet you, Lupita." Jess noticed that Katie hadn't supplied his last name. He wasn't sure whether she was protecting herself or him, but he was grateful either way.

He listened as Lupita and Katie reminisced about building *Star Wars* sets in the garden behind the adobe house. *Katie's grandmother's house.* So that was the connection. Things were starting to make more sense to him now.

Somewhere in the exchange of information Lupita managed to get their orders for the turkey clubs and two iced teas.

"Give my best to your mother when you see her," Katie said when Lupita was about to leave for the kitchen. "She made the best tamales."

"Still does," Lupita said. "Say hi to your grandmother, too. What a kind lady."

"She died fifteen years ago," Katie said. "That's why my grandfather sold the house—he couldn't bear to live there without her."

"I'm so sorry." Lupita paused. "But now you work there. That's cool."

"Yeah, especially if I can continue working there." Katie kept her attention on Lupita as she said that. No significant glances in Jess's direction to lay a guilt trip on him.

Well, that was good, because it wasn't his fault, damn it. He hadn't known he was involved in a project that would destroy her dead grandmother's house. Shit. He should have figured there was something more to it than historical preservation. Katie's stand on the construction had left no room for compromise, and now he understood why.

Of course, not all grandkids felt that passionately about their grandparents' house. There could be more to the story. Panties or no panties, Katie was going to level with him.

Finally Lupita returned to the kitchen.

"So that's it," Jess said. "KRZE is in your grandmother's old house."

"Yes."

"It's a sentimental attachment then."

Her gaze softened. "That house was filled with so much love you could taste it. My parents get along okay, but my grandfather and grandmother had a great love affair, like the kind you read about in books. I used to go there and soak up the good vibrations."

"All those months we dated and I don't remember you ever mentioning this."

She leaned both arms on the table. "Back then I didn't realize how special their relationship had been. I had to grow up and see more of life before I understood that. I don't think anyone else in my family was as affected by the beauty of it as I was. I also realize that saving the house shouldn't be so significant, but…it is."

"You might have **told me.**"

"I haven't told **anyone, especially** after my parents made it clear they didn't **agree that the** house should be saved." She traced some old **water marks** on the scarred wooden tabletop. Then she glanced up. "A personal campaign to save my grandmother's house because she's dead and can't do it herself—that sounds kind of silly, doesn't it?"

"No to me." An emotion more powerful than lust warmed him. If he'd thought he was in this only for the sex, he'd been wrong. "But you can't stop the construction of that building and the parking garage next to it, Katie. The land is too valuable to have a single house sitting on it. That's reality."

"Then what about renovating some of the old buildings downtown instead? You'd have a similar amount of office space without changing our skyline."

"It's less complicated to build something new than bring one of those old relics up to code. What I'm putting up will have all the right wiring, all the right plumbing and all the necessary insulation." He paused. "Besides, the view from the top floor will be breathtaking. Have you thought about that at all?"

"If I want a view, I can drive to the top of 'A' Mountain."

Just a mention of "A" Mountain spiked his hormone level. They'd had some great make-out sessions up there. The buff-colored peak near the edge of town always reminded him of those nights.

He longed for a solution that would give them both what they wanted, but he couldn't imagine what that could be. And so he decided to deal with what they could handle in the here and now. "We're definitely on different sides of the fence."

"Looks that way."

"But I still want you."

She blew out a breath. "Isn't that something? We should be bitter enemies."

"Never."

"No." The blue of her eyes deepened. "So what now?"

"You mentioned some ground rules."

"I did, didn't I? Well, how about—" She paused as Lupita arrived with their iced teas.

"Sandwiches will be up any minute," Lupita said.

"Great," Katie said. "Thanks."

After Lupita walked away, Katie leaned forward. "In case you were wondering, anything that might have happened in this restaurant…won't."

"I figured as much."

"The plan was no longer feasible when I was recognized, but running into someone from my childhood was the clincher."

"Hey, I didn't come here to seduce you."

"Maybe not." She smiled. "But I came here to seduce you."

"Cut that out." Childhood friend present or not, he couldn't take that kind of comment without getting ideas. "Talk about something else. Like ground rules, for instance."

She took a sip of her tea and cleared her throat. "I guess there's only one. We should agree that there's no connection between our personal relationship and the jobs we're committed to doing. Specifically we aren't planning to use sex to influence the outcome of this disagreement between us."

He wanted to reach for her hand. Instead he picked up

the cold glass of iced tea and looked at her over the rim. "I never thought you would."

"I never thought you would either."

"Anything else?" He wondered if she intended to set any sexual boundaries.

"That's basically all I wanted to say. Maybe it wasn't necessary, after all. We're both too ethical to use sex to get what we want."

"So when we're together, it's all about sex."

She smiled. "I guess that's one way of putting it."

As he held her gaze across the table, the sexual energy surged between them. He wasn't going to be able to calmly eat lunch and then take her back to the station while he went on to work. Something more had to happen before they parted ways or he'd go crazy this afternoon.

"What do you have to do after this?" he asked.

Her breathing changed slightly, as if she had a hunch what he was leading up to. "I...uh...need a little more prep time for my show. About an hour or so. A couple of errands. That's it. Why?"

"I have an idea." He pulled his cell phone from the clip on his belt. "If you will excuse me a minute, I need to check in with my foreman."

"Sure." She picked up her iced tea, although her hand didn't look completely steady doing it.

He watched her cheeks grow pink as he told Gabe he'd be taking a longer lunch than planned. Then he put away the phone.

She took a gulp of her tea and set it on the table. "So what's your idea?"

"We get our food to go and drive up to 'A' Mountain for old time's sake."

Her eyes widened. "But it's broad daylight!"

"That's right." He felt his groin tighten. "And not a soul will be up there. We'll have the place to ourselves."

"I thought…" She paused to take a deep breath. "I thought you had a prejudice about vehicular sex."

He felt like a skydiver about to take a jump. "I used to. But thanks to you, I've expanded my horizons."

10

THEY ATE THEIR SANDWICHES on the way, and Katie found hers juicy and delicious. Jess turned out to be talented at eating and driving, but that wasn't surprising. His job involved plenty of driving and he would have become an expert at eating on the way, which was probably why he'd suggested taking the food along.

Katie wasn't convinced she was still in charge of the proceedings, but chickening out wasn't an option. A bad girl wouldn't make up some excuse to get out of parking on "A" Mountain in the middle of the day. Besides, she was curious about what he had in mind.

For one thing, his two-passenger cab was worse than any backseat invented when it came to maneuvering room, and the truck bed was full of construction equipment. With that configuration, she couldn't imagine what kind of sex they could have that wouldn't put them both in traction.

Another factor was the temperature. Inside the air-conditioned truck the weather was balmy. The outside air hovered around ninety today.

Everyone called this conical hill "A" Mountain because of the large stone A that represented the University of Arizona, but it was called Sentinel Peak on the map. Covered by sagebrush and cactus instead of pine trees, it was no cooler than the desert floor.

So was Jess planning to keep the engine on and the air running? Nothing about this episode made logistical sense to her. They had limited options for a close encounter of the sexual kind. Yet she didn't think they were climbing the winding road to take in the view.

They didn't talk during the first three-quarters of the drive. Back in high school they had never talked on the way up here either. They'd both been so full of anticipation that neither of them had felt conversation was necessary. Maybe the situation hadn't changed. She couldn't think of a single topic worth discussing.

Well, except the obvious. "If someone's up there, we can't stay," she said. "Your company's name is on the side of the truck."

"If somebody's there, we won't stay," he said. "But it's one-fifteen on a hot October afternoon. Plus it's Monday. Nobody will be up there."

She was inclined to agree. "This truck isn't exactly a make-out wagon," she said.

"It'll work," Jess said.

"I'm no contortionist, Jess. I reserve the right to—"

"Every single one of your rights is reserved and shining like a neon sign in my brain, Katie. I'll make the suggestion. You have unilateral veto power."

She glanced at him. He looked damned sexy with those dark shades on as he juggled a sandwich, the gearshift and the steering wheel. She had a thing for ambidextrous men. "But you're not going to tell me your suggestion yet, are you?"

"There's no point until we find out if the area is as deserted as I expect it to be."

"Come on. Tell."

He laughed. "You really *are* curious."

"Well…yeah. Before we had cover of darkness and a big backseat. Now we have bucket seats and a console." She jerked a thumb over her shoulder. "And back there is totally out. I'm not interested in crawling around on boards and ladders and tools."

"Don't worry. You won't have to." His smile was infuriatingly confident.

But that was just it. She was worried…worried that curiosity would be her undoing, worried that the combination of Jess and the site of their old make-out sessions would put her at a disadvantage. She didn't want to turn back into that vulnerable eighteen-year-old who could be crushed by a careless word or deed.

On the other hand, the higher they climbed, the more turned on she was. The drive had always meant sex, so taking the curves had become an aphrodisiac in the old days. Apparently the effect of this mountain road hadn't worn off.

Jess wadded up his sandwich wrapper and tucked it in the paper bag sitting on the console between them. "Have you been up here since high school?"

"No."

"Me either."

"We got too old for parking, I guess."

"I suppose." As he rounded a turn, the city spread out beneath them, toasted to a burnished brown in the midday sun. "But I miss that intensity. I miss obsessing over whether I'd be allowed to put my hand under your blouse."

"You obsessed over that?"

"For hours. I almost flunked trig because of it."

"You were never in danger of flunking trig." She'd admired his body, but she'd respected his brain, too.

"Well, I damn near got a B on the final then."

That made her smile. "Because of obsessing about my boobs."

"You have no idea the daydreams I had in class—daydreams about unhooking your bra and then wondering if you'd let me touch you."

Her nipples tightened. "I always wanted you to touch me. I fantasized about it all the time."

"Girls do that, too?"

"I did. I used to lie in bed at night and imagine it. Sometimes I'd touch myself and pretend it was you."

He made a noise low in his throat. "I wish I'd known that."

"I couldn't tell you! I was afraid you'd think I was easy."

"Not easy. Generous."

She wanted to be generous now, unless it involved ending up on her back in a truck bed full of construction equipment. "Semantics. One person's generous is another person's easy. Girls that age are always walking a fine line. And then, when I finally decided to be *really* generous, you—"

"Yeah, I know." He reached over and took her hand. "I'm sorry, Katie. I had no idea what was at stake."

That simple gesture of holding her hand affected her more than anything else he'd said or done since they'd come face-to-face at the radio station. He used to take her hand like that years ago, and her world would click into focus.

It was happening now, too. There was a connection between them, whether she chose to acknowledge it or not. He'd been her first love, and that would never change.

After squeezing her hand, he released it and pulled over

to the low rock wall that bordered the road. Beyond the wall the ground sloped down toward the city that fanned out beneath them. The Fourth of July fireworks display was staged from this spot because the show could be seen all over town.

At night the sparkle of city lights stretching into the distance could knock your eyes out. She wondered how many people came up for the view. She and Jess had been too busy to notice a view.

"Nobody up here," Jess said.

"Nope." Her heart thumped faster as she tried to imagine what he had in mind.

In the old days the routine had been obvious—climb in the backseat, start kissing until they were frantic. Then he'd unbutton her blouse or put his hand under her sweater. She would have let him do more than fondle her breasts, but he hadn't pushed beyond that.

And yet he'd been hard and ready for more. As they'd kissed and pressed their bodies together, she'd known that. In those days she hadn't had the courage to offer to help him out, and he hadn't asked.

She turned to look at him and discovered that he'd taken off his sunglasses and was looking right back at her. He'd left the engine running, but the air conditioner couldn't touch the heat they were generating.

"So we're back here at last," he said.

"Uh-huh." She took a steadying breath. "Now that I'm older and wiser, I realize those sessions must have been painful for you."

"Aw, I didn't care. Besides, you didn't get to come either."

"No. I...I didn't know much about female orgasms then."

"And you thought I did?" He shook his head slowly.

"My God, Katie. If I'd decided to go for it, you could have been in for a major disappointment."

"Maybe not. Sometimes it happens even when people have no idea what they're doing."

"That would have been me. No idea. A clueless idiot who would have come before you were even halfway there."

"I know, but I still wish…" The scent of sagebrush always reminded her of that night. It had felt magical, until Jess had turned her down. "I think it would have been worth taking the chance."

"You know, it was my ignorance as much as the back-seat issue that made me say no. I had some stupid idea that we'd have real sex someday and by then I'd know what to do to make it good for you."

"But, Jess." She didn't want to laugh, but it was funny. "How were you supposed to learn?"

"That was a catch-22." He grinned sheepishly. "I was hoping books would help, but it turns out you need hands-on experience."

Which he now had. She was jealous of those other women, even though she had no right to be. "But you really thought there would be a time when we would—"

"Absolutely. I pictured us in a king-size bed with candles on the bedside table. You in a white lacy outfit."

"And you? What would you be wearing?" She could see a pair of black knit bikini briefs. Mmm.

He blinked. "Nothing, I guess. I wasn't imagining what I would wear. Guys don't really care about that."

"You wearing nothing works for me." Did it ever.

"Anyway, I had a very clear picture of how it would be."

"And it never happened."

"Not then, it didn't." He unsnapped his seat belt.

Heat sizzled through her veins. But there were practical matters to think of. "Unfortunately I don't see any king-size bed around here and I didn't happen to bring a white lacy outfit along."

"Oh, this isn't it. This is a warm-up." He put the truck in neutral, set the emergency brake and left the engine running and the air on. Then he reached for his door handle. "You might want to unsnap your seat belt."

Despite her skepticism, her heart started drumming at the thought that he was about to make his move. "If you think you're going to fit on my side of the cab, you didn't learn much in trig, after all."

"I'm not climbing in with you." He opened the door. "But I am coming around to your side."

"I don't get it."

He glanced over his shoulder and smiled at her. "You will."

He was giving her a taste of her own medicine, and that made her a little nervous and a lot aroused. But whatever he did, she was determined not to melt into a puddle of need and gratitude as she had so often in the past.

As he walked around the front of the truck, he turned, glanced at her and grinned. The breeze ruffled his dark hair and the sun dusted his skin with gold. In that moment she was lost. *Jess.* He'd never stopped being the man of her dreams, not for one second in the thirteen years they'd been apart.

And she thought she could maintain her distance. What a joke.

JESS WAS AMAZING HIMSELF, driving up to "A" Mountain with Katie. And on Monday afternoon, no less. He couldn't remember the last time he'd taken a long lunch hour, let alone one that included sex. Down below him in the heart of the city, earthmovers would be growling away as his crew proceeded with the excavation work. He'd left Gabe in charge.

He trusted Gabe, but that wasn't the point. No matter how much he trusted Gabe, he wasn't in the habit of abandoning the job so that he could take care of personal business. Very personal business.

Yet here he was, with the sun beating down on his head and the tang of sun-roasted sagebrush in the air. A small lizard scurried over the rock wall and down into the desert below, and a cactus wren squawked from its perch on a cholla cactus growing about ten yards down the slope.

Otherwise the hillside was quiet, with only the faint hum of traffic drifting up on a breeze. Noise would carry on the clear desert air, though. That was another good reason to keep the truck running, so the sound of the engine would muffle any erotic noises that might come from the interior of that cab.

By the time he opened the passenger door, he was so excited he had trouble getting his breath. He left it angled so that the door would partially shield them. Maybe she'd refuse what he asked. He didn't think so, but she had the power to do that if she chose to.

She started to climb out of the truck.

"No, I want you to stay there. Just turn toward me."

Silently she faced him. As he looked into her eyes, he saw anticipation and a liberal dose of lust. That was a good beginning.

"You have a little bit of mustard on the corner of your

mouth." His heart racing, he leaned down to lick it off with a slow swipe of his tongue.

She didn't move a muscle. "Thank you."

"Glad to help out. Welcome back to 'A' Mountain." Then he cupped the back of her head and kissed her.

She surrendered to the kiss with a little sigh of pleasure that sent blood straight to his groin. That felt familiar. It had always happened starting with that first kiss up here on the mountain. Back in those days he'd taken the torture for granted, considering it the price he had to pay for kissing Katie.

Today was no different in that respect. He would get no relief up here. But he had big plans for Katie. Kissing her until she started breathing fast was the first step.

Turned out that didn't take very long. Clutching his shoulders, she telegraphed an eagerness that drove him crazy. Soon they were both gulping for air as she angled her head so he could thrust his tongue deep into her mouth. This was a woman who loved to be kissed, and he was happy to oblige.

With his knees braced on the edge of the door frame he had the perfect position to go on kissing her forever. That wouldn't be a bad idea, but it wasn't his ultimate goal. As he continued to splay his fingers over the back of her head to hold her steady for his kiss, with his other hand he began pushing her skirt up…and up a little more.

Her breath caught and she pulled her mouth away. Her voice was unsteady, her breath warm on his face. "Did I say you could do that?"

"You're the one who took off her panties." He slipped his hand between her thighs. *So close.* "Are you going to tell me no?"

She swallowed. "I…"

"Don't tell me no," he murmured, stroking her soft curls with one knuckle. "Move closer. Tell me yes."

"This is a mistake."

The blood pounded in his ears. "You don't really think so."

"I do. But I still want…this." With a moan she slid toward him on the leather seat and opened her thighs.

Anticipation made him dizzy. Leaning forward, he nibbled on her lower lip. "Tell me what feels good." Slowly he began to explore. Ah, she was so wet. So incredibly ready.

She mumbled something he couldn't hear.

"What, Katie?" He slipped two fingers deep as he brushed his mouth over hers. "Tell me."

"Good. Very…good."

Not precise, but he could work with it. Curving his fingers slightly, he probed for her G-spot, all the while placing butterfly kisses on her mouth, her throat, her cheeks. Her groan of pleasure told him he'd found what he was searching for. He rubbed gently and her muscles tightened.

He increased the pressure and the speed of his strokes. "Come for me."

"Jess." Tipping her head back, she gasped. Then she began to quiver.

"That's it." He kissed her throat. Then he nipped her skin lightly with his teeth. "Come, Katie. Now."

"Oh, yes…yes…" Her body arched. Then she cried out as her climax roared through her.

If he'd had a condom, he would have wrenched open his jeans and taken her right there, right where she was balanced on the edge of the seat. If he needed more leverage, he'd loop her ankles around his neck. Her head could rest on the console, and he would keep thrusting until they were both delirious with sensation.

But that wasn't going to happen today, for many reasons. Maybe someday they'd try it, after they'd rolled around on a real mattress first. In the meantime, he had more to accomplish here.

As the shudders from her orgasm lessened, he inched slowly downward until he was kneeling on the pavement.

"Jess." Her voice quivered. "You're not seriously going to—"

"Yes." He glanced up into her flushed face. "Yes, I am." Before she could protest any more, he'd cupped her bottom in both hands and propped his shoulders under her knees.

She grabbed the dash and the back of the seat as her center of gravity shifted. "I don't think—" Then she whimpered as his tongue made contact.

"Don't think. Don't think at all." And he settled in.

11

KATIE WASN'T SURE EXACTLY when she'd lost control of the situation, but one thing was for sure—propped on the edge of the truck seat with Jess's head between her thighs was not the best position for regaining that control. It was an excellent position for enjoying another orgasm, though.

She didn't know where Jess had learned how to do this, didn't want to know. All that mattered was this moment. Frigid air swirled around them as the air conditioner struggled to keep up with the double assault of hot bodies and hot air from outside. The cooling breeze had little effect on Katie.

The fire burning inside her raged through her blood and singed her skin. She moaned and writhed in Jess's arms. That mouth. That talented, incredible mouth. All her attention became riveted on the spot where his mouth touched her. The pleasure grew, spiraling deeper with every stroke of his tongue, every movement of his lips.

The first climax had burst upon her quickly, but this one built more slowly, more powerfully. She rode the crest of it, her breathing shallow and quick, her skin moist with sweat, her vagina drenched with excitement.

Almost there…almost…*now*. Her groan of ecstasy rose from deep in her chest as her body surged upward. Oh, glorious. Glorious! She rocked from the force of it.

He held her steady as the waves crashed over her. The imprint of his fingers became part of her, part of the climax. She wondered if his strong grasp would leave a mark and almost hoped it would. This...this was what she'd been longing for and never found—total immersion, total absorption in the wonder of release.

Her recovery was gradual, eased by his gentle kisses along the inside of her thighs. Limp as a rag doll, she allowed him to slide an arm under her knees and another around her shoulders so that he could lift and settle her back into the seat. Eyes closed, she leaned back and gasped for breath.

Vaguely she realized he'd adjusted her skirt and fastened her seat belt. Then he closed the passenger door. Moments later she heard his door open and a rustle as he climbed into the driver's seat.

"Let me know when you're ready to leave." His voice held no urgency.

Keeping her eyes closed, she ran her tongue over her lips. "How about never?"

"Fine with me."

"I..." She swallowed and tried again. "I liked that."

He chuckled. "Good to know."

"A lot."

"Anytime."

Anytime. Now there was a concept. "Really?"

"Pretty much. All I need is a little advance notice."

Slowly she opened her eyes. With her head still propped against the headrest, she turned to look at him. "You mean...I could just call you up and...ask for this?"

He smiled. "Why not?"

"Because I could become a real pest."

PLAY THE Lucky Key Game

Do You Have the LUCKY KEY?

and you can get

FREE BOOKS and a FREE GIFT!

Scratch the gold areas with a coin. Then check below to see the books and gift you can get!

YES! I have scratched off the gold areas. Please send me the **2 FREE BOOKS** and **GIFT** for which I qualify. I understand I am under no obligation to purchase any books, as explained on the back of this card. I am over 18 years of age.

▶ DETACH AND POST CARD TODAY! ▶

Mrs/Miss/Ms/Mr	Initials	K6II

BLOCK CAPITALS PLEASE

Surname

Address

Postcode

2 free books plus a free gift   1 free book

2 free books   Try Again!

Visit us online at www.millsandboon.co.uk

The Reader Service™ — Here's how it works:

Accepting the free books places you under no obligation to buy anything. You may keep the books and gift and return the despatch note marked 'cancel'. If we do not hear from you, about a month later we'll send you 4 brand new books and invoice you just £33.10* each. That's the complete price - there is no extra charge for postage and packing. You may cancel at any time, otherwise every month we'll send you 4 more books, which you may either purchase or return to us - the choice is yours.

*Terms and prices subject to change without notice.

His smile broadened. "You think?"

"Absolutely. This is way better than chocolate." She paused. "And I really crave chocolate. I could wear you out."

"I'll take my chances."

"Okay, but I'm warning you." She let her eyelids drift closed. "Mmm, what a feeling. I have no stress. Nada. A constant dose of you giving me oral sex and I would live to be a hundred and fifty, like those people in Tibet. I'll bet it's not goat's milk at all. They just can't say what it is, but I'll bet it's oral sex."

"There's more to my routine, you know."

She opened her eyes again. "You can't top this, buster."

"I'd like to try."

Her euphoria began to wear off as she realized she was in a vulnerable position. He thought he could make her even loopier with a complete program. Judging from what had happened this afternoon, he could be right.

That could be very bad. She'd already boosted his ego way too much. If she let him have the ultimate experience, full-body sex, she could end up groveling at his feet. He was the one who was supposed to be groveling. That was the plan she and Cheryl had cooked up.

Unfortunately she wanted the ultimate experience. She craved the ultimate experience. If she said the word, he'd be only too happy to give her that tonight. What was a girl supposed to do?

"Don't overthink it," he said. "Maybe I should leave the ball in your court." He reached across her and opened the glove compartment.

"What do you mean?" She fought not to grab him. All she had to do was catch a whiff of his cologne and she wanted to rip his clothes off.

He handed her a card. "How about you come over to my place tonight if you feel like getting together? Just call my cell and I'll give you directions."

"I don't know." Giving her the decision might look like a concession, but she didn't think it was. Ultimately she'd end up at his place, on his turf. That would work to his advantage.

"I'll show you my yellow rosebush."

Well, damn it, she was curious about his yellow rose-bush—and his house and whether he had a king-size bed. "We'll see." She gazed at the card, which of course advertised Harkins Construction.

She was insane to consider going over to his house. He was the enemy, the man who was willing to tear down her grandmother's house to build a parking garage. But he was also the man who had just given her two out-of-this-world orgasms.

Maybe she could go over to his house, help herself to one round of oral sex and leave. That would be demonstrating that she was a bad girl only out for some fun, wouldn't it?

"You don't have to decide anything now," he said.

She thought about the guest she'd lined up for her show tonight. "Are you planning to listen to my program?"

He gazed at her. "Yeah, I'm sure I will. I'm a glutton for punishment."

"After you hear it, you might not want to see me."

"I *shouldn't* want to see you, but that doesn't mean anything." He leaned closer. "In case you hadn't noticed, you get me really hot."

That gave her some comfort. She glanced down at his crotch. "We're not kids anymore. You don't have to drive back like that. You look as if you could use a little—"

"I could but I won't. Ready to head for town?"

"Jess, don't be noble." Besides, she'd feel much better if she could make him moan and groan a little before they left this mountain. "This isn't a contest."

He studied her for a moment. "Isn't it?" Then he put the truck in gear and started back toward civilization.

IT WAS DEFINITELY A CONTEST. Jess thought about that some more as he was forced to give his men yet another lecture about not allowing the deflating pink balloons to insult their manhood. He and Katie were engaged in a contest over this construction project and they were also competing to see who was in charge of their sex life.

Before today he'd thought he'd have to concede the latter battle to her, but up on "A" Mountain the tide had turned. He knew it and so did she.

He was gratified that she still wanted him as much as she had thirteen years ago. Now that he knew that, he needed to think beyond this little sexual game they were playing and decide what he was after besides sex. He didn't have to think very hard.

They were adults now, adults capable of making a commitment. Jess found himself moving in that direction. He'd like to believe Katie was moving in that direction, too. They might be enacting a strange kind of mating ritual, but he knew how he'd like this to turn out in the end.

The trick was to build on what had happened this afternoon. So after work he stopped by the Tucson Mall and bought a white lace teddy. She might not wear it for him, but then again, she might.

On the way home he picked up fast food and ate it while he drove. Unfortunately doing that reminded him of lunch with Katie, and he started getting hard. His old memories of her had been filled with sweetness and nostalgia, but the new ones they were creating threatened to ruin him for polite company.

The situation worsened when he got home and walked onto the back patio to see if his rosebush needed a supplemental watering. He'd realized yesterday that he'd bought the rosebush because of Katie, and now he had to admit he'd bought a lot that had a view of "A" Mountain. His friends thought he'd planned it that way so he could have parties on the Fourth of July with a ringside seat for the fireworks.

But he was very much afraid he'd wanted that view because "A" Mountain kept those memories of Katie close at hand. She'd been influencing him for years and he hadn't even acknowledged it. Now he knew where he wanted this relationship to go, but there were no guarantees. If it blew up on him, he'd be stuck with his view of "A" Mountain. He might have to sell the house.

That wouldn't please his mother, who was convinced he'd bought it as a first step to getting married and providing her with grandchildren. She didn't believe that he was only in it for the investment. Now that he recognized why he'd picked that particular place, he had to agree with her.

Funny how things worked out. Now that it had finally dawned on him that he wanted Katie back in his life, they were locked in this stupid struggle over one of his construction projects. If he'd contacted her earlier... But he hadn't. He'd allowed the years to come between them and now he was paying the price.

Maybe tonight they would finally get past their disagreements and make that vital connection he longed for. To that end, he spent a ridiculous amount of time setting the scene in his bedroom. This time he used fat pillar candles, not wanting her to launch into her candle routine again.

But he wouldn't light them yet. Everything else was ready, though. The sheets were turned back, the pillows were fluffed, the white teddy lay across the end of the bed and condoms were tucked in the bedside table drawer. He'd loaded the CD player with Sting and Billy Joel, two of her favorites when they'd been dating.

By the time he was ready to hit the shower, it was nearly nine, so he decided to tune in Katie's show on the radio he had mounted inside the oversize shower stall. The news ended just as he was sudsing up. The minute he heard Katie's voice, he knew he'd made a mistake. Listening to Katie while he was naked was a very bad idea.

"Hello, Tucson! It's Crazy Katie on this balmy Monday night in October and we're Talking About Sex! *This is the show that asks that all-important question—what sexual symbols do you have in your life? For example, ever thought about the significance of candles and candleholders? Doesn't take much imagination to see what they represent, now does it?"*

Jess groaned. His penis was making like a candle at this very moment, thanks to the combination of warm water and Katie's voice making that suggestive comment. He was positive her reference to candles was directed straight at him.

"In a few minutes I'll be doing a telephone interview with a special guest who sees that same significance in the tools and hardware of the construction trade. As you all know, our little station is threatened with oblivion because of the construction about to take place next door. I wonder what those burly guys would say if they knew they were handling the equivalent of fertility symbols all day?"

"Katie, damn it! I'm already having trouble with my crew!" He reached for the channel knob on the radio but then decided not to turn it. Better to hear what she had to say so he could plan how to deal with the fallout tomorrow.

"But before we get into that, let me give you your Kama Sutra *tip of the night."*

Ignoring his erection, Jess began scrubbing himself vigorously. He needed to take this shower and get it over with. He didn't need to be hearing the *Kama Sutra* tip of the night while he was scrubbing, but he couldn't make himself switch channels or mute the sound.

"Tonight's tip includes the use of Kegels, those wonderful little exercises women can do while sitting at a desk, driving a car, even walking down the street! No one will even know you're doing them. And as you strengthen those love muscles, your man will thank you."

Jess closed his eyes as the water beat down on his throbbing penis. She'd picked that subject on purpose to torture him. He had no idea if she gripped with her love muscles or not. And he wanted to know. Now.

"He'll especially thank you when you try the Mare's Position. Sit astride your guy with your back to him and squeeze those muscles! Trust Crazy Katie, it's good for you and good for him! We'll take a break and be right back with Dr. Gerald Brewster, who'll be discussing his Ph.D. dissertation, The Nuts and Bolts of Sexual Symbolism. *Don't touch that dial!"*

Or anything else. Jess refused to give in to the temptation to masturbate in the shower. She'd love knowing she'd made him do that. Instead he turned off all the hot water and winced as the cold spray hit him. Between that and the commercial break, he got himself under control.

He left the radio on as he stepped out of the shower and toweled off. God, he hoped she'd show up tonight ready to have real sex. He hadn't been this frustrated in his life.

Gerald Brewster sounded like Yoda. But then, anybody who browsed hardware stores looking for sexual meaning would have to be pretty weird. After walking into the bedroom to get dressed, Jess turned on the radio in there. He'd never stopped to question why all the radios in his house were tuned to KRZE.

If anybody had asked him a week ago, he would have said that he liked the all-talk format, that he learned things from the programs. But in reality he only cared about the program that came on at nine on weeknights. He probably could count on one hand the number of times he'd missed Katie's show.

"Obvious, it is," Brewster said in his Yoda voice. *"Into cavities, bolts slide. Into soft wood, nails penetrate. Into hollow nuts, screws twist."*

"And Dr. Brewster, would you say that those who manipulate this hardware are subconsciously recreating the sexual act?"

Jess snorted. What a load of bull.

"Of course."

"Construction crews are dominated by men, correct?"

"Appropriate, it is."

"Because men feel the need to bolster their manliness by manipulating these objects?" Katie sounded gleeful.

"Of course."

"You are an idiot!" Jess shouted. He didn't feel very adult yelling at the radio, but it released some of his tension, enough that he started to laugh. He hated to think what work would be like tomorrow. Maybe nobody from his crew was listening.

Yeah, right. After Friday night he'd bet they were *all* listening. He wouldn't be surprised to learn they'd gathered at one of their favorite bars specifically to hear what Crazy Katie had to say this time.

They wouldn't be happy to know that he was hoping to welcome her into his bed tonight. They'd call him a traitor to the cause, a traitor to all men everywhere. He was consorting with the enemy by asking Katie to come over here.

And he could hardly wait for her to show up—because her program had given him an idea of how to proceed.

ALTHOUGH KATIE HAD TRIED to convince herself the decision wasn't made, she knew she'd go over to Jess's house after the broadcast. This afternoon she'd programmed his number into her cell phone. Then she'd changed into a gauzy skirt, tank top and lightweight jacket so he wouldn't see her in the same outfit she'd worn to lunch. It was on the wrinkled side anyway, after having sex in his truck.

Yep, she was planning to see Jess again. The barriers between them were coming down, and she felt good about that, although she wasn't quite ready to think of a future with him. The possibility of a life with Jess had taken root in her subconscious, though. She could feel it there, waiting its turn, biding its time until she was ready to consider that kind of commitment. Her heart beat faster as she got into her car and pulled her phone out of her purse.

He answered quickly. That was a good sign.

"Hi." She sounded too eager. Time to tone it down, shoot for casual and breezy. "I'm finished at the studio so I thought maybe I'd stop by for a few minutes, if you're not busy."

"Come ahead. I'm just here bolting a few things to-gether, twisting some screws into some snug little nuts."

So he'd listened. She liked that, too. "Jess, you have to admit that there's something to that theory."

"Katie, I can't deny it. The writing's on the wall—or on the cave wall, more like it. I'm sure your Yoda guy is right."

"Yes, he did sound like Yoda, but his concept—"

"It's fascinating. Makes perfect sense. Early man looked at how neatly he could fasten himself to a woman and—bingo!—next thing you know you have sturdy pegs thrust into knotholes."

"Uh, yeah. Exactly." She hadn't figured on him agreeing with her. "I'm glad you see the similarities."

"I couldn't before but I'm into it now."

"You're teasing me."

"Hell, no! I think it's a revelation. All this time I thought I just liked building things, when I was actually rehears-ing for sex. Who knew? It's a terrific concept. So how soon can you get here?"

Warning bells jangled in her head. He was having way too much fun with this sexual-hardware idea. That could endanger her plan to dominate the proceedings. She prob-ably should make an excuse and go home.

She didn't do that. "All I need is directions to your house." So her curiosity was getting the better of her. Hav-ing a curious nature was both a curse and a blessing.

But she wasn't going to bed with him. She'd already de-cided that, even before her pep talk this afternoon from Cheryl. She'd just ask for some quick oral sex and then leave. He had promised to deliver it anytime she asked.

As she listened to the instructions for finding his house,

she figured out he was in the foothills of the Tucson Mountains. "I can be there in about twenty minutes," she said.

"That should give me plenty of time to penetrate some soft wood with a few ten-penny nails and a rhythmic swing of my big hammer."

"Now I know you're making fun of me."

"Absolutely not."

And he wasn't, she realized. He was trying to seduce her and he was succeeding. The more he talked about sliding bolts into cavities and penetrating soft wood, the hotter she became. He was using her own weapon against her.

Okay, so it would be a challenge. She liked challenges. Besides, there was no way she wasn't going over there. Some temptations were too delicious to resist.

12

EVEN BEFORE SHE SAW THE inside Katie knew Jess's place would be gorgeous. Perched on a small rise that overlooked the city, the single-story house was certain to have a dazzling view from the back patio. She left her car parked in the circular drive and walked through a paved courtyard to reach the massive front door.

To her right a three-tiered Mexican fountain gurgled. To her left a sculpted mesquite tree's feathered leaves rustled in the breeze. No doubt about it, Jess had done very well for himself. Even the doorbell was classy—a deep-throated chime that sounded extremely masculine.

Jess answered the door dressed in a snug white T-shirt and jeans. Safety goggles hung around his neck. "Hi! You made good time." He held the door open.

"Traffic was moving well." And she might have broken a couple of speed limits on the way over. So what? She still wasn't going to bed with him, even if he had manly sawdust on his T-shirt and smelled of freshly cut wood.

In high school he'd worked at Home Depot after class and on weekends. Consequently she'd hung out at Home Depot a lot. She'd forgotten that the scent of sawdust and lumber had once been an aphrodisiac.

He closed the door after she walked in. "I hope you

don't mind, but your show inspired me to get back to a project I kept meaning to finish. I just have a little more to do. Come on back to my shop."

"I can do that." Lured by her Home Depot memories, she looped her purse over her shoulder and followed him through a tiled entry. To the right was a sunken living room filled with cushy leather furniture and sleek wood accent pieces.

He turned left and took her into a state-of-the-art kitchen with granite counters and stainless-steel appliances. "Want something to drink? I have both hard and soft."

He was toying with her by throwing out that line, but she didn't take the bait. "Thanks, but I'm good." She wasn't a soda drinker and she didn't dare have alcohol. Her resistance was already eroding at an alarming rate.

Judging from what she'd seen so far, his master bedroom would also be impressive. She visualized a king-size bed, lights on a dimmer switch, sheets with a three hundred thread count. One step into a bedroom like that and she'd be mattress diving in no time.

"I bought this house primarily because of the wood shop." He opened a door off the kitchen.

One whiff of that shop and Katie was aroused. In the Home Depot days she'd almost gotten Jess fired when she'd dragged him behind a stack of plywood and French-kissed him. But he'd looked so sexy using one of the power saws that she'd been overcome with lust.

The shop was almost as big as her living room. A table saw took up one corner, and the workbench stretched along an entire wall. Tools hung on a giant Peg-Board above it.

Sawdust and curled ribbons of wood littered the floor, and a belt sander sat on top of a slab of wood propped on metal sawhorses. The wood was about eighteen inches wide and four feet long.

"It's a bench for the entryway," Jess said. "I want it to look rustic, so I may just rub it with oil and call it good."

Katie pretended great interest in the piece of wood, because otherwise she was liable to demonstrate great interest in the woodworker. She ran her hand over the silky surface. "Mesquite?"

"Yeah. A huge tree. A guy in the neighborhood was determined to cut it down. I tried to stop him, but when I couldn't convince him to leave it, I bought the wood. I have more in the back."

"Pretty grain." And she had a thing for men who worked with their hands. Years ago she'd loved watching Jess in the lumber department, a pencil behind his ear and a tape measure hanging from his belt. He'd handled the store's table saw like a pro.

This shop vibrated with Jess's personality. It was his space, and he'd invited her into it. She'd never been so aware of another human being than she was of Jess right now—his steady breathing, his voice, the scent of his skin. She avoided looking at him for fear her eyes would betray her.

Instead she examined the wood more closely. "This isn't a bench yet, though. I thought you said you were almost finished."

"I am. The top is planed and sanded." He pulled the safety goggles over his head and tossed them on the workbench. "All I have to do is attach the legs. Want to help?"

"I don't know anything about carpentry."

"You don't have to. I just need another pair of hands." Once he'd crossed to the thick slab, he picked it up and turned it over.

She shouldn't have watched him do that. It made his muscles bulge, and nobody could display muscles better than Jess.

"I've tapered the legs." He picked one up from the workbench.

"So I see." Talk about phallic symbols, that bench leg would definitely qualify.

"So now I have to push them into the holes I've bored out in each corner. I could use someone to hold the top. You know, steady it."

She sincerely doubted that. "Okay." After laying her purse on the workbench, she started back toward the sawhorses.

"You might want to ditch the jacket, too."

She glanced at him, convinced he was up to his ears in ulterior motives. "Oh, really?"

"Or not." He shrugged. "Your choice."

Helping with a construction project would be easier without the jacket. She took it off and laid it on top of her purse. Just because she was going along with his little scheme didn't mean she had to follow it to its logical conclusion. She was still in control. Mostly.

He tucked the leg under one arm. "If you'll hold on here—" he paused to demonstrate "—then I'll screw it in."

She grasped the wood where he'd indicated. "Don't think I'm not onto you, Jess. Your whole approach is transparent as hell."

"What approach? I'm putting together a bench for the entryway."

"Sure you are."

"You're the one who said all this had sexual significance." A smile twitched the corners of his mouth as he positioned the tapered end of the leg in the hole nearest her.

"No, that was the Yoda guy." Their bodies nearly touched. She imagined she could hear his heart beating. Or maybe it was hers, going faster with every second he stood beside her.

Then he began twisting the leg into the hole. He'd created a tight fit, and working the leg in soon had him breathing hard. Katie had nothing more to do than hold on, yet soon she was breathing hard, too. Even though she knew his intentions, knew he was using the subject of her program to taunt her, she was turned on anyway.

"One down, three to go." Jess pulled up the hem of his T-shirt and wiped his sweaty forehead. "No air-conditioning out here," he said with a smile.

She barely heard him. Instead her brain was still processing that sneak peek at his six-pack. She'd never seen Jess naked. Suddenly that seemed like total deprivation.

"You can stay right there for the other corner," he said. "But you don't have to grip quite that hard."

Glancing down, she noticed she was clenching the slab of wood as if it would save her from drowning. "Right." She loosened her death hold.

Jess picked up another leg to the bench and positioned it over the hole. "I think I'm making this too difficult. Let me see if I can ease it in gently. Coax it a little."

Katie swallowed. Her best bet would be to close her eyes. Apparently she was into risk-taking, because she kept both eyes wide open.

He tested the leg one way, then turned it slightly and worked it down about an inch. Then he pulled it back out and tried a different position. "Maybe I should get some K-Y jelly," he said.

"Hey, cut it out."

He gazed at her as he bore down on the leg. "What?"

"You know what."

"I can't imagine what you're talking about." He held her gaze as he thrust downward in one swift movement.

Heat washed over her. "Your cute little game isn't going to work, you know. I'm tougher than that."

"I'm sure you are. Considering your radio show and all." He walked to the workbench and got the other two legs. "Okay, let's move to the other end."

She wasn't tough. As he worked the third leg into position, she ached with longing. She wanted those strong hands peeling off her clothes, stroking her body, urging her thighs apart. Then she wanted exactly what he was pantomiming as he shoved the leg into its socket.

"I've drilled the holes so the legs come in at an angle," he said. "When the bench is right side up, the legs will be spread to provide stability." He started working the fourth leg in.

"Mmm." Where were those snappy comebacks when she needed them? Thinking up snappy comebacks wasn't easy when she was picturing herself with her legs spread as she took his personal phallic symbol right up to the hilt.

"Angles are important. If you can get the right angle, all sorts of good things happen." His biceps stood out against the sleeves of his white shirt as he shoved the leg into place.

Her panties were drenched.

"Now let's turn it over." He glanced at her. "You can let go now, Katie."

"Oh. Right." A red haze of desire blotted out all her fine plans. She wanted him right here, right now, and to hell with playing hard to get. But she vaguely remembered he had some fantasy about a bed. Too bad. In this shop surrounded by tools and sawdust, she'd give him anything he wanted.

After flipping the bench over, he set it down on its new legs. "Should be pretty sturdy. Let's see." He straddled it and sat down.

She barely managed to swallow the whimper that rose in her throat. If he stayed like that and unzipped his jeans, she could—

"Try it out. Let's see if it'll hold both of us." His eyes were dark and unreadable as he patted the wood in front of him.

"That's okay." If she got that close to him, she might lose what little bit of restraint she had left. "I'm…wearing a skirt."

A hint of a smile touched his mouth. "I didn't say you had to sit the way I'm sitting."

No, he hadn't. She'd been the one assuming she'd spread her legs and sit astride, opening herself to all kinds of possibilities.

His voice was low and sensual. "Come sit with me, Katie. Help me test the bench."

Like a moth to flame, she edged closer. "How do you mean that?"

"How do you want me to mean it?"

Desperation drove her. "What if I…asked you to unzip your jeans?"

"Depends on the reason. I'm not in the mood for oral sex." His dark eyes held her captive.

She gulped. "Neither am I."

"I see." Without breaking eye contact, he reached in his back pocket and pulled out a foil packet. "How about something involving this?"

Her heartbeat thundered in her ears. "I thought...I thought you were determined we'd end up...on a bed."

"We will." Still holding her gaze, he laid the condom in front of him and reached for the top button of his jeans. "But I'm willing to start with a bench."

She wanted him so much she was quivering. He held her captive with his gaze as he slowly unzipped his jeans and pushed down his briefs. He was fully erect, and the sight of his thick penis brought a moan of anticipation to her lips.

Putting on the condom with the ease of a man who'd done it countless times before, he silently held out his hand.

Her breath came in short, quick gasps as she put her hand in his. The heat in his eyes flared as his fingers closed around her wrist and he drew her toward him.

"Step over the bench," he murmured. "I've got you."

Yes, he had her. She was his to command so long as he was willing to let her slide down onto that glorious piece of equipment. As she straddled the bench, only one barrier remained—a pair of very wet panties.

Still holding her wrist with one hand, still looking into her eyes, he slipped his free hand under her skirt.

"I should take those o—"

A sharp tug followed by a ripping sound told her that finishing the sentence was unnecessary.

As he caressed her, his voice was husky. "You're so ready for this."

"I guess...I'm not so tough."

"Thank God."

She closed her eyes as his clever fingers worked their magic. "Don't make me come. I want—"

"I know. Me, too." He scooted closer and slid both hands

under her bottom. "Brace yourself on my shoulders. When I lift you, wrap your legs around my waist."

"Are you sure?"

"You used to be a cheerleader. You can do this."

"I'm not worried about me. I'm worried about you."

He smiled. "Katie, with all the adrenaline flowing through me right now, I could lift a car. Ready?"

"More than you know." Clutching his shoulders and looking into his eyes, she moved in concert with him until—oh, joyous heaven—all that lovely length and circumference was deep inside her, filling her to the brim with its bounty.

Closing his eyes, he exhaled slowly. "At last."

She was stunned by the perfection of it. In the past sex had been fun, even satisfying sometimes. But she'd never felt this ultimate connection, as if she'd found some vital part of her that had gone missing. Being locked with Jess this way seemed essential to a complete life.

His eyes were still closed and his expression reflected pure bliss, but maybe he looked that way whenever he found himself buried in a warm vagina. What she considered incredible and unique might not register that way for him. And that could be dangerous.

He opened his eyes. "Katie, this feels so good."

"Uh-huh." *Do you say that to all the girls?*

"I've been a damned fool."

That didn't sound like something he'd say to everyone. "You have?"

He kneaded her bottom. "I could have had this on prom night."

She allowed herself to savor the moment. After all these years of hurt and anger, she wanted to remember he'd said that. Yet it wasn't in her nature to flaunt a victory. "You didn't have a wood shop then."

"I had a backseat."

"It's okay, Jess. Water over the dam."

"I know, but I wish—"

"Shh." She leaned forward and kissed him gently. "Let's not spend time on regrets. Let's enjoy what we have right now."

"All right." He brushed his lips over hers. "But I have a confession. It's about the bench."

She cradled his head in both hands and nibbled on his bottom lip. "I know the whole bench thing was designed to seduce me, if that's what you mean."

"No, not that." He paused to kiss her again. "I mean, yes, it was, but I've never had sex on a bench before. I didn't stop to think how…restrictive it would be."

"Oh." And here she'd thought he'd remembered her *Kama Sutra* tip of the night and wanted to run a test. "Well, I like it here. Wood shops turn me on." She rubbed her breasts against his T-shirt.

His breathing quickened. "We're not leaving. But you could lie back on the bench."

"We can make it work this way."

"But I can't thrust. And I—"

She hit him with a Kegel.

"Whoa."

"Did you like that?" She squeezed her muscles again.

He groaned in obvious delight. "The *Kama Sutra* tip."

"Yeah, baby." Holding his head, she gave him an open-mouthed kiss and thrust her tongue deep as she began a series of rhythmic Kegels.

This was turning out much cooler than it had sounded

in the book. She could totally direct the action. Each time she squeezed those muscles around his stiff penis, they both got a charge.

Jess kept a firm grip on her bottom, his fingers kneading in time with her Kegels. Her climax hovered, ready to sweep down and wash over her trembling body. She moaned, reaching for it.

Jess wrenched his mouth away and leaned his forehead against hers as he gasped for breath. "Are you close?"

She gulped for air and kept squeezing. "Very…close."

"I've never…this is so wild."

"But *good*."

"God, yes. So very good. Kiss me again. Hard."

She plunged her tongue into his mouth as the first spasms danced through her body. Then her orgasm descended like an avalanche, tumbling through her writhing body with such force that Jess exploded with her.

They clung to each other, each swallowing the other's cries as they shuddered and quaked in the grip of a shared climax. Their first shared climax. The thought whirled past at first. Katie was too dazed for it to register, but then the thought circled back around and settled over her, warm and soft as cashmere.

She needed to be careful, though. Jess likely didn't place as much importance on such things as she did, which left her vulnerable. But not long ago he'd called himself a damned fool. Maybe he wouldn't be a damned fool a second time.

13

IF JESS HAD ANY DOUBTS that Katie was more experienced than he was, she'd just eliminated those doubts. Sure, he'd maneuvered her into having sex with him on the bench. He'd thought that was so clever of him.

But she was the one who'd made it work. Man, had she ever. He hadn't been able to keep from coming. Even worse, he hadn't had much to do with her climax. She'd given herself one. And only one, because he hadn't been able to last once he'd felt her contractions. He was disappointed in himself.

As they propped each other up, heads resting on each other's shoulders, he took a long, quivering breath and tried to make amends. "Katie, I'm sorry. I wanted to hold back, but I…couldn't."

She stirred against him. "Why would you want to hold back?"

"So you could keep going. Have another one, at least."

She met his comment with silence.

He didn't think silence was a good thing. "Katie?"

"I didn't know we were keeping score."

"We're not, but I was hoping the first time that I could last longer." *Because a woman like you would probably expect that. You've been studying these things and I…haven't.*

"Jess, trust me, the orgasm I had was fine. I wasn't worried about having a second one."

Damn. Now she was trying to protect his feelings. How humiliating. He needed to beef up his reputation.

Lifting his head from her shoulder, he leaned down to nuzzle her soft throat. "Tell you what. Let's take a shower, have a glass of wine and try this on an actual bed."

She raised her head to look at him. There was no welcome in her eyes. "I don't think so, Jess."

The pain of rejection twisted in his gut. "Was I that bad?"

"You weren't bad at all! Stop saying that!"

"Look, you don't have to pump me up. I'm sure you would have appreciated more control on my part."

"Is that all you care about? Your precious control? I thought we were having a great time together, and all you can talk about is the fact that I only had one orgasm."

Now he was confused. Apparently she wasn't upset about the number of orgasms. She was upset because he'd brought up the subject. "Look, I was only trying to—"

"Never mind. Just never mind, Jess!" She disentangled herself from his lap and stood. Her torn panties fell to the floor.

Which was another thing. He'd torn her underwear without giving it a thought. He'd been so filled with lust that he would have ripped aside any piece of clothing that kept him from her. He didn't usually do things like that either. "I'll buy you a new pair," he said.

"I couldn't care less about new underwear."

Before he'd figured out what she had in mind, she grabbed her purse and jacket and stomped out of the wood shop. He was in no shape to run after her.

As he listened to the sound of her car starting up outside, he tried to figure out what had just happened. Here she was, the host of a show called *Talking About Sex,* and that's what he'd been trying to do! Anyone who'd read the *Kama Sutra* from cover to cover and knew how to work those Kegel exercises would have certain expectations, right?

Right! She'd put on quite a demonstration for him, and he'd responded like an eighteen-year-old. Then he'd tried to apologize for coming too soon, and she'd acted as if that was the worst thing he could have said to her. Women! How were you supposed to figure them out?

KATIE GOT A MILE DOWN the road and turned around. This was stupid. She had the prospect of having some of the best sex of her life with Jess. So what if he wasn't moved by the significance of it all? He hadn't understood her emotional needs thirteen years ago and he didn't understand them now either, but that didn't change the fact that nobody gave her sexual thrills like Jess.

So what if he would never be her happily ever after because he had the sensitivity of a tortilla? Life wasn't perfect. Jess wasn't perfect. Just because she wouldn't ever marry him didn't mean she should deprive herself of the physical joy he could bring her.

Instead of storming off in a huff because he'd been more interested in counting orgasms than rhapsodizing about a mutual climax, she should have taken him up on his offer of a shower, some wine and a romp in his king-size bed. If she didn't expect him to get sentimental, if she went into it looking for great sex and nothing more, then she'd be fine.

Her hazy dreams of a future together were probably doomed anyway, even without this problem. This conflict over the construction would be a bone of contention forever. Even if he considered sex with her to be the spiritual experience of a lifetime, he'd still be hell-bent on tearing down a piece of her history.

So she had a choice between being a martyr to the cause or getting some outstanding satisfaction from Jess. Cheryl had advised Katie to have some fun with this. She hadn't ever insinuated that Jess and Katie were soul mates. Katie should just use this guy for some mutual mindless sex. It was a fair exchange, wasn't it?

After parking in his driveway, she tucked her keys in the pocket of her skirt and left her jacket and purse in the car. Then she locked the car and walked through the courtyard again. As she rang his doorbell, she thought of what she wanted to say.

He opened the door wearing running shorts and the same T-shirt he'd had on earlier. He was also barefoot and looked understandably surprised to see her. "Is something wrong? Did your car break down?"

"No. Everything's fine. Can I come in?"

"Sure." He stepped aside. "Listen, I know I said something wrong a few minutes ago. I've never been good with words. I didn't mean to upset you."

"I shouldn't have flown off the handle." She turned to him. *Live for the moment,* she reminded herself. Soon she and Jess would be naked and writhing on a king-size bed. That was her only goal right now.

"Why did you?" He looked genuinely puzzled.

So he was clueless, but he was also yummy. She'd be a fool not to take what he so obviously wanted to give her. "It doesn't matter," she said. "Let's not make this complicated. I like having sex with you."

Heat flared in his eyes. "I'm glad, but—"

"Do you like having sex with me?"

"You'd better believe I do."

Desire tightened within her. Maybe it wouldn't be so bad having a man intent on giving her multiple orgasms. "Then let's do it."

"That's all? No conditions? No special instructions?"

Only to myself. "None. I know I've been playing hard to get."

He rubbed the back of his neck. "That's putting it mildly. But I guess I should expect that, seeing as how you have that show and everything."

"What does my show have to do with it?"

"It's obvious." He waved a hand in the air. "You're an expert in the field, so you'd want to try stuff out, test a guy to see what he can take."

"You think you're some sort of lab experiment?" That blew her away. He really didn't know her at all.

"In a way, yeah. That's fine, though. I'm not complaining."

"You *like* being a lab experiment?"

"It's been pretty damned exciting, Katie. Yeah, I like it."

Apparently she'd played the bad girl a little too well. He seemed to be attracted to her because she was, as he put it, *an expert in the field.* No wonder he hadn't gotten all warm and fuzzy over their first mutual orgasm.

Well, that made this very easy. "Jess, the experiment's over. I just want to have hot, sweaty sex with you. No more games."

He gazed at her as if he couldn't quite believe it. Then he reached out and clicked the dead bolt, locking them in. "I'm not about to turn down a chance like that. Come with me." He took her hand and laced his fingers through hers.

An *expert in the field* would be nonchalant about walking with him down two steps to the living room and across to a wide hall. But Katie's heart was pounding as they neared the end of the hall where a pair of double doors stood open. The dim light revealed the corner of a bed, a four-poster in dark wood. His bed.

This is only for sex. She needed to keep chanting that to herself so that she wouldn't start imagining that they were headed for something more. Maybe she should have suggested they go to a hotel after all, to underline the impersonal nature of this event.

Yes, a hotel would have been better. Once she stepped into his bedroom, she could feel his personality there almost as strongly as in the wood shop. The bed, end tables and armoire were massive and telegraphed the virility she'd always associated with him. A leather chair and a floor lamp made an equally bold statement of masculinity.

"I suppose my bedposts are phallic symbols," he said.

"Classic." The thick posts definitely qualified. Maybe she was susceptible to that kind of suggestion because she'd always liked sturdy four-posters. The delicate spindly ones didn't appeal to her, but this…oh, yeah.

Then she noticed the white teddy lying on the comforter and the unlit pillar candles on the dresser and both bedside tables. She gestured toward the teddy. "For me?"

"Yeah. But after I heard the first part of your show, I decided the wood shop was where we should start out."

At that moment she realized this was the scene he'd pictured years ago when he'd imagined how they would eventually make love. Maybe he had a tender, sentimental side after all. Maybe… No, she'd been down that road one too many times.

He'd set this up because he'd wanted to seduce his field

expert and he thought white lace and candles would do the trick. After listening to her show, he'd switched to a different venue. He'd been trying to outthink her.

She'd intended to make him work for everything she gave him, and he'd done that. Presenting him with challenges had given her a sense of power which had served her well the past few days. She hadn't been easy for him, and that was okay with her.

But now that she'd cured herself of sentimental longings, she didn't have to throw obstacles in his way every five minutes. The process had been sort of exhausting, come to think of it. She was ready to relax and enjoy some no-strings sex.

She picked up the teddy. "Would you like me to put this on?"

He glanced from her to the teddy, then back at her, his gaze already growing hotter. "Yes."

She noticed another set of double doors standing open on the far side of the room. "The bathroom?"

"Uh-huh."

"Then I'll be right back."

"I'll be here." There was something in his tone—something rich and deep. Appreciation, maybe, or gratitude, as if he truly valued having her there.

Damn, she was doing it again. She had no solid evidence that he was gaga over her. Therefore she would not go gaga over him. End of story.

She wouldn't even allow herself to go gaga over his bathroom, although it was the kind of bathroom she'd always dreamed of having. Closing the double doors to give herself some privacy, she looked around and gave a little sigh of pleasure.

The white marble and white tile might have looked stark, except that he'd chosen deep purple towels and glittering gold faucets, so the bathroom looked as if it belonged to royalty. The scent of his aftershave hung in the air, and one of the oversize towels on a hook by the shower felt damp.

On an impulse Katie stripped down and stepped around the tiled wall into the shower. Of course he had multiple showerheads. Of course. When she turned them on and was engulfed in an invigorating spray, she moaned in ecstasy. A shower like this was almost foreplay.

Consequently by the time she'd toweled dry with another one of those thick purple bath towels, she was feeling very sexy. Slowly she stepped into the white lace teddy, and as she did, she caught a glimpse of herself in the large mirror behind the marble counter.

She looked like a *Playboy* centerfold.

Was that the image Jess had of her? She'd certainly never had that image of herself. She wouldn't have bought this teddy, thinking that it belonged on a woman with more cleavage. But the way the teddy fit, she seemed to have plenty of cleavage.

Seeing herself in this outfit reminded her of catching her first glimpse of the publicity shot KRZE had used on the billboard ad. That couldn't really be her. She'd given credit to the wonders of digital photography, which could make anybody look great with a few clicks of the mouse.

Lo and behold, a white lace teddy seemed to have the same effect as Photoshop. She looked *good*. With one last glance in the mirror, she walked out to meet Jess.

ONCE HE HEARD THE SHOWER going, Jess knew he had a little time. Heading for the living room, he grabbed a butane lighter out of a drawer and went back to light the pillar candles. The shower was still on when he finished that, so he acted on another inspiration.

His bedroom opened onto the patio through a pair of curtained French doors, which gave him access to the yellow rosebush. Fortunately he'd left the pruning shears on the patio table next to the bush. Choosing a rose in full bloom, he snipped it off and quickly pruned off the thorns.

Then he carried it back inside and laid it across the pillows. They wouldn't want to bother with covers, so he threw those back, bunching them at the end of the bed. He was so excited he was shaking. For years he'd dreamed about this moment, and now it was finally here.

The candles gave plenty of light, so he turned off the lamps. And that was that. He couldn't think of anything else to do. Wait—he could get a few condoms out of the box and leave them loose in the drawer. There, that was better. More accessible.

Music! He'd nearly forgotten. He hurried over to the armoire where he kept his CD player, opened the doors and punched the power button. Nostalgia filled the room. He and Katie had listened to these songs on the radio when they'd driven up to "A" Mountain to make out.

And now he really was out of things to do. He couldn't imagine himself stretched out on the bed when she returned. Even if he did that, would he leave his clothes on or take them off? Neither option seemed good. Lying there naked was too obvious, and yet his T-shirt and shorts wouldn't look particularly erotic.

He finally decided to sit in his leather armchair on the far side of the bed and wait for her to come out. The longer he sat there imagining her naked in his bathroom, the more aroused he became. But he wouldn't go in there. He'd waited too long for this moment to spoil it by jumping the gun.

And another thing—no matter how good she looked, he would take this lovemaking slow and easy. He'd make sure that she had several orgasms before he came. She might not have liked his mentioning that, but he couldn't believe she didn't want multiple orgasms. All women did, especially ones who spent five nights a week talking about sex.

He'd been concentrating so hard on those double doors that when they opened at last, he had to blink to make sure he wasn't imagining things. No, the doors were open, and Katie stood there pink and rosy from the shower. The tips of her hair were damp, and the light from the bathroom created a halo around her body. He'd never seen anyone look so beautiful.

Speechless, he rose to his feet. The wide expanse of the bed lay between them. He wished he'd decided to stretch out on it after all. Then he'd be that much closer to her.

"Here I am." She reached back and turned off the bathroom light before starting toward the bed. "Boy, that music brings back memories, doesn't it? I hope you didn't mind, but I decided to take a—oh." Her gaze fell to the rose on the pillow.

Slowly she reached for it. "I—I'd forgotten you had that rosebush." She put the blossom to her nose and sniffed.

For the rest of his life he would remember how she looked standing there in the white teddy and holding the yellow rose he'd picked for her. She was everything he'd ever wanted, but he didn't know how to tell her that, was afraid if he tried that he would break the spell. She was here. She wanted him. That would be enough for now.

"The teddy fits," she said.

"You look…wonderful in it." *Wonderful* didn't begin to describe how she looked, but her beauty was frying his brain cells.

"Thank you." She stretched out on her side on the pale green sheets and laid the rose in front of her. "And thank you for the rose."

He nodded, too overcome to form a complete sentence.

"Are you coming to bed?"

"Yes." But he didn't want to move just yet. He needed to absorb the picture of her lying in his bed—Katie, white teddy, nostalgic music, flickering candles, yellow rose. Heaven.

She smiled. "Sometime in this century?"

He had to laugh at himself. She must think he was a complete dork. "I'm sorry. It's just that…never mind." He reached for the back of his T-shirt.

"What?"

"Nothing." He pulled the T-shirt over his head and tossed it aside.

"Talk to me, Jess."

"You look like you should be on a calendar or something." He shoved his running shorts and briefs down in one swift movement.

She gazed at his erection. "From your reaction, I have a good idea what kind of calendar you mean."

"If I've insulted you I take it back." Slightly dizzy from the anticipation of what was about to happen, he climbed onto the bed.

"No insult taken. I feel like a calendar girl in this outfit." She picked up the rose and stroked it over his penis.

He groaned. He'd never felt anything quite like the tickle of those soft petals. "Is that a move in the *Kama Sutra?*"

"Not that I know of. I made it up." She stroked him again with the rose. "When I do that you twitch."

Much as he enjoyed the velvety rose, twitching could lead to other things, and he didn't want to let loss of control ruin this episode. Time for some bold moves. He was determined to acquit himself.

He took the rose from her. "Let's see if I can make you twitch."

"By doing what?"

"I don't know. Lie back and let me make something up."

14

KATIE WASN'T SURE IF SHE should let Jess take over. The sight of him naked and aroused was playing havoc with her decision to make this an impersonal encounter. He was so gorgeous she couldn't see straight. And he had that music from their dating days playing in the background.

She couldn't seem to get her footing with Jess. Right when she thought she understood him and could play by his rules, he put a yellow rose on the pillow and Billy Joel on the CD player. Having no-strings sex with a guy was tough when he did things like that.

"Come on, Katie. Relax." Jess brushed the rose once across her lips. "I won't bite." His smile looked slightly wicked. "Or if I do, I promise you'll like it."

She wanted to abandon herself to the experience. She really did. Those carpenter's hands would feel outstanding. But while he was touching her all over, she didn't want him fooling with her heart. Every other part of her was fair game, but her heart was off-limits.

Unfortunately he might capture her heart without realizing it. If he didn't even know he had it in the palm of his hand, he could get careless and break it into a million pieces. She didn't trust him not to do that.

Then she had an idea. She would pretend she didn't

know this man in bed with her. She wouldn't say his name at all. In her mind she'd turn him into a handsome, virile and very naked stranger. She wouldn't get emotionally involved with a stranger.

With that thought in mind, she turned on her back and stretched out on the soft sheets. A stranger was about to seduce her. How delicious. She closed her eyes.

"Don't go to sleep on me now." The stranger stroked the rose over her eyelids.

She pretended she'd never heard that husky baritone before. "It's up to you to keep me awake, isn't it?" Thinking of him as a stranger made her feel sassy.

"I'll take that challenge." The rose drifted down to her mouth again.

She nipped at the soft petals. The petals had the same silkiness as the skin covering his penis. She ran her tongue over her lips. Except he was a stranger, so she wouldn't know that fact about him. Not yet. She could only imagine.

As he drew the rose away and nestled it between her breasts, he kissed her on the mouth. She struggled to keep her image of a stranger, but the kiss felt much too familiar. It would be so easy to open her eyes and discover exactly who was using his mouth to heat her blood and soften any remaining resistance.

Eyes still closed, she turned her head to one side, away from his seductive kiss. "Blindfold me," she said.

He hovered over her, his breath warm on her face. "Why?"

She couldn't tell him why. But she'd have to give him a reason that he'd accept. "If you lose one sense, the others become stronger."

"I want every single one of my senses tonight."

"And I want all but one." She felt his hesitation.

At last he spoke. "I'll be right back." A few feet away a drawer slid open, then closed again. He returned and lifted her head to slip something underneath.

Moments later a smooth strip of material covered her eyes and tightened around her head. She thought it might be a silk necktie. Now she could open her eyes and it didn't matter.

"How's that?"

"Perfect." Not being able to see helped enormously with her fantasy.

"Did you…" He paused and cleared his throat. "Did you want me to tie you up?" Although he sounded a little uncertain, there was a trace of excitement there, too.

Somehow she managed not to laugh. Give a man a little taste of kinkiness and he was off to the races. "Let's save that for another night." She was assuming there would be another night, and if she was only using him for sex, why not?

"Another night then." The rose moved again as he trailed it down the inside of her arm. "Tonight I want to memorize every inch of you, from the tips of your fingers to the tips of your toes." He traced the line of her other arm all the way down to her palm, which lay facing up.

Next he used the rose to tickle her inner thighs. She discovered that what she'd told him was true. Now that she couldn't see, she could feel the individual petals curling and bending against her skin. Her thighs became increasingly sensitized the longer he touched them with the rose.

She heard him breathing and knew he was aroused from the tempo of each inhale. Reminding herself that he was a stranger, she imagined him watching her as he teased her with the rose, imagined him getting harder and more desperate as he gazed at the softness of her inner thighs.

Then he moved down over her calves and on to the soles of her feet. There he traded tickling for a soft brushing motion. As the petals traveled over the curve of her instep and whispered across the base of her toes, the caress seemed to travel up her body, kissing all her nerve endings and making them hum.

Trailing the rose back up her body, he shifted his weight. One strap of her teddy slid down her arm. The other strap followed. The rose found its way between her thighs and lay there as he tugged the straps down, peeling the white lace from her breasts.

Cool air touched her nipples. The straps had effectively pinned her arms to her sides. Her blindfold suggestion had obviously started him thinking. Slowly he circled each breast with the rose while her nipples grew tighter with each turn.

Then he centered in, brushing the rose rapidly across each nipple until the petals began to fall. She felt each individual one, a yellow thumbprint on her quivering breasts. She expected him to follow the path of the rose with his mouth, but instead his weight shifted again and in one quick motion he'd unsnapped the crotch of her one-piece teddy.

She gasped at the suddenness of it and gasped again when he drew the rose between her thighs and settled it firmly into her moist cleft. The outer petals had fallen away, leaving a stronger bud that made perfect contact with her trigger point. Slowly he began to wiggle the rose.

Surely she wouldn't come that easily. After all, he'd only been stroking her gently with a flower. That shouldn't be enough to…but then again…maybe she'd misjudged her level of arousal, because…oh, my…

He wiggled the rose faster, and she began to pant.

Maybe it was the blindfold. Maybe it was telling herself that he was a dashing stranger who had appeared to seduce her. But in no time she was quaking in readiness, nearly there and then…coming in a rush, her hips lifting off the bed with a soft cry of surprise.

With a gentle murmur of approval, he eased the rose free. Using it like a paintbrush, he drew circles around her breasts with the damp petals and at last brushed the rose over her mouth once again. She tasted the wildness of her own desire, which inflamed her even more.

The moisture from the rose was replaced by his tongue, his mouth, feasting, sucking, nipping. He moved from her lips to her throat, from her throat to her shoulder, from her shoulder to her breasts.

He covered her with kisses, moving ever downward, peeling the teddy away on his descent. Pausing briefly to swipe his tongue over her still-quivering flash point, he pulled the teddy over her thighs, past her knees and then her feet. It hit the floor with a soft plop.

Her blindfold made her conscious of every layered sound. In the far background was the music, make-out music from high school. Closer yet was his breathing and the lap of his tongue and mouth as he started his journey back, beginning with her toes.

The most immediate sound was her own breathing and the rapid thump of her heart. That thump grew louder as he made love to her toes, sliding his tongue into each crevice as if he could make her come that way. Maybe he could. With the blindfold on, her entire body was an erogenous zone.

When he sucked on her toes, she felt the tightening begin. She could almost will herself into a climax—she was that far into this fantasy. When he moved on to the backs of her knees, bending her leg so that he could thoroughly lick her there, she thought maybe that would be enough to trip her switch.

Before she could find out, he kissed his way back up the inside of her thighs and found the spot that would surely take her anywhere he wanted her to go. She'd thought that having oral sex in his truck on the top of "A" Mountain was the best it could get. She'd been wrong.

Lying on fine sheets, blindfolded, wrapped in the pretense of anonymity while he gave her the most incredible tongue bath ever known—that was the best. She was helpless in the face of his assault and she came once before he'd really gotten started. Moaning and thrashing about, she discovered she wasn't going anywhere. He held her fast and continued to nibble and suck until she produced another writhing, whimpering orgasm.

As she gulped for air, he slid back up beside her and kissed her, flavoring her mouth yet again with the taste of her climax.

Then he lifted his head and sucked in air. "I could keep that up forever, except for one thing. If I don't get inside you in the next few seconds, I'll go crazy."

"I want you there." Amazingly she did. She didn't need another orgasm, but she definitely needed the solid length of his penis buried deep in her vagina. There was a reason phallic symbols showed up everywhere and bolts fit smoothly in their assigned holes. That interlocking concept was what kept civilization going.

She waited impatiently as he opened a drawer and tore open a condom packet. The sound of latex snapping against skin had never seemed so erotic. It was a distinctive sound, but she'd never have paid attention without the blindfold.

She felt like melted candle wax ready for the press of a golden seal.

At last the mattress dipped as he moved over her. Leaning down, he placed a gentle kiss on her lips. "Now." And with one smooth thrust he was there. He groaned softly.

She grasped his hips. "We fit so well."

"Of course we do." He began a slow, steady rhythm. "I've always known we would."

She tried to block that comment. A stranger wouldn't say it. She tried to convince herself that she didn't know this man who was stroking so firmly, touching all the right places, creating a new and different tension within her.

His breath feathered across her cheeks. "God, but you feel good. So warm, so yielding. I hate having this damned latex between us."

Her breath caught. She'd been thinking the same thing. She longed for the slide of his bare penis. "That would be crazy."

"That doesn't mean I don't want it." He picked up the pace and his breathing grew ragged. "Just because something's crazy doesn't mean...it wouldn't be wonderful."

"No." She gripped him tighter, rising to meet his thrusts.

His voice rumbled in her ear, heightening every sensation. "I want to feel your slick, wet vagina, feel you start to contract."

She moaned. "I'm going to come again."

"I know. I can tell." He began to gasp for breath.

She edged nearer to her release. Any second she'd be lost in the whirlwind. Soon...soon...

"I want to feel the rush of moisture when you come." He groaned. "I want to feel myself pouring into you."

She was losing her grip on her fantasy. The closer she came to her climax, the less he seemed like a stranger.

"Katie, let me see your eyes."

"Noooo." She felt herself falling into that dangerous place where she cared too much.

"I want to see your eyes when you come. While I'm inside you, thrusting. I want to see that, Katie. I've dreamed of it forever."

Her body began to shake.

"Please, Katie." He pumped faster. "Let me take off the blindfold. Let me watch you come."

"Jess, no." The minute she said his name, she knew her fantasy had slipped away.

"Yes." His voice, warm and rough, coaxed her as his body urged her higher. "Give me that."

With a wail of surrender she lifted her hips and took that final stroke that sent her over the edge. The moment the spasms hit, he pulled off the blindfold.

She looked into his eyes, those hot, dark eyes, knowing he would see far too much, helpless to conceal the powerful emotions that rocketed through her body. He was no stranger. He never would be.

"Oh, Katie." With a deep groan he surged forward, his body shuddering in release. "Katie," he murmured again as he quaked in the aftermath of his climax. "We finally made it."

She held on tight, not knowing what he meant, not knowing if this was an ending, the final phase of a conquest he'd longed for, or the beginning of something new. Words had never been his strong suit.

But his body talked beautifully. She'd never experienced anything remotely like this in another man's arms.

Yet life wasn't all about sex. Although with someone like Jess, she was tempted to believe it could be.

JESS KNEW HE HAD A BAD habit of falling asleep after sex. He didn't want to let that happen this time, but he'd been up early this morning and he'd put in a long day. Add to that all the sexual activity and two orgasms, and he couldn't help feeling groggy. Half-asleep and fighting to stay awake, he was vaguely aware that Katie had wiggled out from under him, but he thought she was still there in the bed.

Any second now he'd rouse himself and get up. He could make them a pot of coffee. Now that he had her in his bed, he wanted to make up for lost time. They could talk, really talk. And then make love again. Hell, he could sleep anytime. Anytime at all...

At dawn he woke with a start and discovered Katie was no longer in the bed. He called her name, but when he got no answer, he knew for sure she'd left, probably hours ago. Damn it! This was not how a woman like Katie should be treated.

Then he noticed his red silk tie lying on her pillow. She'd found his pad of yellow sticky notes in the kitchen and attached one to the tie. In the gray light of early morning he squinted at the writing, which was bold and curvy, like Katie.

Jess, thank you for a great time. Katie

That was it. No mention of seeing him again. He studied the note some more. She did say she'd had *a great time.* That should count for something. A woman who'd had a great time would want to repeat the experience, wouldn't she?

Climbing out of bed, he noticed that she'd left the teddy

lying on his leather armchair. He'd meant for her to take it, but he hadn't spelled that out, so maybe she thought it had been on loan. Yeah, right. Like he'd ever let another woman wear it.

He picked it up and felt an immediate rush of desire. She'd looked fantastic in the teddy. She'd looked even better as he'd slowly peeled her out of it. Half in and half out of that scrap of lace had to be the sexiest pose he'd seen on any woman.

So now what? He couldn't very well keep a white teddy hanging in his closet or folded in his underwear drawer. Just his luck he'd get in an accident, end up in the hospital, ask a buddy to bring him some clean clothes and be branded a cross-dresser.

Then he had an inspiration. The teddy was the perfect excuse to see Katie again. He wouldn't even call, which would give her an excuse to turn him down. He'd just show up at the station after her show tonight and say he had something that belonged to her. Excellent.

As he showered he thought about the night before, how Katie had stormed out and then come back wanting more sex after all. That was encouraging. Sure, he'd fallen asleep on her, but the evening hadn't been a total bust. Once he was face-to-face with her again, he'd be able to tell which way the wind blew. But he thought she'd want more sex. He sure as hell did.

The big question was whether she wanted more than sex from him. He couldn't get a handle on that. He'd finally admitted to himself that he wanted more than sex from her. A steady relationship would be nice and then…well, he'd start with the steady relationship and see how that went.

As he arrived at the job site, he was reminded of the

issue that might make a steady relationship with Katie problematic. The Value Our Roots gang was loving Katie's on-air campaign. Somewhere they'd located a fifteen-foot plastic screw-and-nut combo, which they'd mounted on a wooden platform on wheels so they could roll the thing back and forth along the construction fence.

The inflating and deflating balloons were still there, too, but now more picketers carried signs that said simply Screwed. A few signs read Save Crazy Katie's Station, as if she owned the whole damned thing.

The number of picketers told him the movement was gaining ground. He didn't think the developers would scrap their plans for the building, but stranger things had happened. Because it was now at least a possibility, he had to ask himself how he'd feel about Katie if she robbed him of the chance to complete this project.

Not good. No matter how much he wanted to forget it, he doubted that he'd be able to. Even though Harkins Construction wouldn't be responsible for the project going belly-up, his company's name would be associated with the failure. The reputation he'd worked so hard to build would suffer to some extent.

His company was on the hot seat now, but once the building was completed and everyone could see how beautiful it was, the protests would go away. After the KRZE building was torn down, people would eventually forget that, too.

Katie wouldn't, though. Unfortunately if he got what he wanted, she wouldn't get what she wanted. She might blame him for losing her grandmother's house forever.

Funny, but when he was in bed with Katie he forgot all of that. He liked to think that she did, too. But they couldn't stay in bed all the time, and once they each got to work, the problems became huge.

Gabe was in the construction trailer drinking coffee when Jess walked in, and Jess had the feeling Gabe had been waiting there specifically until he showed up.

"I guess you've seen the latest," Gabe said. He didn't smile.

"Yeah." Jess got his personal mug and retrieved some coffee from the battered two-gallon pot he'd bought at a garage sale the year he'd started the business.

"I decided to listen to Crazy Katie last night after all, to see if she'd changed her tune. But I guess you didn't have any luck yesterday talking her out of this campaign of hers."

Jess felt a stab of guilt. He hadn't tried to talk her out of it. According to their ground rules, he wasn't even supposed to try. She'd stuck by those rules, too. At no time had she implied that she'd have sex with him if he'd work to save her grandmother's house.

Because he'd been so desperate to have sex with her, he'd given up his right to change her mind about her protest. At the time the decision had seemed logical, and that was scary. Now he had no idea what to tell Gabe.

He made a great production out of stirring powdered creamer into his coffee while he considered his options. "I'm afraid I overestimated my influence on her," he said at last.

"Seems like it."

Jess tapped the wooden stirrer on the edge of his cup and dropped it in a plastic trash can next to the coffeepot. "She's a very stubborn woman."

"I'm sure." Gabe cleared his throat. "Okay, what's going on, Jess?"

Jess glanced at him in surprise. His foreman had never used that tone with him. "What do you mean?"

"You took a long lunch hour with her yesterday, so I thought you must be getting somewhere. Then I listened to the show and found out she was on the same kick as before. Hardware sex. That's quite a stretch."

"I suppose." But Jess didn't think so, not anymore. Symbols were powerful. He'd proved it by shoving the legs into the bench he'd made and turning her on in the process.

"Anyway, I was out last night running errands, so I came by your house to ask you what was up with her. But you had company, so I didn't stop."

"Um, yeah, I did." Feeling guiltier by the minute, Jess met Gabe's gaze.

"It was her, wasn't it?"

Jess tried one last dodge, although he figured it was no use. "Why would you think it was her?"

"I doubt there are two people in town whose license plate says KRZ KTY."

Jess closed his eyes. He was no good at this secrecy business. He'd never noticed that she had a personalized plate, but he still should have told her to park in the garage in case someone recognized her car.

"Look, man, I don't blame you for having a thing for her. She's a babe. But the timing sucks."

"Yeah, it does." Jess stared glumly at Gabe. "Have you...mentioned this to anyone?"

"No. And I won't."

"Thanks."

"But I have to tell you, if the guys found out, you'd have a real problem with morale. They hate what she's doing to this project and they're not all that fond of her either. If they thought you guys were shacking up, then—"

"I hate what she's doing, too. But she…has her reasons." Jess wasn't going to defend his behavior by revealing Katie's sentimental ties to the house. That was personal information.

"I sure hope she has reasons! Jess, I'm not going to try and tell you what to do, but…getting involved with her isn't the best idea you've ever had, unless you can somehow make her shut up."

Jess's smile was bleak. "That's not an option, buddy."

"Then be careful. Be very, very careful."

15

"I NEED AN EMERGENCY LUNCH meeting." Katie had speed dialed Cheryl's office and been lucky enough to find her in.

"I can't do lunch," Cheryl said, "but I can meet you right away over at La Placita for a quick cup of iced coffee. I can't stay long because I'm due back in court, and this trial is turning into a circus. The defendant claims he's channeling Clarence Darrow so he doesn't need a lawyer, but personally I think he's channeling Elvis. You should see the hair on this guy. Straight out of the fifties. And his clothes are—"

"It's about Jess."

"'Nuff said. See you."

Katie made it to the cozy plaza right across from the court buildings in record time. Perpetually late Cheryl was nowhere in sight. Katie made use of the time she knew she'd have to get two iced coffees from her favorite little shop on the plaza.

By the time she'd carried the drinks to a wrought-iron table under a mesquite tree, Cheryl came striding briskly along, a large purple tote slung over her shoulder. Cheryl wasn't a tiny-purse sort of woman. She liked to haul large chunks of her life with her, including her day planner, a water bottle, various snack foods, a generous makeup case, her morning paper and a paperback novel in case she finished the newspaper and was stuck with nothing to do.

"I'm glad you called." She sat down in the wrought-iron chair opposite Katie and took the iced coffee Katie pushed in her direction. "I've been dying to know what's happened, but I've been working late—although I took time out to listen to your show and I *love* the nuts and bolts guy. He sounded just like Yoda. Didn't he? I closed my eyes and pictured this little wrinkled guy with big pointy ears. I—"

"We don't have much time, right?"

Cheryl glanced at her Mickey Mouse watch. "Right. You talk. I'll drink my coffee."

Now that she was sitting here with Cheryl, Katie didn't know where to start. "He planted a yellow rosebush," she said.

Cheryl looked at her as if she'd lost it. "Is that significant? I know rose colors are supposed to mean different things, but I never can remember what they are. Red is good for passion. Are you afraid he's not passionate?"

"Yellow roses were our special thing in high school. I guess you wouldn't remember."

"He was *your* first love, not mine. I don't remember a thing about yellow roses." Cheryl's gaze sharpened. "Do you know this because he told you or because you saw it for yourself?"

"I—"

"You went to his house, didn't you, you little devil! Was it gorgeous? A guy with his own construction business would have a gorgeous house, that's what I'm thinking. Did you go to bed with him?"

"Yes." Maybe all she'd have to do was wait for Cheryl to ask the right questions. That would make this easier.

"Wow. Now what? Was he good? Was he better than

Stewart What's-his-name, the guy you dated a year ago? Personally I thought Stewart was too bland to be a good lover, but Jess—he has potential."

"Cheryl, he was too good. That's the problem."

Cheryl reached over and patted her hand. "Trust me, too good is not a problem. Too good is a woman's dream come true. Are we talking multiple orgasms?"

"Yes." Katie could still feel the imprint of his hands, his mouth and his tongue on her skin.

"Woo-hoo." Cheryl fanned herself. "I thought he'd be a powerhouse, and I was right."

"But that's just it! I'm right back where I was, with me wanting him so much I can't stand it, and he...he fell asleep on me! But then I think of the yellow rosebush and Billy Joel on his CD player and I wonder if maybe he's really into me."

"Sounds like it." Cheryl looked as if she wanted to say something more, but instead she went back to drinking her iced coffee.

"But what if all those things are only his way of getting sex? And don't forget that he fell asleep right after!"

Cheryl put down her drink. "Guys do that. I wouldn't read too much into it." Then she grinned. "Maybe you wore him out."

"I'm scared, Cheryl. I'm scared I'm going to do something stupid like blurt out that I love him or something."

"Do you?"

Katie hesitated, turning the concept over in her mind. "Yeah," she said. "I've tried really hard not to, but it looks like I might. I'm having all these white-picket-fence yearnings, too."

"What about your grandmother's house?"

"Exactly! How can I be in love with someone who's ready to put up a parking garage on the property?"

"Katie, it's not his decision. He was hired to do a job. I'll bet he doesn't even know it's your grandmother's house."

"Yes, he does. He found out yesterday. But he didn't say anything to me like *Oh, in that case, I'll see what I can do to save it.* So he can't have those same kinds of feelings for me, can he?" She needed Cheryl to put her logical lawyer's brain to work on this question.

"I don't know what he could do to save it. He could jeopardize his career by refusing to build the parking garage on the site, but that seems like a stupid sacrifice. They'd fire him and hire somebody else. You don't want him to fall on his sword for no good reason, do you?"

"No." Katie couldn't see a way out. "But if he goes ahead with it, I can't pretend he wasn't involved. I'd always remember that, which could be a real deal breaker. If I win and he can't finish the project, he'll be just as upset with me. So I think I have to stop seeing him. That's aside from the fact that he fell asleep on me."

"Oh, dear." Cheryl frowned. "You're really going to stop seeing a guy who gives you multiple orgasms? I think that goes against the Women's Code of Reasonable Conduct."

Despite her misery, Katie laughed. "You made that up."

"Well, if there isn't such a thing, there should be, and you'd definitely be in violation of it. He hasn't started building that parking garage, has he? How about you wait to get mad at him until he actually does that?"

Katie's spirits lifted as they usually did whenever she talked to Cheryl. "And in the meantime I soak up all that great sex?"

"That's what I'm thinking."

"What about this falling-in-love business?"

"Maybe you are and maybe you're not. You're operating under the influence of all those terrific orgasms, which could be skewing your thinking. If you end up losing your grandmother's house, which I hope you don't, but if you do and you still have feelings for him, then it's probably love and not just sex."

"And if I succeed and his project isn't built, then he'll dump me."

Cheryl looked at her over the rim of her plastic drink glass. "Unless he's falling in love with you."

Katie couldn't pretend she hadn't thought of that. There was a moment last night as he'd pulled off her blindfold when she could have sworn she'd seen something in his expression, something deeper than mere lust. But she didn't trust herself. She might be indulging in wishful thinking.

JESS SPENT MOST OF HIS spare moments debating what to do about Katie. He'd planned to take the lace teddy to her at the station after her show. If he handed it to her in something like a bag or a box, it wouldn't be embarrassing for her. He'd spent a fair amount of time wondering what he should put it in.

If she'd never worn it, he could get some kind of a box and tissue paper, the way you did with new clothes given as a gift. But he wasn't sure that was appropriate under the circumstances. A brown paper sack was too tacky, and he obviously couldn't just hand it to her.

The teddy was his reason for seeing her again, so he had to handle the presentation right. After listening to Gabe's mini lecture, he'd realized he couldn't go over to the station tonight and risk being seen there again. From now on he had to keep his relationship with Katie under wraps.

So long as Gabe was the only one who knew what was going on, Jess figured he was safe. He worried some about Gabe's opinion, but not enough to stop seeing Katie. She might be through with him—no guarantees on that—but at least he would give it another shot on the pretense that he'd intended the teddy as a gift and wanted to give it to her.

Finally he could find no alternative except to show up at her apartment. He wouldn't pick the lock this time. Once would qualify as an interesting stunt to get her attention. Twice was venturing into stalker territory.

Because her apartment was a fair distance from his house, he decided to drive the Jag over and listen to her show on the way. It wasn't the wisest choice, because hearing her voice made him hot. That was even before she began describing her *Kama Sutra* tip of the night.

"Tonight we'll talk about the role of biting in sexual play," she said.

"Biting?" He turned up the volume. Sure, he'd nipped her skin a few times, but he'd never considered an actual bite. Maybe that was a mistake on his part.

"I'm sure most of the women out there have been given a hickey at one time or another. You probably think men are more likely to use their teeth on a partner. Not so."

Jess had never given Katie a hickey. He thought guys who had to mark their girlfriends had to be insecure dweebs.

"Surprisingly women actually do more biting than men. One theory is that men express their passion with larger movements, like...shall we say...vigorous thrusting."

Due to his growing erection, Jess decided to pull into the

right-hand lane and slow down. Speeding along while Katie talked about thrusting could end badly for him and his fellow motorists. Unfortunately that put him behind a motor home from Illinois going ten miles under the speed limit.

"Biting can increase the sexual tension, but we're not talking werewolves and vampires here, folks. Let's not break the skin. Let's not draw blood. Little nips at key times can be exciting for both of you. Immediately prior to or during orgasm, for instance. It can be a signal that you're really turned on by what's happening."

Katie sounded as if she wanted more of that. He'd remember to keep that in his routine. Come to think of it, he wouldn't mind a few love bites from her. Maybe she didn't do that unless a guy drove her wild. That was a depressing thought.

If she'd let him into her apartment tonight, he could try to get her worked up enough that she'd feel like biting him. Damn, now it seemed like a mark of excellence. If he didn't leave her place with tooth marks, then he hadn't done his job.

"Where to bite? I'll leave that up to you, but here are a few guidelines. Guys—concentrate on her erogenous zones, primarily her breasts and thighs. As you move up her thighs in search of that all-important buried treasure, take it easy when you reach X marks the spot. And ladies— nibbling on his package works fine, but don't get rough or the fun will be all over."

If he didn't know better, he'd think she was giving him suggestions for the next time they had sex. But she hadn't indicated there would be a next time. He'd thought about calling her today and had chickened out.

He didn't want to hear bad news over the phone. If she

didn't want to see him again, she'd have to tell him to his face. And then he'd try to talk her out of it.

"We have to take a short commercial break, but don't go away. I'll be right back with tonight's featured guest, Dr. Edna Reid, who will tell us why little boys dig huge holes in the ground and why some continue that obsession as adults, using tractors and earthmovers for the same infantile satisfaction. Don't touch that dial!"

Jess couldn't believe there were this many weirdos in the world and that Katie knew how to get in touch with all of them. During the commercial he got back into the passing lane and gunned the engine to get past the motor home.

So Katie was into biting. He had to face the fact that she was way more experienced than he was. For example, there was the blindfold thing. At the moment she'd suggested it last night, he'd wondered if she'd want to go from there to some kind of bondage game.

Her answer drifted through his already fevered brain. *Not this time.* She obviously liked to spice up her sex with a little adventure, and here he was, going over there empty-handed except for the teddy in a little gift bag he'd bought today. Maybe he'd better stop somewhere and pick up…something.

He'd have to miss part of her show, but if he expected to come out at the end of the evening with teeth marks, he needed a plan. He needed props. He needed a copy of the *Kama Sutra*.

Thirty minutes later he was back on the road, headed for her apartment. Katie and her wacky sociologist were now in the call-in segment of the show.

"Hi, this is Gabe," said a familiar voice. *"I want to get this theory straight."*

Jess swore under his breath. Gabe was doing this on purpose, knowing Jess was probably listening. Gabe had obviously appointed himself as Jess's conscience tonight.

"What's your question, Gabe?" Katie asked in her radio-perfect voice.

She did have the perfect voice for radio, too—sassy and sweet yet with a firmness and authority that made people believe what she was putting out there. Shoot, Jess even found himself starting to believe her nonsense about his construction urges being tied in with his sex drive.

He loved hearing her voice on the radio, but mostly he loved hearing it when he was deep inside her or when he settled his head between her thighs and made her come. She didn't use her radio voice then. What came out of her mouth was much more wild and untamed.

"Dr. Reid says guys dig holes in the dirt because we're trying to get back to the womb?"

"That's correct," said a woman who was not Katie. Obviously the good professor.

"And guys have sex for the same reason?"

"Exactly," said Dr. Reid.

Jess sighed. He could see the protest signs now—Go Home to Mama, Little Boys. His crew would be furious.

"So why do women have sex then? Are they wishing they had a di—"

"Oh, my, we're late for our commercial break," Katie cut in. *"Thank you, Gabe, for calling in."*

Jess pulled into the parking lot of Katie's apartment complex. This situation was getting out of hand. He sure didn't need to have his foreman calling in to Katie's show to heckle. Maybe the crew expected someone to defend them, and Gabe had appointed himself to the job.

Tomorrow the crew would be giving Gabe high fives for the comment he'd almost made, the one the audience would know he'd been about to make before Katie cut him off. Jess didn't like the direction this was going. Emotions were running way too hot on this issue.

He knew trying to get Katie to back off would be doomed to failure. This was a personal fight for her, and in the end he had no leverage to force her to do it. But Gabe worked for him, so he should be able to convince Gabe that he wasn't helping by stirring up more controversy.

Under the circumstances, Jess knew he should turn his car around and leave this parking lot. He was literally sleeping with the enemy. But when he was in bed with Katie, she didn't feel like the enemy. She felt like paradise.

In any case, he needed to give her the teddy. After work he'd bought a red gift bag—a compromise between a plain paper sack and a box with tissue paper—and he'd folded the teddy and put it inside. If he didn't give it to her tonight, he might as well throw it in the Dumpster, and he couldn't bear to do that.

His more recent shopping trip had netted a few other goodies, including an illustrated edition of the *Kama Sutra*. Katie's show was almost over, thank God, but she wouldn't be home for another fifteen or twenty minutes. He might as well wait in the parking lot and read.

Switching the ignition to alternate current, he rolled the car windows down and left the radio on so he could hear the last of her show. Then he took a flashlight out of the glove compartment in order to read the book. He should have picked up a copy three days ago. Then he might not be lagging behind so much.

"Not only do men like to dig holes," Dr. Reid said, *"but*

they love muddy holes even better. If that's not an indication of their mind-set, I don't know what is."

Jess shook his head. Dr. Reid had some twisted theories going on. Opening the book, he switched on the flashlight and started looking at the pictures.

"*I used to like playing in the mud when I was a kid,*" Katie said. "*Was I trying to get back to the womb?*"

"*Of course, but you don't play in muddy holes now, do you?*"

Katie laughed. The sound teased Jess's nerve endings. He wanted her to come home so he could hear her laugh, hear her sigh, hear her moan.... Even with all the problems she was causing, he just plain wanted her.

"*I don't play in mud holes anymore,*" Katie said. "*But I've had some interesting experiences with fudge sauce.*"

"*That's a whole other topic, food and sex,*" said Dr. Reid. "*Ask a man to slice a cucumber and watch his face. They don't like doing it.*"

"*Give a woman a cucumber and some vegetable oil and she doesn't need a guy,*" Katie said.

"Oh, yeah?" Jess muttered. He was feeling sexually frustrated and more than a little cranky. Plus the pictures in the *Kama Sutra* were extremely arousing. "Try getting a cucumber to go down on you. See how that works out."

"Okay, buddy, out of the car!"

Startled, Jess looked up into the bright glare of a much bigger flashlight than the one he was holding. "What?"

"Security!" The guy sounded big and mean as he opened the driver's-side door. "Out of the car, and keep your hands where I can see 'em. Don't bother zipping up either."

"I don't know what..." But then he figured it out.

What an idiot he'd been. He'd been so engrossed in his multiple problems that he hadn't realized how it would look with him sitting there with the radio tuned to Katie's show and a book full of naked people on his lap.

Obviously by doing that he'd attracted the attention of a gung ho apartment-complex security guard who thought he was sitting in his car playing a tune on his personal flute. Worse yet, he had a woman's lace teddy in the bag on the passenger seat. And that wasn't all.

In the other bag, the one from the adult store where he'd shopped on his way here, was an X-rated video. But the video wasn't nearly as damning as the pair of fur-lined handcuffs he'd added to the purchase just in case Katie wanted to try them out. And then there were the nipple clips.

Wasn't this a peachy situation? And if he didn't handle it carefully, he was liable to be arrested for public indecency.

16

WHEN KATIE PULLED INTO the front parking lot of her complex, she noticed that Ted, the security guard, was busily interrogating someone. Ted's golf cart was parked next to the intruder's car, and Ted's new Taser was deployed and ready to drop the man standing in front of him if he made a wrong move.

Katie slowed down to take a closer look. A couple of shopping bags sat on the hood of the guy's car. Could it be drugs? She'd always wondered if the complex was wasting money on a security guard, but maybe not. He'd actually found some weirdo to point his Taser at, although not too many weirdos drove Jags.

There was something familiar about the set of the guy's broad shoulders, and the style of his hair reminded her of—*Jess.* Oh, dear God. Jess had been collared by the fuzz. She hoped to hell he hadn't tried to break into her apartment again. He'd been damned lucky Ted hadn't caught him at it the first time.

She'd better get over there and save his butt before Ted called in Tucson's finest. But she was pleased that Jess had chosen to come over here tonight. That was a good sign. She had decided to wait and see if he'd make the next move. If he'd done nothing, she'd have done nothing. She wasn't about to run after him. If he seemed willing to show up and have sex with her, fine and dandy. She'd take whatever she could get.

Cheryl had made a good point. Jess might build a parking garage where her grandmother's house now stood, but he hadn't done it yet. Until the wrecking ball arrived, Katie might as well scoop up as many orgasms as possible. No telling if she'd ever find anyone who could pass them out as abundantly as Jess.

Parking her car one space away from Ted and his quarry, she got out of her car. "Hi, Ted! What's up?"

"I have the situation under control, Katie." Ted kept the Taser pointed at Jess. "Don't worry. This guy won't bother you while I'm on duty."

"I'm not here to bother anyone," Jess said. "I—"

"Oh, sure," Ted said. "That's why you're sitting in your car with a sex book on your lap and a bag full of pornographic items on the seat next to you."

What an interesting development. Had Jess decided to study up? "You don't want to arrest this guy, Ted," she said. "He's my research assistant."

Jess groaned. "Katie, please don't help."

"Research assistant?" Ted glanced at her in disbelief. "That makes no sense. This here's Jess Harkins, the owner of the construction company putting up that building next to your station. You hate that construction. How can he be your research assistant?"

Jess rolled his eyes. "I'm not—"

"He prefers to keep his side job quiet," Katie said. "For obvious reasons. Jess and I have known each other for years. We happen to be on opposite sides of the fence on this construction issue, but we aren't letting that affect our friendship or our research into human sexuality. Right, Jess?" She gave him a bright smile.

He didn't smile back. "Katie, I appreciate the effort, but you're only making things worse."

"You'd rather be arrested?"

"Well, no."

Ted lowered the Taser. "I suppose you could be a research assistant, considering what you had in the car."

"All in the name of research," Katie said. "What did you bring for me to take a look at this time, Jess?"

Jess glanced heavenward. "Oh, the usual kind of stuff."

"There's a white lace teddy in the red bag," Ted said helpfully.

"Oh." Katie had wondered if she'd ever see it again. Although he'd bought it for her, she hadn't felt right taking it last night. She glanced at Jess. "Thanks."

He shrugged. "No problem."

"Then there's the sex book, of course," Ted continued, "which he was reading while he listened to your program. It's got pictures of real people, and they're in color, which I personally think is better than black-and-white or drawings."

Katie nodded in agreement. "Definitely better to have real people in color." She glanced sideways at Jess. "The more colored pictures of real people, the better."

Jess's jaw muscles clenched, and he gave her a subtle shake of his head, as if to warn her to stop talking. She wasn't about to. This was almost as much fun as having sex with him.

"So, Jess, what's the name of the book?" she asked.

He cleared his throat. "The *Kama Sutra*."

"Right!" Ted snapped his fingers. "I thought I recognized the name. That's where you get your tips from, isn't it?"

"Yes, it is." She found it extremely interesting that Jess had decided to buy his own copy.

"That book was what grabbed my attention in the first place," Ted added. "Mr. Harkins, you must've been concentrating really hard on that book, because I stood next to the car for a good thirty seconds and you never noticed."

"I have great powers of concentration." Jess stared at Katie, his expression unreadable.

"I'll vouch for that." Ted shoved his Taser into the holster strapped to his waist. "Anyway, in the other bag is a pornographic video that looks really hot, a box of flavored condoms, some fur-lined handcuffs, and I think those other little things are nipple clips, although I've never seen what they look like myself."

Whoa. Katie did her best to look unfazed, but her brain was sizzling. She could barely believe that Jess had walked into a store and bought those things. He might not be falling in love, but he was certainly falling deep into lust if he wanted to venture that far out of his comfort zone.

"I see," she said in what she hoped was a normal-sounding tone. "It's good to keep abreast of these things." When Jess snorted, she realized what she'd said. "Ha, ha. Pun intended."

Ted grinned. "I knew that. You're Crazy Katie. Nobody knows what you'll say next." He gazed at Jess with obvious envy. "Must be nice being her research assistant."

Jess opened his mouth as if to take another stab at contradicting the story. Then he sighed. "Yeah, it is. Well, Katie, I guess we'd better get started."

She wasn't about to tell him, but she'd gotten started the

minute Ted had mentioned the items in the shopping bag. She could hardly wait to find out what Jess intended to do with them.

JUST CALL HIM MR. SMOOTH. Jess locked his Jag, picked up the bags and got into Katie's car for the ride to her parking spot. Neither of them bothered to fasten their safety belts, and he put the seat back as far as it would go to give him room for his legs. That way he could also put the bags at his feet instead of holding them like some dweeb who'd just been to Circle K.

If he'd hoped to impress Katie with his worldliness, getting detained by the security guard wasn't the best way to go about it. At least the guy hadn't decided to use his Taser, or Katie might have driven up to find him twitching on the ground. Even so, knowing that she'd felt obligated to rescue him added insult to injury. Plus he was worried about her cover story, which could do some real damage if it leaked out.

Maybe he should offer to bribe Ted. That could backfire, though. If he made too much of a deal out of this, Ted could decide to blackmail him for the rest of his life. Wouldn't that be terrific?

"Fur-lined handcuffs?" Katie drove around the complex and parked in a numbered space under a canopy.

"Research assistant?" he countered. He didn't want to *discuss* the handcuffs lying in one of the bags at his feet. He wanted to *use* them to make her become so crazed with passion that she left teeth marks on his body.

"It was the only thing I could think of to explain what you were doing with fur-lined handcuffs and nipple clips."

The whole security-guard episode had been a fiasco from the beginning. "And how do you think Ted pictures this research being done?"

She turned off the ignition. "About the way it will be done, I guess."

"And what if Ted is a blabbermouth?" All he needed was for this *research assistant* thing to somehow make its way to his work crew.

She glanced at him and smiled. "Relax, Jess. We don't have tabloid journalism here and it's a big town. The chances of Ted getting us into trouble are slim to none."

"I'm already in trouble."

"In what sense?"

In every sense. "My foreman Gabe drove by my house late last night and saw your car parked out front."

She stared at him in the darkened interior of the car. "I don't know which is scarier—that your foreman has your house under surveillance or that he took the time to figure out it was my car."

"He doesn't have my house under surveillance. I—" Jess paused to take a breath. In the close confines of this car he was way too aware of her. Being near Katie after a twenty-four-hour absence had put him on sensory overload, bombarding him with the scent of her perfume, the sound of her breathing, the rustle of her clothes. He was having a tough time containing his hunger for the body under those clothes.

"Do you want to go inside?" she asked gently, as if she could read him like the *Kama Sutra.*

"Is it that obvious?"

"To me." She leaned toward him. "But then, I know how your breathing changes when you want sex."

His gaze took in her parted lips, just inches away. "Yours is changing, too." He met her halfway and claimed her saucy, sexy mouth. She kissed him like a woman who was ready for anything.

When he cupped her breast and stroked her taut nipple through the material of her blouse, she whimpered against his mouth. He must be insane, because he'd started evaluating whether they could do it right here, just to take the edge off.

To buy himself some time to decide if he dared suggest that, he broke away from that steamy kiss and leaned his forehead against hers. "We should be able to make it to your front door, don't you think?"

"I don't know." Her breath came in shallow gasps. "I didn't expect to come home and find you waiting with fur-lined handcuffs and nipple clips."

"We don't have to use them." He didn't care so much about them at the moment. He just wanted to ease this unbelievable ache.

"I know." Her voice grew husky. "But the very fact that you bought them..." Easing away from him, she reached under her skirt.

"Katie..." It was half warning, half plea. If she took off her panties again, he couldn't be responsible for what happened next.

She didn't take off her panties. Instead she found an equally effective way to blow his mind. "This is what you've done to me," she said as her fingers emerged and she brushed the tips over his upper lip.

He moaned in desperation. The scent of her arousal eliminated all remaining common sense. Grabbing her hand, he licked and nibbled her fingers, starved for the taste of her, the feel of her closing around him. His voice was harsh with the force of his need. "I want you. Now."

Her breath caught. "Here?"

"Right here. It's no more complicated than a mesquite

bench." He thought briefly of Ted, who might drive by in his golf cart, but then he dismissed Ted as irrelevant. Everything was irrelevant except being inside Katie.

"I guess you'd like me to take off my panties?" Her question trembled with excitement.

"Unless you want them ripped." Releasing her hand, he fumbled in the bags at his feet and located the box of flavored condoms.

She wiggled in the seat next to him and tossed something lacy in the back seat. "Panties are gone."

His heart hammering with anticipation, he handed her a condom packet as he started unfastening his jeans. She was right about how his breathing changed. Right now he was dragging in great gulps of air and praying he wouldn't hyperventilate before he was finally buried deep inside her.

Her soft chuckle added another erotic sound to the mix. "These are the flavored ones. What flavor are they?"

"Who cares?" Hurriedly he lifted up and shoved his jeans and briefs down to his knees.

"I care. I'm curious." She tore open the packet and put the condom in her mouth. "Raspberry," she said as she took it out of her mouth and handed it back to him.

He'd never put on a condom that was already wet. The effect was so sensuous he was afraid he might come right then and there. By some miracle he didn't. One hurdle crossed.

As he thought of how they could do this, he gave thanks for his short study period in the car. He'd learned only a few things, but one of the pictures and its explanation would come in very handy. "If you climb over here and kneel on the seat facing forward—"

"Mare's Position," she murmured. "You really were concentrating on that book."

"A guy has to stay current." He held her hips to steady her as she clutched the dash and hiked up her skirt so she could sit astride him. For a second or two he thought maybe it wouldn't work, but then...oh, yes...she eased down, taking his throbbing penis in deep.

"Oh..." She lifted up a fraction before settling back down, firmly connected to him, her skirt bunched up around her waist. "That feels really, really..."

His voice rasped in the darkness. "Incredible."

"Yeah." She gulped for air. "Really incredible."

Her bare bottom nestled right up against his stomach. He pulled his shirt up so they were touching skin to skin.

"Even better." She did a little wiggle.

"Mmm." He fought down his climax. Not yet. He wanted more contact. Pulling her blouse from the waistband of her skirt, he slid both hands up to her lace-covered breasts. In no time he'd unhooked the front catch of her bra and had filled his hands with her plump softness.

She moaned softly. "Better yet."

Leaning forward, he nuzzled her earlobe as he lightly pinched her nipples. "Who needs clips?"

"Not me." She shivered in his arms. "All I need is...to come. And that shouldn't take long. I'm going to... start...pumping."

"Good."

And was it ever. Gripping the dash and balancing on her spread knees, she lifted up and eased back down again. She had the control, and all he had to do was hold on and enjoy her rhythmic strokes. In no time he was panting as the pressure of his impending climax built like steam in a boiler.

Her sweet bottom caressed his skin, and his fingers

flexed against her breasts. If one *Kama Sutra* position could give him such a thrill, he might have to memorize the whole damned book. What a joy ride.

She seemed to be loving it, too. Her movements grew faster. Soon her bottom slapped against him with enough force to create the most wonderful sound—the sound of lovers moving closer to nirvana. People could have their ocean waves. Jess would take this beautiful sound any day.

"I'm almost there," she said in a breathy voice.

He loosened his restraint a notch, wanting to follow her down that path. He wasn't trying to give her more than one climax this time. They'd come together. And soon. Very…soon. Oh, yeah. The tidal wave was nearly upon him.

"Now," she said, gasping. "Now…squeeze my nipples…oh, good…*good.*" Pumping wildly, she cried out as her orgasm overtook her.

Her muscles clenched around him and then the ripples of her climax massaged his straining penis until…there… *yes.* He said her name and then he kept saying it as the spasms shook him. *Katie.* She'd challenged him, taunted him and completely bewitched him. Somewhere in the past few days, without him realizing it was happening, she'd become the center of his world.

As his dazed brain was trying to process that truth, she stirred in his arms. "Jess."

"I'm here." And he wanted to be here—close to Katie— for a very long time. He had no idea how he'd get that accomplished with all their conflicts, but he'd look for a way. It wasn't only the sex either. It was—

"I hear Ted's golf cart coming."

"Oh." That information certainly didn't add to the ambiance. Logically he should have guessed that Ted would

be along eventually. His job was to patrol the area and look
for anything unusual. Jess wondered if Ted would consider
this scenario unusual.

"I'm going to slide back into my seat." She lifted away
from him.

Jess felt as if he'd lost his hold on all things wonderful.

"Just act natural," Katie said as she pulled down her
skirt and settled into the driver's seat. "If he stops and
shines his flashlight around—which he might because he's
so darned curious about us—we'll tell him we were sitting
here talking."

"I have to say, Katie, that you're one hell of a conver-
sationalist." Jess grabbed the shopping bags and positioned
them on his lap to hide the evidence.

"You hold your own, too." There was laughter in her voice.

Sure enough, there was a tap on Katie's window and
Ted's flashlight beam invaded the car.

She switched on the alternate current so she could roll
down her power window. "Hi, Ted."

"Is everything all right, Katie?" Ted asked.

"Perfectly fine, Ted. We got into a heated discussion and
ended up staying right here to hash things out."

Jess clenched his jaw to keep from laughing.

"Okay then," Ted said. "Just wanted to make sure you
two were safe and sound."

"We're definitely safe." Katie glanced over at Jess.
"Right?"

Jess knew she was thinking of the raspberry-flavored
condom they'd just used. He cleared the laughter from his
throat. "Right."

God, this was fun. The thrill of trying to get away with
something added an element of excitement he hadn't felt

since…hell, he'd never tried to get away with a damned thing. He'd been sickeningly good all his life.

"Glad to hear everything's okay. Have a nice night." Clicking off his flashlight, Ted hopped in his golf cart.

"Thanks! You, too!" Katie called out the window as Ted putt-putted down the access road.

Ted waved in reply.

Katie clapped one hand over her mouth to muffle her whoop of laughter as she used the other to push the automatic-window button. Once the window was closed, she looked over at Jess and they both lost it.

"A heated discussion!" Jess wiped his eyes. "How do you come up with these things?"

She grinned at him. "I guess you inspire me."

He gazed at her, his heart full of an emotion he hesitated to name. Once he gave that emotion a name, his world would change forever. "Same here," he said softly.

17

"THAT WAS FUN." KATIE reached under her blouse to fasten her bra. She needed to be a bit more presentable before they made the trek to her apartment door.

"Yeah, it was." Jess buttoned and zipped his jeans. "Which surprises the hell out of me. For a guy who didn't want to do it in cars, I'm turning into a real convert."

"Maybe denying yourself as a teenager has made you crave it as an adult."

"I don't know, but I'm sure you could find somebody who's written a book on the subject."

"Was that a crack?" She tucked her blouse back into the waistband of her skirt.

He gazed at her innocently. "Nah."

"It was, but I'm going to ignore it because you've given me a great idea. I could do a show on vehicular sex."

"Sounds good to me." He opened the passenger door and picked up both shopping bags in one hand. "The sooner the better."

Grabbing her purse and panties, she climbed out of the car and punched the button on her key ring to lock the doors. "Because then I won't be doing a show about your construction project?"

"Bingo."

"Sounds like you're more worried than you want to admit." She stuffed her underwear in her purse as she led the way across the access road to the outside stairway that would take them to her second-story apartment.

"I'm not worried that your programs will cause the project to be dumped, if that's what you mean." He followed, swinging the bags as he walked.

Thinking of the contents of those bags, she began heating up all over again. "You should be worried." She started up the stairs, intensely aware of Jess right behind her. They might be talking about her campaign against his project, but her body was speaking a whole different language.

"Katie, it's only a bunch of talk. In the end, I promise you the building will go up."

"I don't think you're quite as sure of yourself as you were a few days ago. Besides, the station manager is a hundred percent behind me, which means he thinks we can win."

"He's wrong."

Even though they were on the brink of an argument, his voice teased her nerve endings, warming every part of her body. Soon they'd be behind a locked door. And Jess had brought fur-lined handcuffs. She looked back over her shoulder. "If he's so wrong, why do you care what I say on the show?"

"Because you're infuriating my work crew. If they could see me now, they'd think I was the biggest turncoat in the world."

She reached the landing and took her key out of her purse. Then she paused to look at him. She wanted him inside that door so badly she could taste it, but they had to get one thing straight. "I'm not going to stop my campaign, Jess. If you're hoping to convince me otherwise, then—"

"I told you that my foreman knows you were parked outside my house last night."

She remembered now. He'd been about to elaborate when they'd surrendered to a mutual case of lust. "Tell me about that. Why was he driving by?"

"I mentioned that I was meeting you for lunch and that I'd...see if I could get you to tone down your protest. When your show was as inflammatory as ever, he came by to find out what had happened to my plan."

"What do you mean, *your plan?*" She clutched the keys tighter.

"I'd told him I'd try—"

"Wait a minute. I thought we agreed that we'd keep our relationship separate, that we wouldn't use sex as leverage to get the other one to change positions."

His jaw tightened. "We did. During lunch. And you may have noticed I didn't bring up the subject while we were together."

No, he hadn't. Instead he'd given her an orgasm on top of "A" Mountain. And there had been more where that had come from. She wanted another one very soon.

She took a deep breath. "Okay, you're right. You didn't ask me to tone down anything."

"But Gabe didn't know that. He assumed the long lunch meant I was getting somewhere."

Despite the tense discussion, that made her smile. "You were." He still was. All she had to do was look at him and her body tingled in readiness.

He gripped the railing and studied her. "What a hell of a situation this is. You're making life extremely difficult for me, and I still want you so much I can't see straight. Right now, even while we're arguing about this problem with my foreman and my crew, I want to get inside that door and strip you naked."

Moisture gathered between her thighs. "I'm sorry for your situation with your work crew, but I'm not going to stop my campaign."

He blew out a breath. "Yeah, I know."

"So what do you say?" Her heart hammered in her chest. Either he'd go inside with her and they'd have more amazing sex or he'd decide she wasn't worth risking his reputation for.

Despite his shopping for handcuffs and nipple clips, despite his eagerness when they'd had sex in her car, she had no idea which he'd choose. She still didn't know for sure where she fit in his list of priorities. And that made her vulnerable, whether she wanted to be or not.

Fire burned in his dark eyes as he continued to hold on to the railing as if to keep himself from reaching for her. Then he let go and stepped toward her. "Open that damned door, Katie."

A STRONGER MAN WOULD HAVE walked away. Jess wasn't that man. Maybe in the back of his mind he thought that if they had enough sex, everything would work out. Maybe he thought that if he made love to her often enough, she wouldn't reject him when he finally had to build that parking garage on the site of her grandmother's house.

Or maybe he was in the clutches of a desire that blasted reason right out of his brain. That was the most likely explanation for why he walked through the door, why he dropped the shopping bags to the floor and pulled her fiercely into his arms the moment the lock snapped into place.

Her laugh was low and intimate as he bunched her skirt

up around her waist and backed her against the nearest wall. She knew she had him enslaved. Knew he couldn't keep his hands off of her.

And her mouth—he couldn't get enough of it. Kissing her hungrily, he reached beneath her skirt with one hand and pulled her blouse free with the other. Finding her wet and ready inflamed him even more. He might be fixated on her body, but thank God she was fixated on his, too.

He couldn't resist shoving his fingers deep and hearing her muffled groan of surrender. Massaging her slick heat, he lifted his mouth from hers. "Like that?"

She gripped his shoulders and shuddered. "Yeah, I like that."

"Then let's make something happen." After snapping open the catch of her bra, he stroked her breasts with a firmness of purpose, wanting to push her fast and hard.

"No. This is silly. Let's go…to the bedroom." She gasped and arched her hips toward him, silently contradicting herself.

"Later." Giving her a climax had turned into his favorite thing, and he would do it now, before they got two feet past the front door, because her body was begging for it. "Come for me."

"I just did." She tipped her head back and gulped in air. "In the car."

"Do it again." He pressed his fingers upward, caressing her G-spot rhythmically as he increased his speed.

"Oh…Jess…" She began to tremble. "It's…so…*good.*"

"That's the idea." He felt the first ripple against his fingers. "Let go," he murmured. "Let go, Katie."

"I…I…oh, there! Right *there.*" She welcomed the convulsions with a lusty cry of release.

Jess closed his eyes and concentrated on the feel of her climax against his fingers. He didn't really need kinky sex toys or X-rated videos or *Kama Sutra* positions. All he really wanted was a naked Katie, a big, soft bed and…the rest of his life to enjoy making love to her. That realization hit him hard.

Yet he wasn't caught totally by surprise. On some level he'd known he was playing for all the marbles. He hadn't allowed the thought to surface until now because it would likely have depressed the hell out of him. A few days ago he wouldn't have believed that he had any chance of ending up with Katie, so why even wish for it?

But they'd been through a lot since Friday night. And tonight, as she trembled in the aftermath of her orgasm, he believed a lifetime of loving Katie was possible. Achieving it wouldn't be easy, but then, the best things never were.

KATIE'S PLAN TO GRAB ALL the sex she could before the relationship fell apart was working beautifully. After that special moment in the foyer, she and Jess had picked up the shopping bags and headed back to her bedroom. Their clothes had come off quickly, considering all the kissing and fondling that had taken place during the process.

Eventually they ended up tangled together on her mattress, and it occurred to her that he'd never been there before. They'd had all kinds of sex recently, but none of it had taken place in her bedroom. His presence there in the midst of her white wicker and romantic flower prints made quite a statement.

As a general rule she didn't invite men into an area she thought of as her private bower. She hadn't consciously thought about whether she should invite Jess here either. If she had, she might have nixed the idea. She would have instinctively feared the possibility that once he'd invaded her most personal space, her defenses would be in shambles.

That realization prompted her next move. "About those handcuffs," she murmured between kisses.

He leaned down and nuzzled her breast. "Want to see if they fit you?"

"I have a better idea." She rolled on top of him, pinning him to the mattress. "Let's see if they fit *you*."

His eyes widened. "That wasn't what I—"

"I know." She loved catching him off balance.

"I mean, isn't that why they're fur-lined?" He looked nervous. "Because they're for a woman?"

"Is the fur pink?"

"Black."

"There you go. Unisex." She reached down and stroked his erect penis. "Come on. Let's try it."

His voice was husky with desire. "When you touch me like that, you can get me to do just about anything."

"Good to know." She caressed him with great thoroughness, making sure that she paid special attention to the sensitive tip.

His breathing grew ragged. "Just don't…ask the impossible."

So he was afraid she'd bring up the construction project. She couldn't blame him. "Then I'd be violating my own ground rules, wouldn't I?" The taut skin covering his penis was silky under her fingertips. Amazing that something so delicate enveloped such rigid power. "That wouldn't be fair."

"No." He took a deep, shuddering breath.

"Too bad you're not the kind of man who allows sex to

change his mind, though." She stroked upward, extracting a small bead of moisture that quivered there like a drop of rain.

He moaned softly. "Because you'd try it?"

"Darn tootin' I would." She wiped the drop away with her thumb.

He closed his eyes and sighed. "If I thought I could change your mind with sex, I'd try it, too."

"So we're both like…the Untouchables."

His chuckle rasped in the stillness. "You're very touchable."

"You know what I meant."

"Yeah…I know. God, Katie, that feels great."

"Ready for those handcuffs?" She gave him a gentle squeeze.

He gasped as another shudder ran through his muscled body. "You don't need them. I'm putty in your hands."

"Humor me."

He opened his eyes to reveal the intense passion glowing there. "When it comes to sex, you can have anything. Anything at all."

Excitement surged through her. The kinds of sexual adventures she'd only talked about on the air could become reality with this man. The reason for that wasn't lost on her either. Somewhere along the way he'd given her his trust.

She was the suspicious one, the person who'd kept herself on guard to make sure he didn't break her heart. Yet he'd given her no reason to think that he would. Maybe it was time for her to get over those irrational fears and consider the possibility that Jess wanted her at least as much as she wanted him.

Easing away from him, she left the bed and located the shopping bag containing the handcuffs. She pulled them out and noticed two little gold keys on a tiny ring were hanging from the lock. As she imagined the power wielded by the person holding the keys, adrenaline shot through her. Adventure could be very scary. Trembling, she walked back to the bed.

He lay there watching her, his gaze intent.

Slowly she held them out. "You can put them on me if you want."

JESS REALIZED THAT WITH Katie's offer something significant had changed. When he'd bought the handcuffs, he'd imagined they would be part of some wild and crazy episode that might drive both of them to distraction, might even get them into this biting business she'd been talking about tonight.

He hadn't thought about the handcuffs representing loss of control. But when Katie had proposed putting them on him, he'd understood exactly what those handcuffs meant. His first reaction had been good old-fashioned panic.

Then he'd figured out that she needed to have that kind of control over him for some reason. He'd decided it was in his best interests to give it to her. And why not? She had a firm hold on his heart, so she might as well be in charge of the rest of him.

Now she was giving up that chance. Even more important, she was turning that control over to him. Maybe the invisible wall between them, the one he'd sensed her hiding behind whenever they were together, was finally coming down.

He'd always imagined her as a free spirit who had tried plenty of sexual variations with the men in her life. Her radio show led him to believe it and then she'd asked for a blindfold the first time they'd had full-body sex. He'd assumed she was used to kinky toys.

But the way she was quivering as she held out the handcuffs made him think he'd been wrong about that. Maybe the blindfold had only served to help her hide from him. In any case, he'd be willing to bet that no man had ever put fur-lined handcuffs on her.

So he would be the first. If miracles came true, he would be the last.

Sitting up in bed, he took the handcuffs. He resisted the urge to ask her if she really wanted to do this. She might say no. And then the impulse that had caused her to bring him the handcuffs would be buried under another round of sex.

He didn't know how other guys viewed a sex toy like this, but he knew exactly how he saw it. He would use it to prove to her that she could trust him not to abuse the power she'd given him. He would use it to get closer to her than he ever had before.

"Lie down," he murmured.

She stretched out on the bed beside him, her gaze never leaving those handcuffs. Her throat moved in a swallow.

Once again he fought the urge to tell her they could forget the handcuffs. If he did that, he would be depriving her of a chance to take a risk. Love was all about risk. And love was at stake here, whether she understood that or not.

Before he put the first handcuff on, he made a quick survey of his resources. If they'd been in his bed, he'd have a bedpost to work with, but her wicker headboard didn't have the same advantages. Then he noticed a tasseled gold cord tying back the drapes at each side of her bedroom window.

He glanced down at her and she was still watching him. Her cheeks were pink and so was the rest of her. He loved the way her whole body blushed when she was excited. Her excitement right now had an edge of fear. He could see it in her eyes.

That fear would dissolve as he won her trust. But first he had to push her a little farther out on that ledge of fear. Once he'd opened the handcuffs, he picked up one slender wrist and closed the fur-lined cuff around it.

She drew in a sharp breath.

He didn't reassure her. The experience had to feel a little threatening or it wouldn't be worth doing. Fitting the small key in the lock, he turned it. "Raise both hands over your head."

Slowly she did as he asked. Her breasts quivered, and he longed to bend down and kiss those tempting nipples. But then he might get distracted and not finish what he needed to accomplish. He couldn't give in to his passion until he had her completely in his power.

After clamping the other handcuff on, he locked it, too. Then he left her lying there with her arms over her head while he walked to the window and untied the cord from the drapes. He wouldn't ask if he could use it. She'd put him in charge, and that's the role he'd play.

As he returned to the bed, he could tell that she was getting very nervous, but she didn't protest when he looped the cord through the golden chain linking the handcuffs together. The wicker was an open weave, and he managed to work one end of the cord through it and back out. In seconds he'd knotted the cord and Katie was tied to the headboard, helpless to stop him from doing whatever he wanted.

And he wanted…everything. This would be the defining moment for them, and he planned to wring every ounce of pleasure out of it. He wanted both of them to remember this experience, this coming together of two bodies and two souls, for the rest of their lives.

She was breathing fast—her breasts rose and fell in a tantalizing way. He memorized the shape of them, appreciated anew the dusky color of her nipples against the creamy skin of her breasts.

She had such a slender waist and a satisfying flair to her hips. He wondered how she felt about children. Someday soon he'd have to ask. His gaze lingered on the golden triangle of curls he'd soon explore...for as long as he liked.

Her thighs still had a tinge of gold from her summer tan. He loved her knees and the delicate bones in her ankles. Her toenails were painted the same color as his favorite mocha drink.

He longed to touch her but he held back. Each time they'd been together they'd been in constant motion. He'd been in a frenzy to kiss her, caress her, plunge deep inside her. He would do all those things soon, but for now he would wait.

"Jess?" Her voice was breathy with anticipation. "What are you doing?"

"I'm looking, Katie." He let his gaze travel over her, inch by glorious inch. "Just looking."

18

SEXUAL TENSION COILED inside Katie. She should be embarrassed by having Jess studying her so thoroughly, but embarrassment didn't even come into it. The heat in his eyes melted any trace of shame. Warmed by his gaze, she felt like a priceless work of art.

No, that wasn't quite right. She felt like a goddess, one who wanted to be worshiped with his hands and mouth as well as his eyes. She burned for his touch. Yet she was helpless to pull him to her.

At first that had frightened her. Once he'd cinched her to the headboard, her heart had started pumping so fast she'd grown dizzy. She hadn't imagined her powerlessness would be this complete.

Yet she knew he wouldn't hurt her. It wasn't fear of harm that made her stomach churn. It was her loss of control. She'd never allowed that with anyone. What had possessed her to offer that control to Jess?

But then he'd looked at her, really looked at her, and she'd known why. Relinquishing control to him had been a gift that only she could give. It was more precious than anything she could have offered him. He seemed to know that.

"You are so beautiful." Stretching out beside her, he began a slow caress beginning with her mouth. He traced the outline of her lips with his forefinger. "At eighteen you were pretty, but now…now you're the kind of woman who brings a man to his knees."

So she'd won. Even now, bound to the headboard, she had him in her power. And it no longer mattered. "I don't want to bring you to your knees," she said.

"What do you want?" Smoothing his palm over her collarbone, he cupped her breast.

Your love. But she wasn't quite that brave. "An equal give-and-take."

A smile tipped the corners of his mouth. "You want me to take a turn in the handcuffs?" He brushed his thumb over her nipple.

"Maybe." She shivered as he continued to move his thumb back and forth over her nipple, making it stand smartly at attention. She'd always loved his hands on her, but her helplessness intensified the pleasure in a way she never would have guessed.

"I will, you know," he said.

"I believe you." She drew in a breath as his hand glided over her ribs. "But I wasn't only talking about that. I meant—"

"I know what you meant." He stroked the damp curls that revealed how thoroughly he'd aroused her. "A straightforward exchange. Not being afraid to say how much we crave each other."

She swallowed. "Free to want it all."

"With no holding back," he murmured.

"No holding back." She moaned as he dipped his fingers into her vagina.

He lifted his hand to his mouth and ran his tongue over his fingers. "Anything goes."

"Right." Her heart raced. "Anything goes."

"Now it's my turn to take what you have to give." He moved over her and began to lick the pulse point on the inside of her wrist.

"I know." And she'd never given like this, never been so open, so vulnerable.

"I want to taste the salt on your skin." With his tongue he traced a path along the soft underside of her arm. "I want to feel the blood surging through your veins and your muscles clench with desire. I want to breathe you in, drown myself in all that is you." He looked into her eyes. "I want to know you, Katie."

Somehow she found the courage to meet his gaze. "Yes," she whispered. "Yes."

The glow in his eyes took her breath away. "Beginning now." His mouth found hers.

As many times as he'd kissed her, no moment had ever been quite like this one. His lips conveyed an intensity of purpose she'd never felt before. She didn't feel merely kissed. She felt *claimed*.

She was a modern woman who should be horrified by the sense of possession she felt in his kiss. Instead she was thrilled. Some primitive instinct took over, and she felt driven and desperate, ready to mate.

And her mate was here, inciting her to even greater desperation. She bit his lip.

He lifted his head to gaze at her. "You bit me."

"Did I hurt you? It's not bleeding. I—"

"You bit me." He sounded delighted. "That's excellent."

"It is?"

"Yeah, it is." A flame burned in his eyes. "And now…it's my turn."

His mouth and tongue traveled the length of her body. And every so often he'd nip at her skin, marking her as his, touching off bonfires that blazed long after he'd moved on. By the time he was finished, she was writhing and panting, ready for him in a way that she'd never been before. If he didn't penetrate her soon…she would go insane.

She didn't even realize that she'd begun to beg until he responded with a murmured promise and unlocked her wrists from the handcuffs.

"Not that," she said, gasping for breath. "I want you inside me."

"I know." His voice was rough with desire. "And I want you free to participate." He left the bed. In no time he was back and she heard the snap of latex.

Then he was there, between her thighs, lifting her hips. "Ah, Katie." And he pushed deep.

Grasping his hips, she groaned in relief as she gazed up at him through a haze of passion. "I need you. I need you right there, Jess."

"I need to be there." He eased back and thrust forward again. "Right there."

Her gaze locked with his. They'd passed some sort of milestone tonight, and they both knew it. The games were over. What was happening now was for real.

Words seemed unnecessary. Looking into her eyes, he stroked deliberately. He seemed completely sure of his right to be between her thighs making that all-important connection. He belonged there.

As his steady pumping took her ever closer to the moment of truth, she absorbed that feeling of rightness. No man would ever be what Jess was to her. Maybe nothing mattered but this magic they created. As her climax drew near, all the reasons why they shouldn't be together disappeared.

One more rhythmic movement of his hips and she was there. Her orgasm rolled through her like a tidal wave, sweeping aside everything but the wonder she found in his arms. As he shuddered in the grip of his own climax, he held her gaze. It was all there, all the words. He didn't have to say them for her to know. This was no longer simply a matter of lust. Love was now on the table.

JESS WAS SHAKEN BY THE heavy-duty emotions stirred up by their most recent bout of sex. He knew exactly what was happening, but he wasn't quite ready to have a discussion about it. From Katie's uncharacteristic silence as they lay recovering from their mutual and extremely powerful orgasms, Jess concluded that she wasn't ready for any life-changing discussion either.

After all, they'd made no progress in solving their work-related conflict. Sure, they'd knocked down all the personal barriers between them, and in a perfect world that would be enough. But they didn't live in a perfect world and they couldn't ignore the external issues they both had to deal with.

He had to believe they'd deal with them better after a night like this, though. Surely the silent understanding they'd reached while making love would carry them past their other difficulties. He wasn't sure how, but feelings that big had to be of some use.

He brushed the hair back from her flushed face. "I have an idea."

Her voice was soft and yielding. All the prickliness seemed to have been burned away by what they'd shared. "What?"

"That was…pretty close to perfect."

"Uh-huh."

"I feel like if I say much or do anything, I might screw it up."

Her mouth curved in a smile. "I know what you mean."

"So I'm thinking I should head on home before I spoil this feeling. And I could use some time to process what just happened."

"Me, too."

He sighed in relief. They really were in sync. That felt incredible. "Let's have dinner tomorrow night."

"You mean like a date?"

"Yeah." He leaned down and kissed the tip of her nose. "Like a date. Fancy restaurant, reservations, candles on the table, stuff like that."

"Sounds like an occasion."

"I'd like it to be." He had some ideas about what he wanted to say to her as they held hands across that candle-lit table. But he needed to think about it and make sure he had the words in the right order. "Can you make it?"

"I can." Her expression was warm and open.

"Good. I'll pick you up at six, so we'll have plenty of time before you have to go on the air."

"I'll be ready."

As he gazed down at her, he began to reconsider leaving. She looked so sweet and tousled, so welcoming and sexy. But if he stayed, they'd start to talk, and he wasn't ready to do that.

"Sleep well." He gave her a lingering kiss. If she asked him to stay… But she didn't. He eased away from her.

Moments later he left her apartment and bounded down the outside stairs. Life was great. He was crazy about a woman who was crazy about him. They hadn't had the commitment talk yet, but that would come tomorrow night over dinner.

As he walked around the complex headed for his Jag in the front parking lot, he debated which restaurant to choose. Not Anthony's. That place would remind him of the disastrous date with Suzanne. But there were plenty of other good choices. He wanted a romantic atmosphere. He'd pull out all the stops.

Too bad she had to do her show, because he'd like to go from dinner straight home to bed, where they could seal the deal in an appropriate way. But she had a job to do. He wondered if she'd be able to continue with her campaign after tonight.

He felt guilty thinking like that, because his motivation had never really been to influence her about the show. Well, okay, maybe he'd thought it would be nice if she'd decide to lay off on her own. If tonight wouldn't encourage her to do that, nothing would. Yet he had no doubt she'd continue to cling stubbornly to her cause.

And just like that, his good feelings began to disappear as he considered the tangled mess they had to deal with in the outside world. Damn it. He knew in his heart she was going to lose, and that didn't feel good. But in order for her to win, plans for a perfectly good urban-renewal project would have to be scrapped. That didn't feel good either.

The parking lot was quiet as he approached his Jag. Just as he thought he might escape without encountering Ted, the golf cart came puttering toward him. So what? He had no obligation to hold a conversation with the security guard.

Yeah, but he didn't want the security guard to spread rumors either. At least not until his relationship with Katie was out in the open. Then Ted could take out an ad in the *Arizona Daily Star* for all Jess cared.

So he paused beside his Jag and waited for Ted to drive up.

"Research over?" Ted asked.

Earlier Jess had decided that the guy probably had no life. He'd bet that Ted was divorced and pretty much dateless. The security guard was on the homely side and didn't seem particularly sharp.

"Finished for tonight at least," Jess said. Talk about a ridiculous conversation. They both knew that funny business had been going on in that apartment. "I wonder if I could ask you a favor, man-to-man."

"Don't see why not." Ted seemed pleased to be asked.

"I realize Katie and I aren't exactly celebrities, but—"

"She is. I wouldn't say that you are particularly, but Katie's definitely a celebrity in my book."

"Well, sure, you're right. In any case, we'd both rather not broadcast our relationship at the moment."

Ted puffed out his chest. "Ha. I guess not, with that protest she's leading against your building."

"The thing is, in spite of that, we're getting serious about each other. I'm sure you've figured out that I'm more than her research assistant."

"Pretty obvious."

"I knew you'd see through that story right away. But I'd count it as a personal favor if you wouldn't tell anybody what you've observed here tonight."

Ted eyed him warily. "I'm supposed to write up a report if I detain someone."

"Of course you are, especially if it turns out they were up to no good, but I was here to visit Katie." Jess pulled out the only bribe he could think of on the spur of the moment. "We'd both really appreciate it if you'd keep what you know to yourself. And by the way, Katie and I would love to have you come to the wedding."

"The wedding? You're getting married?"

Jess prayed this wouldn't come back to bite him in the butt. "Yes, but nobody knows that yet." *Not even the bride. In fact, the groom is still in the thinking stages.* "You're the first."

"Wow. I'm honored that you told me. I'll have to give Katie my best wishes."

"Uh, better not do that. She might be upset that I leaked the info to you. I mean, she hasn't even told her parents."

Ted nodded. "Sure, sure. I can see how that would be a problem. How soon do you think the word will be out?"

"Soon," Jess said. "I'll definitely make sure Katie notifies you and gets your address so we know where to send the invitation."

"That'll be fine."

"Well, see you later, Ted." Jess held out his hand. "And thanks."

"No problem. Guess I can congratulate you at least."

"Sure."

"You're one lucky son of a bitch, if you don't mind my saying so."

"That I am, Ted. That I am." Jess got in his car and drove out of the parking lot. So he'd announced a wedding before he'd even decided for sure whether to propose. That was a first.

KATIE FELT AS IF SHE'D developed a split personality. One of her selves was falling in love with Jess and enjoying incredible sex whenever they got together. Her other self was searching for every means possible to stop construction on the building that Jess held dear.

As she headed toward KRZE on Wednesday morning for another appointment with Edgecomb, she could see progress on both fronts. She and Jess had become very close, close enough that soon they might start using the L-word in normal conversation. Tonight's dinner promised to be all about commitment.

Ironically the protest against the office building had gained momentum from last night's broadcast. Besides the deflating balloons and the giant nut-and-screw display, protestors now carried signs showing burly construction guys sucking their thumbs and clutching blankies.

Go Home to Mama, read one sign. Back to the Womb, Big Boy, read another. As she pulled into the KRZE parking lot, she thought of how Jess must have reacted when he'd arrived at the site this morning. No doubt she was making life harder for him, but if she wanted to win this battle, she had no choice.

And she planned to win. Jess wouldn't enjoy abandoning his project, but he didn't seem like the kind of guy who would hold a grudge, especially after the kind of bonding they'd been doing recently. All in all, she felt quite positive as she walked into the lobby.

"Hi, Ava!" She gave the intern a big smile. "Looks like we're getting more support for the cause."

Ava's expression was glum. "Like that matters."

"Of course it matters."

"Edgecomb didn't tell you why he wanted to see you, did he?"

Uneasiness replaced Katie's optimistic mood. "I was assuming that he wanted to congratulate me on our ratings, which have to be through the roof. Everyone is talking about—"

"You'd better go see him. And listen, I don't have any classes this afternoon, in case you want to get margaritas or something after you talk to Edgecomb."

"You're scaring me, Ava." She told herself not to panic. "Is the news that bad?"

"Go see him. I'm not supposed to say anything. He told me that specifically, so I decided to be good for a change."

"Then I'd better get in there and find out what's up." As she walked down the hall, Katie tried to figure out what might have happened. Two days ago she'd been encouraged to continue her campaign. The results had been fantastic. Surely the owners hadn't changed their minds about selling when everything was going so well. That didn't make sense.

Edgecomb was working on his computer when Katie tapped on the open office door. "Be right with you," he said. "I need to finish this e-mail. Have a seat."

She settled into one of the low-slung chairs and tried to stay positive. Maybe she was imagining things, but he acted nervous. His little fringe of hair looked as if he'd been ruffling it with his fingers, and he typed at a frantic pace, as if desperate to get his thoughts out into the world.

Finally he punched a button and turned to her. "Katie."

"Mr. Edgecomb."

"The owners are very pleased with you. They even authorized me to offer you more money. Everyone can always use more money, right?" His smile seemed forced.

"I'm not about to turn down more money. Is that why you wanted to see me?" There had to be more. Ava wouldn't be upset about that.

"Because of your campaign, they've been able to ask a much higher price for the property. And this morning they got it."

She looked at him in stunned silence. Maybe she'd misunderstood. "I'm confused. I thought they'd decided not to sell."

"They've already sold, Katie."

Her ears buzzed. "Sold? I thought the owners were committed to hanging on to the property!"

"No, they were committed to your program once they realized how it could drive up the price. Negotiations have been going on since last week, and early this morning Livingston Development delivered a substantial offer if we promised to muzzle you. The owners accepted the offer."

She felt numb. Eventually the news would sink in, but right now she couldn't process it. She'd lost. Worse than that, she'd never been in the game.

"We've found a great new location over on Main, and the station will be moving there within two weeks. The demolition crew needs to get started as soon as possible."

"Demolition crew." She repeated the words like a robot.

"Right. Harkins Construction will handle that. Apparently Harkins snapped up the demolition contract this morning before the ink was dry on the sale of the property. He must figure he can make use of some of the heavy equipment he already has at the site next door."

Betrayed. And by the very man who'd penetrated all her defenses, the man she'd trusted above all others. She didn't think there was enough tequila in the world to drown that kind of heartbreak. But she'd give it the old college try.

19

JESS'S MORNING HAD BEEN beyond frantic. Thank God some-one at Livingston Development had thought to leave him a message that they'd closed the deal on the KRZE property. He'd been able to contact them immediately and put in a bid for the demolition work. His bid had been ridiculously low, which was why Livingston had grabbed it.

No doubt they thought he was out of his mind, but they had no idea how insane he really was. The job would cost many times the amount they would pay him. And he didn't care. Money was the least of his worries.

Now he had to find Katie. He'd left messages on her cell, but either she wasn't checking them or she didn't want to talk to him. If she'd found out about the sale, she might not feel like having a phone conversation with him about it. If she'd found out about the demolition contract, she might not feel like have a conversation with him, period.

But he hadn't wanted to tell her his plan until he'd known that it might work. He'd had the brilliant idea this morning in the shower, where he got most of his brilliant ideas. Unfortunately he hadn't had the luxury of time to investigate his options. He'd had to bid on the demolition and get information about his idea afterward.

Based on what he'd discovered, he now knew there was

a chance his idea would work. It was time to find Katie and tell her about it. He'd already checked at the station, but she wasn't there. Neither was Ava, the punk-rock receptionist. Jess had an idea they might be together, but he didn't know where.

Or maybe he did. He pointed his truck in the direction of Jose's. Under the circumstances, Katie might be sucking down margaritas. He could hardly blame her. She was convinced that her grandmother's house would soon be rubble.

He couldn't guarantee that wouldn't happen. But he could guarantee that he would give everything he had to keep it from happening.

KATIE WAS ON HER SECOND margarita, and the booze wasn't working. She'd hoped by now she wouldn't give a damn about much of anything, but instead she was more enraged with every minute that passed. She could have handled the disappointment of seeing the property sold. Maybe not right away but eventually, especially with the help of her exciting new relationship with Jess.

But Jess, bless his black villain's heart, had leaped at the chance to demolish the house. In so doing, he'd descended to the level of whale poop, and revenge would be hers. She and Ava, who had opted for iced tea as the designated driver, were busy plotting Jess's downfall.

They'd chosen to sit inside with air-conditioning instead of out on the patio. The October sun was blazing down, and Katie had enough problems without adding sweat to the list. Cheryl was due any minute.

"Remember that old Dolly Parton movie, *Nine to Five?*" Katie asked Ava. Then she waved a hand in dismissal. "Forget it. That came out before you were born."

"That's okay. I saw it on video." Ava looked eager, as if she wanted to prove she was worthy of being part of the revenge plot. "I'm picking up what you're putting down. We could do what they did to the boss, chain him up in a room somewhere."

"Exactly." Except that reminded Katie of the handcuffs she'd worn last night, and she definitely didn't want to think about that. Not ever again. "Nah, that's not horrible enough for him. Let's think of something worse."

"Sand in the gas tank of his car?"

"That's a start. And it would definitely have to be the Jag. Keep thinking. Oh, good. Here comes Cheryl."

Cheryl hurried over and reached down to wrap her arms around Katie. "I'm so sorry, pumpkin! I didn't think he'd turn out to be such a bastard."

"A gold-plated bastard," Ava said, nodding. "We're working on a suitable revenge."

"I'm in." Cheryl sat down and eyed Katie's margarita. "I'd love one of those, but I'm due back in court at one-thirty, so I don't dare. I'll just get some lunch."

"I'm drinking my lunch." Katie took another gulp of her margarita.

"I don't blame you," Cheryl said. "It's one thing if Jess's company ends up building the parking garage, but I can't believe he went after that demolition contract. He knows it's your grandmother's house, right? I can't imagine that he would do that, knowing—"

"Her grandmother's house?" Ava leaned forward, eyes wide.

"Yes." Cheryl gazed at Katie. "I remember going over there when we were kids. I used to love those big heavy doors. And we'd play hopscotch on the tile floors. Remember how we—"

"How about we stake him out on an anthill?" Katie didn't want to talk about her grandmother's house. "Only instead of burying him with his head sticking out, we bury him lengthwise with his tallywhacker sticking out."

Cheryl laughed. "Let's try for something that won't result in jail time, shall we?"

"If he's bulldozing your grandmother's house, he deserves the anthill," Ava said.

"Oh, he deserves it." Cheryl patted Katie on the shoulder. "Don't get me wrong. I like the anthill. But I'm in favor of something that would cause him major embarrassment and wouldn't send us to the slammer."

"I need more caffeine," Ava said. "I can always think better when I—uh, oh." She focused on the doorway of the restaurant.

"What?" Katie didn't turn around, though, because she knew what she'd find. She could sense Jess was there. Fury burned hot in her belly.

"The anthillworthy guy is on his way to the table," Ava said.

Katie swore softly.

Cheryl stood. "Don't worry. He won't get past me."

"No, I think you should let him come over," Katie said. "My margarita will look great dripping down his face."

"I'm heading him off," Cheryl said. "Ava, stay with Katie."

"Don't head him off!" Katie stood and turned. Sure enough, here came Jess, looking disgustingly gorgeous in a snug knit shirt and worn jeans. Her body, a traitor to the cause, reacted to seeing him by getting all tingly and warm.

Screw that. Her brain knew that he was no better than a glob of chewing gum she had to scrape off the bottom of her shoe. He might think he was going to come over and convince her that her grandmother's house wasn't worth breaking up over. Ha. That man was Dumpster-bound.

He looked into her eyes with that sweet puppy gaze of his. He probably expected her to go all gooey inside when he did that. Unfortunately she did go all gooey inside. She'd work on that.

Yet the longer she looked into his eyes, the more she found herself hoping it was all a mistake. Maybe she'd been misinformed. Maybe he'd come here to tell her that Edgecomb had gotten his facts wrong and some other company would handle the demolition.

Cheryl stood on one side of Katie and Ava stood on the other. Her troops, Katie thought with affection. Just as Cheryl had said last Saturday, men might come and go, but girlfriends were forever. She wished that looking at Jess didn't hurt so much, though. If he'd waited until she'd had another margarita, maybe the pain wouldn't have been so bad.

"You're not welcome here, mister," Cheryl said.

Jess's gaze flickered. "Nice to see you again, Cheryl. Congratulations on your career."

Ava's chin lifted. "She doesn't need congratulations from someone who can hardly wait to tear down Katie's grandmother's house."

"Ava's right, Jess," Cheryl said. "I thought it wouldn't do any harm for Katie to get involved with you, but now I can see it's hurt her. You used to be nicer back in high school. Now I wish I hadn't signed your yearbook and I definitely wish I hadn't said all those sweet things. I wish I'd—"

"Shut up, Cheryl," Katie said gently.

"I didn't grow up with Katie or anything," Ava said, "but I can smell a rat when I see one. We know everything, and what you did stinks."

"You don't know everything." Jess gazed down at Katie. "Hey, Katie," he said softly. "Please tell me you're not going to judge me and declare me guilty before I have a chance to defend myself."

Katie finally found her voice. "Did you get the demolition contract?" She prayed that he'd tell her that he didn't have that contract, that his foreman had acted for him and he'd since canceled the deal. She wanted to hear that he could never bring himself to demolish her grandmother's house.

"Yes, but—"

"Then there's nothing more to say, is there?"

He drew in a sharp breath. "You are ready to convict me just like that, aren't you? Doesn't matter what I have to say, does it?"

She swallowed. "Not really."

"I thought we'd moved beyond that stage. I thought after what we've shared you might be willing to give me the benefit of the doubt, listen to my side of the story."

She was trembling, but somehow she managed to get the words out. "I don't see that there's any doubt to give you the benefit of, Jess. And I know your side of the story. The property's sold, and you grabbed the chance to destroy that house. I hope it's lucrative for you." God, this was horrible. She hadn't known she could suffer like this.

His expression stiffened. "I thought you trusted me more than that."

"How can I trust you when you—"

"Apparently you can't." Then he turned and walked out of the restaurant.

She didn't realize she was crying until the room began to blur.

Cheryl wrapped an arm around her and got her back into her chair. "I'm reconsidering the anthill," she said.

JESS HAD EXPECTED HER TO be upset about the sale of the property. After all, she'd lost the battle she'd been fighting so fiercely, and that had to hurt. But as for his role in the demolition, he'd expected disbelief, not a rush to judgment.

Instead she'd heard the news and immediately thought the worst of him. It was prom night all over again. She hadn't wanted to hear his reasons for doing what he'd done on that night long ago and she didn't want to hear them now. She might lust after his body, but she didn't seem to think much of him as a person.

And here he'd believed they could build a life together. Although he hadn't had time to make the reservations, he'd planned that tonight would be special, the beginning of a commitment. He wasn't quite ready to propose, but he was damned close. Or he had been before he'd discovered that she didn't trust him.

Back at the job site he walked into the construction trailer and found Gabe eating a fast-food lunch. Jess knew Gabe being here was no accident. He was the only one who knew that Jess had gone to find Katie.

Gabe put down his hamburger. "I'll take a wild guess that things didn't go well with Crazy Katie."

Sinking into one of the plastic chairs scattered around the trailer, Jess sighed. "Nope."

"So she doesn't think you can move that house?"

"She didn't give me a chance to tell her that's what I

plan to do. She heard about the demolition contract and decided I was slime. End of story."

"Geez, I'm sorry." Gabe studied him. "She means a lot to you, doesn't she?"

Jess shrugged.

"Hell, if she didn't even give you a chance to explain, that's pretty cold. I say good riddance."

"I could've forced an explanation on her." Jess stared into space as he replayed that ugly scene in the restaurant. "But once I saw that she'd already made up her mind about me, I didn't feel like it."

"No kidding, man. I hate to think what moving that house would have cost you. At least now you don't have to do it."

"Oh, I'm still going to do it."

"Why?"

Jess didn't want to answer that question. "I just am. It's the plan, and I'm sticking with the plan."

"Come on, Jess. You know it's a dicey proposition to begin with. She obviously wouldn't appreciate the effort and you could still end up with a pile of debris. Expensive debris, at that."

"Ah, it'll be a challenge." Jess mustered up a grin. "We can always use a challenge."

"You are one crazy son of a bitch." Gabe shook his head. "But it's your money. Me, I'd bulldoze the place."

Jess knew that was the practical thing to do, especially now. But Gabe was right about him. He was crazy—crazy in love with Katie. He couldn't demolish the house she loved when he knew how that would hurt her.

Moving a house was a tricky maneuver, though. Sometimes it slid right off the flatbed and ended up trashed anyway. What he proposed to do wasn't a guaranteed fix, but it was the best he could do.

AFTER THREE MARGARITAS, Katie switched to coffee. She had a show to do tonight, whether she felt like it or not. Her days of broadcasting from her grandmother's house were numbered, so she might as well make the most of them.

Ava drove her back to the station. They'd temporarily abandoned the revenge plot against Jess to brainstorm ideas for Katie's show.

"I suppose I have to cancel the interview with the guy who wrote *Naked High-Rise Windows and Voyeurism.*"

"That sucks," Ava said. "I'd like to hear what he has to say. I'm always looking in windows of tall buildings hoping to see something good. The best is if you're in the building right across from it. If I lived in New York, I'd own a telescope, no question."

"Well, Edgecomb made it clear that if I didn't change my tune on the show, I'd be fired. Besides, there's no point in continuing my campaign anyway."

Ava turned into the KRZE parking lot. "It was good while it lasted."

"Yeah."

"Listen, I know a retired porn star, if you need someone to fill the slot tonight."

Katie sighed. "That would be great, Ava."

"I'll keep thinking about the revenge plot, too. We could order a hundred pizzas delivered to his house tonight."

Katie gave her a tired smile. "I'll think about it. For now, let's go inside and you can hook me up with your retired porn star."

Once Katie had the new interview lined up and had jotted down the questions she wanted to ask, she had time on her hands. A practical person would use that time to sketch out ideas for future shows, now that her assault against high-rises was officially over. She wasn't feeling practical.

Instead she returned to her car and drove away from the station. She had no particular destination in mind, except that she needed to leave the construction site where Jess was working. In some ways changing locations in two weeks would be a blessing. She wouldn't have to confront Jess's project every day.

When she found herself on the winding road up to "A" Mountain, she wasn't surprised. As she and Jess had discovered the other day, hardly anyone went up there during the day, so it would be a good place to be alone. She had to get a grip on this new reality, and soon.

Several times in the past few hours she'd been on the verge of tears. She couldn't afford tears, especially when nine o'clock rolled around and she had a show to do. Therefore, if she planned to have a good cry, "A" Mountain was the perfect place for it.

Once again the area was deserted. If she'd had some romantic idea that Jess would get some sort of telepathic message and meet her up here, she'd been watching too many chick flicks. And what if he met her up here? So what? They'd be in the same fix as before.

Parking her car near the rock retaining wall, she gave in to some self-pitying tears. Eventually that got old, so she found a tissue in the glove compartment and blew her nose. Then she climbed out of the car and walked over to the wall.

Good thing she didn't want to end it all, because this would be a rotten place to jump. If she stood on top of the low parapet and leaped, she'd only land in a bunch of bushes and cactus about three feet below her. Then she might roll a ways more, but she'd never heard of someone rolling to her death.

She didn't want to end it all anyway. She still loved her job and her friends. Unfortunately she also loved Jess Harkins, and he'd turned into a first-class jerk. She should have known better than to think they could start over.

Once again he'd let her down at a critical time in her life. Once again he'd been a part of ruining something special. Oh, sure, he probably had some explanation for it, just as he'd had an explanation for rejecting her on prom night. But she couldn't imagine what he could say that would make any difference.

She hadn't given him a chance to say it, though. She sort of wished she had. As she stared at the downtown skyline, she picked out the spot where Jess's building would go up once the foundation was finished. Although she couldn't see him, she could imagine him down there, yellow hard hat on as he directed his crew in work that he obviously loved.

What had he wanted to tell her when he'd shown up at Jose's? He'd answered her question about the demolition contract with a *yes*. There had also been a *but* attached to it. She'd cut him off. She had judged him without listening to his reasons, exactly as he'd accused her of doing.

He could have insisted that she listen to him, but that wasn't Jess. He was too proud to do that. Thirteen years ago he'd wanted to explain about prom night, and she hadn't listened then either.

Then she faced another hard truth. She hadn't been willing to listen thirteen years ago because she'd been afraid of what she'd hear—that he didn't love her enough. It was the same today. She was afraid that he'd say that her feelings about her grandmother's house weren't that important in the grand scheme of things.

Life was easier if she got on her high horse, and she was riding high on it now. But damn it, he *had* snapped up the demolition contract. How could any discussion of that turn out well? Better to leave things as they were.

Returning to her car, she drove back down the mountain. Stupid as it was, she watched for Jess's truck the entire way. Of course she never saw it. She really had been watching too many chick flicks.

20

BECAUSE IT WAS A WEEKNIGHT, only a few cars were parked on "A" Mountain when Jess arrived a little before nine. Anybody who knew the situation would call him a masochist for driving up here, but he'd been going stir-crazy at home and he wasn't in the mood for company. So here he was, parked a distance away from the other cars.

He noticed that a few windows were rolled down to catch the evening breeze, and he didn't want to eavesdrop, so he switched on the radio. Oh, who the hell was he kidding? All along he'd known he would listen to Katie's program. Listening to it up here on "A" Mountain seemed stupidly appropriate.

Maybe she wouldn't be on tonight. The last time he'd seen her, she was headed for Margaritaville. KRZE might have a canned program they could plug in if Katie wasn't up to broadcasting her show. Once the news was over, he held his breath, waiting to hear her voice.

"Hello, Tucson! Crazy Katie, here, broadcasting from the beautiful downtown studio of KRZE talk radio on this gorgeous Wednesday night. All you lovers up on 'A' Mountain, do you know where your condoms are?"

Jess let out his breath in a rush. If he'd been worried about Katie, he didn't need to be. She was tough, tough enough to make a reference to "A" Mountain as if it held no special meaning for her.

Then again, she might be hoping he was listening. At this point, she wouldn't be above giving him a dig or two—or a couple dozen. Imagining her trying to get in a few personal jabs at him while she did her show was some comfort. He'd rather have her mad at him than not thinking about him at all.

As for him, he was thinking about her constantly. He didn't know what to do about that. It just happened on a regular basis, like breathing. If he knew how to stop obsessing, he would go that route, but he was clueless. He'd never been in this situation before.

"Are you all ready for your Kama Sutra tip of the night? We'll deal with a basic this time—kissing. Are all your kisses the same? They shouldn't be."

He might not be able to listen to Katie talk about kissing. It brought up some potent memories, and the way things were turning out, he wouldn't be kissing her ever again. But he left the radio on.

"Vary the pressure of your kisses and don't forget to use your tongue. Guys, if you are in the mood to give your lover an all-over tongue bath interspersed with playful kisses and love bites, you'll reap the rewards. Speaking from recent personal experience, I can vouch for the effectiveness of this move."

Jess drew in his breath so sharply he choked. She was talking about last night! He couldn't believe it. Not only was she talking about it, she acted as if she held fond memories of the event. How could she, considering how she felt about him now?

Hell, he would never understand women. If he didn't

know better, he'd think she was inviting him to come over tonight after the show. She wasn't, of course. She'd made it clear today what she thought of him.

"I need to take a short break for one of our marvelous sponsors, but don't go away! When we come back, I have a real treat for you. The star of more than twenty X-rated movies is in the studio, ready to tell us what life is like be-hind those cameras. He's speaking to us anonymously, so we'll simply call him Dick Johnson. Stay tuned!"

As Jess sat in the car, dazed and confused, he wasn't thinking about the coming attractions. Instead he was try-ing to figure out why she'd made such a pointed reference to having sex with him last night. Had she guessed that he might be listening? So far, her comments seemed totally aimed at him.

What that meant, he had no idea. If she was hoping he'd show up at the studio the way he had last Friday night, she would be disappointed. And if she thought they could pick up where they'd left off, sexually speaking, that wouldn't be happening either. He'd progressed beyond the point of having sex for its own sake. He wanted commitment or nothing.

"I'm back! And before we start talking with Dick, I have a brief comment concerning the construction project in the KRZE neighborhood. It seems that the building next door will go up, after all. The KRZE studios will move to a new location on Main Street and this building…will be torn down. Those are the facts, and I thank all of you for your support."

So that was that. Jess couldn't believe how calmly she'd delivered the news. She believed her grandmother's house would be demolished in two weeks and she'd announced it on the air as if giving a weather report. Jess admired that. He admired it a lot.

"And now let's hear from our distinguished guest. Dick, how did you get involved in making these films?"

"I learned to be flexible." Dick laughed. *"I mean mentally flexible. I was already flexible physically. Still am."*

Dick didn't sound all that old. Jess wondered if Katie would be attracted to a retired porn star. God, he hoped not. He didn't want her to be attracted to anyone. But if he didn't do something, she would drift out of his life again.

Thirteen years ago he'd let his pride keep him from contacting her to explain his actions. She'd blown up at him, and he'd decided not to give her any more information. If that was the way she'd wanted it, then he wouldn't lower himself.

As a result, he'd lost thirteen years. Now he was repeating the same damned pattern and he stood to lose…the rest of his life. Maybe she wouldn't take him back if he told her about the plan to relocate the house, but he should at least give her another chance to hear him out.

"Please tell us about that mental flexibility," Katie said.

"I'd planned on being a Hollywood leading man. When it became obvious that wasn't going to happen, I had to consider other options. I found a director I could trust—a woman, as it turns out—and we did a bunch of films together. Got married along the way. We had fun and made enough money to retire to Tucson."

Jess relaxed a little. The guy was married. But Katie wouldn't always meet happily married men. Jess decided a visit to the station was in order.

"Sounds like a success story," Katie said.

"It is. But I could have had a miserable life if I hadn't been willing to bend, rearrange my goals, face reality."

Jess turned up the volume to catch Katie's reply. He would love to know if she agreed with that philosophy. But just then a car with no muffler cruised past, and whatever Katie had said was drowned out.

Maybe it didn't matter. He was going to the station, and that was that. He would talk her into listening to what he had to say. If necessary, he would beg her to listen. To hell with his pride. Their future was too important to let that get in the way.

On the way down the mountain he listened as Katie delved into the juicy details of Dick Johnson's movie roles. He discussed his most favorite positions and least favorite. Then he gave some examples of porn-film bloopers that were hilarious.

When he described how a woman fell forward off a table during oral sex and almost broke his nose, Jess found himself laughing. It felt great to laugh. He hadn't thought he'd ever laugh again after that scene with Katie today. At that point he'd thought holding on to his pride was everything.

It was nothing. So what if she didn't trust him completely yet? They'd had only a few days to build that trust. The evidence against him had been damning, and he couldn't blame her for thinking the worst. She didn't know him well enough to question what she'd been told.

When the call-in portion of the show started, he decided to give her some warning that he'd be showing up at the station. After grabbing his cell phone from the holder on the dash, he punched in KRZE's number.

As he expected, he had to wait in line behind several other calls. She got a huge response from her listeners because she was good at what she did. And she made it look easy, which was the mark of real talent.

Maybe he and Katie were supposed to have this thirteen-year break in their relationship. They'd each had a chance to grow into the people they were meant to be. Speaking for himself, he hadn't been mature enough to handle being with Katie until now. Hell, he hadn't been mature enough until about thirty minutes ago.

"This is Crazy Katie. You're on the air."

"Hi, it's Jess." It was very weird to hear himself on the radio.

"Hi, Jess. What's your question?"

He wondered if the listeners could hear the quiver in her voice. "No question, just a comment. This mental flexibility thing sounds like a great idea."

"I agree. Thanks for calling, Jess."

It wasn't much to go on, but he'd take it. He pulled into the KRZE parking lot a little before ten. Might as well go in and face down Ava. He wanted to be in the lobby waiting when Katie came out.

He wasn't surprised when Ava gave him the evil eye. She was loyal to Katie, and he liked that.

She finished up with a caller and sat up very straight in her chair. "I'm in my official position here, which means I have to be nice to you. But if you start any trouble, I'm calling the cops."

"I'm not here to start trouble." Two barrel chairs upholstered in pigskin sat against the lobby's far wall. He chose one and sat down. Then he glanced around, checking for cracks in the walls. They looked solid. He hoped to hell they were.

Ava glared at him as she took another call. Then she folded her arms on her desk. "Tell me, how does it feel knowing that you'll be responsible for sending this whole place to the landfill?"

"That might not be the outcome."

"Aha! I knew it. You're going to sell it off in pieces, aren't you? Get people to haul off the adobe bricks and the doors and windows before you bulldoze the foundation. The house will die a long, lingering death instead of a quick one. Won't that be special?"

"You know the house can't stay here."

"That doesn't mean you have to be the one to destroy it."

"Better me than a stranger." He glanced at his watch. Katie should be coming out any minute.

Then he heard her voice in the hall, along with a deep baritone. Dick Johnson was still in the building. Jess stood.

Dick Johnson turned out to be a tall, silver-haired guy of about fifty-five. Katie was turned toward him, and she was laughing at something he'd said as she walked into the lobby. When she caught sight of Jess, she stopped laughing and froze.

Jess stepped forward. "Katie, I need to talk to you."

"I can have the cops here in five minutes," Ava said. "Just say the word."

Katie swallowed. Then she glanced at Dick. "This is a…friend of mine, Jess Harkins. Jess, this is my guest on the show, Dick Johnson."

"Actually it's Benjamin Creighton," the man said, extending his hand. "I see your name all over town, Harkins."

"I've been fortunate." Jess returned the actor's firm handshake. "I enjoyed your interview."

"You called in, didn't you? I remember a Jess who made a comment about mental flexibility."

"That's right. It's a worthy goal." From the corner of his eye he watched Katie. She was breathing as if she'd just climbed a flight of stairs and her hands were clasped tightly in front of her. His heart wrenched as he thought of how relaxed they used to be with each other.

"Well, Katie, I need to shove off." Benjamin took Katie's hand. "It's been a pleasure. I'll be in touch."

That's when Jess noticed the guy wasn't wearing a wedding ring. "I suppose your wife is waiting for you," he said. Not every man wore his ring.

"Unfortunately no. About two years ago she decided Tucson wasn't exciting enough for her, so she moved back to LA. We had a friendly divorce."

Jess had the insane urge to yank Katie's hand out of Benjamin's cozy grip. Yikes, a former porn star! He might be old enough to be her father, but he looked sleek and fit. And he'd know all the right moves. Jess hadn't arrived a minute too soon.

"Goodbye, Benjamin." Katie smiled.

That smile was entirely too friendly for Jess's taste.

"Nice meeting you, Harkins."

"Same here." Jess's jaw clenched and stayed that way until the guy walked through the heavy oak door and into the night.

Katie turned to him. She looked wary but not totally unfriendly. "You had something to say?"

"Are you going to see him again?"

"Who?"

"Dick. I mean, Benjamin! Whatever his name is."

Behind him Ava blew out a breath. "She can do that, you know. You have no claim on her."

"Yes, I do! Katie, I love you!"

Her eyes widened.

Jess groaned. "Damn. I didn't mean to say that."

"B-because it's not true?"

Man, if he'd had a blueprint for screwing this up he couldn't have done a better job. "It's true. But before I said that I wanted to tell you—"

"Wait." She moved closer and her expression softened. "I have something to tell you. It's okay. It's okay about the demolition. You tried to explain the whole thing to me, but I wouldn't let you. I should have trusted you to have a good reason for jumping on that contract."

"That was a rotten thing to hear, and I don't blame you for being—"

"And one more thing." She put her hands on his chest. "I love you, too."

His jaw dropped. "How can you?"

"I can't seem to help it."

Ava sighed. "Oh, brother. Katie, you need a serious intervention. This is the creep who's going to bulldoze this old house that you love!"

"That's okay, Ava." Katie gazed up at Jess. "I love him a lot more than I love this house."

"Sheesh." Ava blew out another loud breath. "There goes the revenge plot. And I was coming up with some really good ideas, too."

Jess barely registered what Ava was saying. He was too busy looking into Katie's eyes and trying to process what she'd just said. He put his hands around her waist. "You love me? For real?"

"Yeah." She smiled, and it was a much warmer smile than she'd given the porn star. "For real."

"But I haven't even told you what I'm doing about this house!"

"Doesn't matter."

Ava cleared her throat. "Excuse me, but it does matter to some of us in this room. I love the house, too, you know. I want to hear what this genius has in mind."

So Jess told Katie about moving the house.

Astonishment sparkled in her eyes. "Jess, that's brilliant!"

"It's not a bad idea," Ava said. "It might work."

"And it might not," he said. "It could fall off the flatbed during the move and then it really will be a pile of rubble. I can't guarantee that won't happen."

"But knowing you're going to try…" Katie's eyes misted. "You have no idea…."

"I think I do." He drew her close.

"I guess you do, at that." She gazed up at him, love in her eyes.

"If you two are going to start with the kissing, you might want to move into the conference room," Ava said.

Jess continued to hold Katie's gaze. "For what I have in mind, even the conference room isn't private enough."

"Oh, for crying out loud," Ava said. "Get out of here, you two. Get a room."

"Consider us gone." Jess wrapped an arm around Katie's shoulder and started toward the door.

"So I take it you won't be meeting Cheryl and me for margaritas later on?" Ava called after them.

"Good guess," Katie said, laughing.

"Don't forget, men come and go, but girlfriends are forever!"

Jess glanced back at Ava. "Just for the record, this man

is staying." Then he hustled Katie out into the warm October night.

"For how long?" Katie asked as he helped her into his Jag.

"How long what?"

"Are you staying?"

Leaning down, he kissed her gently. "Forever."

Epilogue

"I SHOULDN'T HAVE HAD coffee this morning. Something more soothing would have been better. Maybe warm milk." Katie's tummy quivered as she rode in Jess's truck. A sign announcing Wide Load had been attached to the roof of the cab.

Ahead of them shimmied the wide load itself, her grandmother's house. Jess was humming "Over the River and Through the Woods."

"You're not helping, you know, with that humming," Katie said.

"Who says? It's helping me."

"So you admit you're nervous? While they were jacking it up and loading it on the flatbed, you looked cool as a Sno-Kone. You even made jokes with Gabe." Katie gasped as the flatbed rounded a bend and the house swayed.

"I'm nervous. I've never moved a house before."

"But you think it'll work, right? I mean, getting it on the truck was the hard part, wasn't it?"

He hesitated. "All of it's the hard part. That's a very sharp curve we have to navigate before we get to the property."

"Maybe we should have picked a different lot."

"You love that lot."

"I do." It was a mile down the road from Jess's house,

and the view of "A" Mountain was even more spectacular than Jess's.

"Okay, here we go." Jess sucked in a breath as the flatbed started up the winding road leading past Jess's house. "Come on, baby. Hang on."

"Are you talking to me or the house?"

"Both. If you have any influence with your grandmother, now would be the time to use it."

"Funny you should say that. I've been thinking about how happy she'd be right now."

Jess nodded. "Let's keep it that way."

"Right." Katie crossed the fingers of both hands and concentrated on the house, balanced so precariously on the flatbed. But much as she wanted the building to make it to the lot in one piece, she was prepared for failure, too.

Whenever she thought of the love Jess had shown by deciding to move this house, she got a lump in her throat. If he managed to save the house, she would be forever grateful. If the house tumbled into a ditch, she would be forever grateful. He'd tried. That was all that mattered.

They passed Jess's house with the Sold sign in the yard. He'd put it on the market as a show of faith that moving the house would work. They'd have their wedding in the backyard and live in it until they were old and gray. He'd told her that keeping his house as backup was the chicken's way out, and they didn't want to start out as wimps.

But the curve looked ten times worse than it had when they'd driven the road last night. And the house looked ten times bigger and more unstable than she'd imagined.

As the flatbed entered the curve, Katie glanced at Jess. "I love you."

"I love you, too." He didn't take his attention off the house.

"No matter what."

"That's good to know. Oh, shit. Look at the way it's tilting."

Katie didn't want to look, but she made herself. If the house went down, she should have the courage to watch it go. Holding her breath, she willed the house to right itself.

"Straighten up, damn it," Jess murmured. "Straighten up."

The curve seemed to go on forever, and the house tilted even more. Katie groaned and fought the urge to cover her eyes. She should have picked a different lot, one that didn't have a curve like this. She should have—

With a rumble the house straightened.

Jess blew out a breath. "Thanks, Grandma."

Katie looked at him in surprise. "You really do think she's watching over this move, don't you?"

"I don't know, Katie, but that house is what brought us together after all these years, and when I got the brainstorm of moving it, I knew I wanted us to live in it together. You said that your grandmother and grandfather had a—what did you call it?—a great love affair. And so do we."

Her heart swelled. "Yes," she said softly. "Yes, we do."

"So it seems as if this house move has to work. Your grandmother would want it that way."

"It's going to work." And suddenly Katie was absolutely sure it would.

Hours later, when the crew had eased the house off the flatbed without incident, she wasn't surprised. After everyone else left, she and Jess stayed on, arms around each other as they gazed at the little adobe.

"Think it'll be big enough?" Jess asked.

"For two of us? Of course."

"I was thinking three, maybe four of us."

She turned into his arms. "If this is your subtle way of asking if I want kids—"

"It is."

"The answer is yes. Kids, dog, play set in the back-yard—"

"I can build that for them, you know." He pulled her closer.

She wiggled against him, teasing him into responding just because she could. "Don't you mean you're going to *erect* it?"

"Exactly." He cupped her bottom and settled his hips firmly against hers. "And it'll have lots of levels, because I feel the urge to erect it so it's thrusting skyward. I'll use lots of screws and nuts and bolts, too, not to mention my big ol' hammer."

She batted her eyelashes at him. "Jess, are you talking about sex?"

Leaning down, he brushed his lips over hers. "No, you're the one who talks about sex, Crazy Katie. I'm the one who takes action. Let's go back to the truck and I'll show you my tools."

"You want to do it in the truck?" As usual, all it took was a light kiss and a sexy suggestion and she was willing and eager.

"Yeah." He nibbled on her lip.

"It might be a little cramped."

"No problem." Lifting his head, he gave her a smile so sexy it took her breath away. "I've memorized the *Kama Sutra*."

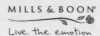

SILHOUETTE®
Desire™ 2 in 1

BOSS MAN by Diana Palmer

Stubborn, smart Blake Kemp, the town's tough lawyer, hadn't looked twice at his dedicated, gentle assistant Violet before but, when she left him, Blake mounted a campaign to win her back!

TANNER TIES by Peggy Moreland

Estranged from her family, Lauren Tanner was getting her life back on track. But she hadn't counted on Luke Jordan, who was determined to bring her back to the fold by any means possible —even seduction…

THE MILLIONAIRE'S CLUB

BLACK-TIE SEDUCTION by Cindy Gerard

Christine Travers had no time for flirtatious millionaire Jacob Thorne. But he was confident that only he could satisfy her needs. So he decided to show her just how good he could be…

LESS-THAN-INNOCENT INVITATION
by Shirley Rogers

Years had passed since Melissa Mason had thrown Logan's marriage proposal back in his face and left town. But the burning anger and desire he felt seeing her again made him demand answers…

APACHE NIGHTS by Sheri WhiteFeather

Though Joyce Riggs and combat trainer Kyle Prescott were as different as night and day, they entered into a no-strings affair… But what would happen if Joyce confessed her secret hope?

BEYOND BUSINESS by Rochelle Alers

One look at sultry secretary Renee and Sheldon Blackstone knew he would make her his mistress. But he hadn't bargained on her vulnerability and charm chipping away at the shell that encased his heart.

On sale from 15th September 2006

Visit our website at www.silhouette.co.uk

FREE!

2 Books
and a surprise gift!

We would like to take this opportunity to thank you for reading this Mills & Boon® book by offering you the chance to take TWO more specially selected titles from the Blaze™ series absolutely FREE! We're also making this offer to introduce you to the benefits of the Mills & Boon® Reader Service™—

- ★ **FREE home delivery**
- ★ **FREE gifts and competitions**
- ★ **FREE monthly Newsletter**
- ★ **Exclusive Reader Service offers**
- ★ **Books available before they're in the shops**

Accepting these FREE books and gift places you under no obligation to buy, you may cancel at any time, even after receiving your free shipment. Simply complete your details below and return the entire page to the address below. You don't even need a stamp!

YES! Please send me 2 free Blaze books and a surprise gift. I understand that unless you hear from me, I will receive 4 superb new titles every month for just £3.10 each, postage and packing free. I am under no obligation to purchase any books and may cancel my subscription at any time. The free books and gift will be mine to keep in any case.

K6ZEF

Ms/Mrs/Miss/Mr ....Initials ....

Surname .... **BLOCK CAPITALS PLEASE**

Address...

....

....Postcode ....

Send this whole page to:
UK: FREEPOST CN81, Croydon, CR9 3WZ